D.G.

DATE DUE			
MY 29 07			
8/4/08 JAN 16 2013			
DEC 3 X 2015			

LP
F
ALB
 Albert, Susan Wittig.
  Lavender lies

LAVENDER LIES

*Also by Susan Wittig Albert
in Large Print:*

Hangman's Root
Mistletoe Man

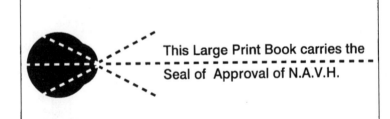

LAVENDER
LIES

A CHINA BAYLES MYSTERY

Susan Wittig Albert

Thorndike Press • Thorndike, Maine

Copyright © 1999 by Susan Wittig Albert.

Published in 2001 by arrangement with The Berkley Publishing Group, a member of Penguin Putnam Inc.

Thorndike Press Large Print Mystery Series.

The tree indicium is a trademark of Thorndike Press.

The text of this Large Print edition is unabridged. Other aspects of the book may vary from the original edition.

Set in 16 pt. Plantin by Minnie B. Raven.

Printed in the United States on permanent paper.

Library of Congress Cataloging-in-Publication Data

Albert, Susan Wittig.
    Lavender lies : a China Bayles mystery / Susan Wittig Albert.
        p. cm.
        ISBN 0-7862-3162-9 (lg. print : hc : alk. paper)
        1. Bayles, China (Fictitious character) — Fiction.
    2. Women detectives — Texas — Fiction.   3. Herbalists — Fiction.   4. Texas — Fiction.   5. Large type books.
    I. Title.
    PS3551.L2637 L38 2001
        813'.54—dc21   00-065767

To my daughter Robin, on her marriage:
here's lavender for devotion, dear heart

Acknowledgments

I am especially indebted to Bertha Reppert and Betsy Williams, who have taught me a great deal about the traditions of wedding herbs and the fragrant meanings and delightful uses of lavender. Sadly, Bertha has died since the writing of this book, but her memory will remain ever green as the rosemary she loved.

And as always, I am inexpressibly grateful to Bill Albert, comforter, computer wizard, and co-author. His love and constancy not only makes writing a long series possible, but a great deal of fun, too.

Author's Note

The Texas Hill Country setting of the China Bayles books is a fictional one. (This doesn't make it any less real, of course, for imagination and memory are closely allied and our recollections of fictional places we love are often as vivid and delightful as those of places we have actually visited.) The people aren't real, either, except for Bertha Reppert and Betsy Williams, who have graciously consented to allow their fictional counterparts to appear in these pages. However, the herbs definitely *are* real, and their uses may have both favorable and adverse consequences. The medicinal and therapeutic uses of plants I mention in this book are documented by scientific research or by long practice, but please don't take my word for their appropriateness in your particular situation. You should do your own research or seek advice from a qualified practitioner before treating yourself with any plant medicine.

Chapter One

Traditional Bride's Cookies

1 cup butter, softened
1/2 cup sifted powdered sugar
2 cups flour
1 cup finely chopped pecans
1 teaspoon mace
1 teaspoon vanilla
Powdered sugar for dusting
Tiny silver balls for decorating

Cream butter and sugar. Add flour, pecans, nutmeg, and vanilla. Shape into 2-inch crescents and decorate with a row of silver balls. Bake on a greased cookie sheet at 325° for 20 minutes. Dust with powdered sugar while warm and store in an airtight container. Makes about 4 dozen.

"You're not practicing that hocus pocus on me," I said. "If you have to tell fortunes, Ruby, start with Justine."

Across the table, Justine Wyzinski looked

up from the lavender stems she was attempting to braid. "Palm reading is only a parlor game, China. Just superstition. Play along — it won't hurt you." She tossed the braid onto the table with an impatient gesture and leaned back in her white wicker chair. "Isn't there something else I can do besides making these ridiculous lavender hearts? Ruby's are perfect. Mine are hideously deformed."

"Justine," I said, "you only admit to being incompetent when you don't want to do something."

Ruby put the heart she had fashioned into the box in the middle of the table and swatted away a bee. My front porch isn't screened, and the fragrant honeysuckle draws bees from three counties. "For your information, Justine, palm reading is not a game, it's one of the great mystical arts. And as for superstition —"

I picked up one of the four dozen cookies Ruby and I had turned out earlier in the afternoon and began to taste-test it, while Ruby launched into a lecture on palmistry, her latest occult passion. As the owner and manager of the Crystal Cave, the only New Age shop in Pecan Springs, she has to know about such psychic oddities as astrology, tarot, and numerology.

10

But weirdness is right up Ruby's alley, which is clear from the moment you meet her. She is a wild and wonderful six-foot-tall redhead with her own wacky brand of outrageous exuberance. Today, she was wearing a long, slim, yellow knit dress, yellow sandals, and a yellow upper arm bracelet. She looked like a luscious lemon popsicle topped by a frizz of carroty hair. Her eyelids were shadowed to match the green of her contacts and she had applied mascara and eyeliner with a dramatic hand. If I went out in public looking like that, people would double over in hysterical giggles. But when Ruby wafts past, there are murmurs of awed admiration.

"Well," Justine said reflectively, when Ruby had finished her lecture, "all I've got to say is — *yee ha!*" And with that, she leaped from her chair, yanked both my hands onto the table, and pinned them there, palms up. "I'll hold her, Ruby. You read."

"This is assault," I said, and closed my hands into fists. "And you've made me drop my cookie."

My third taste-test had fallen onto the porch floor, right under Howard Cosell's nose. Howard is a crochety old bassett hound whose favorite exercise is lurking

11

under chairs in anticipation of falling cookies, bits of bread and jelly, and other delectable doggie treats. Unfortunately, these goodies have done a number on his liver. He's been under the weather, and the tests show that his liver enzymes are out of alignment. Every day now, Howard gets his dog food with a topping of milk thistle seeds and a sprinkling of turmeric. We'll see what the retest shows.

"Don't be a sore loser." Justine straightened my fingers. She is a large person with a strong will. I yielded the point.

"Okay," I said. "Ruby, you can read my palm — first. Then it's the Whiz's turn. Her palms have lots of lines. But I'm on record as saying that this is all a bunch of hooey."

Justine relaxed her hold. "Of course it's hooey." She let go of my hands and pulled her chair next to mine. "But if Ruby's going to engage in this mystical claptrap for hire, she needs to practice. How else is she going to be able to fleece her unwitting victims?" She leaned over and said, in a stage whisper, "When they threaten to sue, refer them to me. Consumer fraud is such fun." She reached for another cookie. "What's the flavoring in these? Is it legal? They're pretty tasty."

"Mace," I said.

12

Justine sputtered and Ruby laughed.

"Not that kind of mace," I said. "This one is a spice. The dried covering of the nutmeg fruit, which looks like a pear. Cut the fruit open, and you'll find a seed. That's the nutmeg itself, which is covered with a sort of fibrous stuff. That's the mace. It —"

"Spare me the botanical details." Justine yawned. "I get the picture."

When Justine and I were in law school together a million years ago, she earned the nickname the Whiz because she was so damned smart. Her brown hair might not have been combed for a day or two, she might have spinach on her teeth, and she had the social savoir-faire of a three-toed sloth, but nobody doubted that, intellectually, this woman was light-years ahead of the rest of the class. After graduation, the Whiz hung out her shingle in San Antonio, where she is now one of the city's most respected renegades, still fast, still tough, and still very, very smart. I joined the law firm in Houston where my father had once been a partner and began a career as a criminal defense attorney. Unlike Justine, though, I didn't stay with it. A few years ago, having concluded that the herbs growing in the greenhouse window of my

13

condo were far more interesting and less stressful than the career I was cultivating, I turned in my boardroom key, cashed in my retirement plan, and opened an herb shop called Thyme and Seasons in Pecan Springs, a small Texas town halfway between Austin and San Antonio. It hasn't been the uneventful life I anticipated and I'm certainly not reaping bushels of money. But my earnings don't grow out of somebody else's grief, and I'm doing what I want to do. What's more, I can enjoy the luxury of closing the shop on Mondays and sitting on my porch with friends, making lavender hearts and getting my palm read. It isn't a bad life.

"I'll try not to commit any fraud," Ruby said, with a glance at Justine. She studied my right hand as if it contained the secrets of the universe. "Palmists say that the shape of a person's hand tells a lot about her character," she remarked. She looked at my hand for a few seconds longer. "Yours is square."

"So far so good," I said. "I am an extremely square person. In bed every night at ten, nose to the grindstone from dawn to dark. No hanky-panky."

Lately, at least, this was true. Back in June, following the annual Cedar Choppers Chili Cookoff, I'd had the misfortune of breaking my femur, cracking an ankle socket, and getting generally scraped when I got stuck — and nearly incinerated — in an abandoned barn. I spent June and July and part of August in a traction rig and then in a cast. When I finally limped back to the shop, I was so far behind that I've had to work double time to catch up. And for the past three weeks, I've been getting ready for a wedding — mine. I haven't had a spare second for hanky-panky, even if I were inclined in that direction.

"People with square hands are successful in business," Ruby went on. "They enjoy making money. They're good partners because they are scrupulously honest, although their independence sometimes gets in the way." Her fingers traced a line on my palm. "See this? This is the money line. It ends under your index finger — which means that you will make a lot of money in business."

"Good deal," the Whiz said approvingly. "I'm all in favor of making money. The more the merrier."

"She isn't reading my palm," I said, "she's speculating." Ruby and I are partners in a soon-to-open tearoom called Thyme for Tea, which is located behind my herb shop, which is next door to the Crystal Cave. All very convenient for a partnership, although I confess that I haven't quite gotten used to the arrangement. Ruby won the lottery, you see — not the Big Sweet One, but big and sweet enough to yield a very substantial annual income. She might have retired to Jamaica for the rest of her life, but for some weird reason she had set her heart on having a tearoom. I was opposed to the idea at first, because . . . well, because I *am* independent, damn it. I've lived forty-five years without a partner, and I don't function well when I have to ask permission. But one of the lessons I learned this summer is that even fiercely independent people sometimes have to ask somebody else to help them get into their pantyhose. We can't fly solo all our lives. So I signed the partnership agreement and Thyme for Tea is about to open. Ruby is providing the capital, I'm furnishing the space, and both of us are contributing ideas and labor. We may argue violently over the details — the menus, the decor, the kitchen layout — but we haven't gotten a divorce yet. I'm not one to make optimistic predictions, but it just might work out.

"The fingernails tell a lot about you,

too," Ruby said, turning my hand over. I tried to jerk free, but it was too late. Ruby gave a disapproving *tch-tch*. "I hope you have a pair of decent gloves for the ceremony."

"I am a gardener," I said with dignity. "I garden in alkaline soil that eats fingers to the bone. If McQuaid doesn't like my hands, he can find himself another wife."

The Whiz gave me a curious look. "Are you going to call him McQuaid even after you're married to him?"

"Yep," I said. I was a criminal attorney and he was a cop when we met, and our friendship began on a last-name basis. He could call me China if he wanted to, but to me, he'd always be McQuaid. "I intend to keep my own name too," I added. "I may be getting married, but I'm not losing my *self*."

Ruby turned my hand over. "Now, about the heart line."

"Does she have one?" the Whiz asked. She propped her feet up on the porch railing, leaned back in her chair, and clasped her hands behind her head. "I've always thought of China in terms of head, not heart."

"Of course she has a heart. It's right there." Ruby pointed with a gorgeous, gold-painted nail. "See that line? It ends between the middle and index fingers, which indicates a realistic approach to relationships. She's not exactly a romantic."

"Tell us something we don't already know," the Whiz said. "China does not have one ounce of romance in her soul. How McQuaid ever persuaded her to marry him, I don't know."

"It was the other way round," Ruby replied, before I could open my mouth. "China was the one who decided it was time to get married, after all those years of saying no every time he asked her. And McQuaid was the one who —" She stopped, biting her lip. "Who said yes," she went on. "See? Right there? That's the marriage line."

Ruby's general outline was okay as far as it went, but it left out eight months of painful detail. McQuaid had gotten involved with a young, pretty law enforcement officer just about the time he accepted a temporary assignment with the Texas Rangers. He ended their brief relationship before I discovered it, but the job with the Rangers nearly ended him. In February he was badly wounded in a gunfight with a carload of dope dealers on a deserted South Texas highway. At first, the doctors were afraid that he might not make it — and then that the injury to his spine would leave him in a wheelchair for the rest of his life.

But an indomitable will and a therapist who is as stubborn as a Texas mule enabled him, at last, to stand and walk. He wears a brace on his left leg and uses a pair of lightweight aluminum canes, but he came home from the convalescent center in August. He has even accepted an interim appointment as Acting Police Chief of Pecan Springs — Bubba Harris had been the chief until he got mad and quit in June. McQuaid gets around slowly and he tires easily, but being back in law enforcement (he's a former homicide detective) has been good for his morale, and things are definitely looking up. When you total up all the pain we've been through, add the months McQuaid was out of commission, and factor in my six miserable weeks in an uncomfortable cast, it hasn't exactly been the Best Year of Our Lives. But it has taught us that we want to spend the rest of it together, and that's got to be worth something.

The Whiz made a skeptical noise. "So what does China's marriage line have to say about her future with McQuaid?"

"It says . . . It says —" Ruby scrutinized my palm. "Actually, it doesn't say much. It's a pretty short line. Not very definite, either." She frowned. "Which is not to suggest that — I mean, it doesn't necessarily indicate that —"

"That our marriage is doomed?" I asked. "That the wedding might not come off?"

"Ridiculous," the Whiz said. "Don't be a nervous Nellie. Of course the wedding will come off." She looked at her watch. "In exactly six days and one hour, you'll be taking McQuaid for better or worse. Until death do you part. Which is not to say," she added judiciously, "that the marriage will be a success. Into every marriage a little rain must fall."

"Good *grief*," I said.

But Justine was right about the nerves. While I loved McQuaid without qualification, the jury was still out on marriage. After all, we didn't require the blessing of the State of Texas to live together comfortably (we'd been doing that for over a year), and no marriage certificate under the sun is going to make me a better mother to McQuaid's son, Brian. I've been doing that more or less well already — although he's discovered girls now, and all bets are off. But McQuaid and I had finally persuaded one another that we were in this for the long haul and that it was time to make a stronger and more binding commitment. So it was too late for second or third thoughts. There was no way I could back out now, even if I wanted to. Which was only between the hours of midnight and four a.m., five or six nights a week. Well, maybe seven.

"Only six days left?" Ruby cried. She turned anxiously to me. "Have you heard from Betsy and Bertha? *When* are they coming?" She gestured toward the box of lavender hearts. "When we get done with these, there are the sachets to make and the greens to cut and the bows to make." Her voice rose. "And that isn't even considering the flowers and food and —"

"Relax, Ruby," I said. "They'll be here on Wednesday, and the Merryweathers have agreed to help them."

Bertha Reppert and Betsy Williams have written books on herbal weddings and both were in Texas for a meeting of the Texas Herb Growers and Marketers Association — which I had to miss because I already had my hands full. When they heard that McQuaid and I were getting married, Betsy offered to help with the flowers, Bertha agreed to supervise the table decorations, and the entire membership of the Myra Merryweather Herb Guild volunteered to be their assistants. The Merryweathers promised to bring baskets of fresh flowers from their gardens to supplement mine, and Holly and Merry Christmas, who operate the Christmas Flower Farm near New Braunfels, offered to let us come and pick what we needed at the last moment. Justine produced the invitation list on her computer and Sheila Dawson was taking care of the music. Ruby was putting the final touches on the garden and the tearoom, where the wedding was scheduled to take place. Theoretically, all McQuaid and I had to do was show up.

"They won't be here until Wednesday?" Ruby fretted.

"That ought to be plenty of time," Justine said. She doesn't do teamwork any better than I do. If it had been her wedding, she would have planned it with the efficiency of a quartermaster and conducted it with the aplomb of Leonard Bernstein — all by herself. I doubt that the groom would have been asked to do anything but say "I do."

"It may seem like plenty of time to you," Ruby said, "but not to me. Between this wedding and the opening of the tearoom,

I'm a nervous wreck." She glanced at her watch. "In fact, I should be at the shop this very minute, checking on the painters. They're finishing up this afternoon. And after that, the pantry shelves have to be installed before the inspector can come out and tell us we're legal."

"If you'll recall, you were the one who wanted to have the grand opening two weeks after the wedding," I pointed out self-righteously. "You were also the one who kept adding on to the guest list. *I* was the one who suggested that McQuaid and I could ask Maude to marry us at her house." Maude Porterfield has been a JP in Pecan Springs for over forty years and still leads a busy life marrying people, holding traffic court, and signing death certificates.

"Oh, *hush*," Ruby said. "Do you think I'd let you sneak off and get married in Maude's back parlor? No way. We are all going to enjoy your wedding. Then you can go on your honeymoon, and when you get back we'll have the grand opening to look forward to." She glanced up as a red Ford Explorer pulled into the circular drive. "Oh, look — it's Sheila."

Sheila Dawson, a.k.a. Smart Cookie, was slim, blond, and gorgeously chic in her working clothes: silky red blouse, smart navy blazer and skirt, medium heels, and gold jewelry. But while Sheila might look like Miss Dallas, I wouldn't mess with her. She's an experienced cop with ten years of law enforcement, culminating in her current position as chief of security at Central Texas State University. Smart Cookie is also one of the three candidates the City Council is considering for Bubba's job as Pecan Springs's police chief, the position McQuaid is temporarily filling. The Council was supposed to make a decision on the chief's position several weeks ago, but it's apparently in no great hurry to make up its collective mind. Several members have said privately that chief of police is an unsuitable job for a woman and have been pressuring McQuaid to accept a permanent appointment. McQuaid has already told them that he intends to go back to his teaching job in the Criminal Justice Department at Central Texas State, and after that gunfight in February, I am definitely opposed to being a police chief's wife. But listening between the lines when he talks about what's going on at headquarters, I think I hear a hankering after his old calling. I hope not. Anyway, I'm rooting for Sheila.

As Sheila came up the steps, there was a

unanimous chorus of *hi*'s followed by a round of "Did you bring the CDs for the reception?" (from Ruby); "Are you still in line for the chief's job?" (Justine); and "How's everything going?" (me).

Sheila dropped into a chair. "What are you doing out on the porch? Isn't it cooler inside?" Howard Cosell, who is madly in love with her, rose from his reclining position and licked her calf, mooning up at her with his big, sad eyes. She patted him on the head, handed Ruby a stack of CDs, and took a newspaper out of her large bag. "Have y'all seen today's *Enterprise*?"

"Celtic," Ruby noted approvingly, shuffling the CDs. "Perfect."

"Wonderful," the Whiz said. China's marriage may be doomed, but the wedding reception is shaping up nicely. "Have a bride's cookie," she offered, and passed Sheila the plate. "They're flavored with mace."

Sheila blinked. "Mace?"

"Tiny shavings of the wooden staff carried by figures of authority," the Whiz replied. "Symbolic of female dominance over the male, which is the appropriate distribution of power in a marriage."

"Ignore her," Ruby told Sheila. "She's showing off. Mace is a spice, sort of like nutmeg, only sweeter. There are chopped pecans in the cookies too, but no shavings. No splinters, either." She looked down at the CDs. "These are fine for the reception, Sheila, but what about the music before and after the ceremony?"

"I was thinking maybe Pachelbel's *Canon*," Sheila said. "Then the *Bridal Chorus* and the *Wedding March* at the end."

"That's a heavy dose of classical," Ruby said. "How about some contemporary love songs? How about 'All I Ask,' from *Phantom of the Opera*? I love that line about let me be your freedom." She sniffled. "It always makes me cry."

"Of course it does," I said firmly. "It should. That song isn't about love, it's about co-dependency."

"I told you," the Whiz said, shaking her head. "Not an ounce of romance. How about 'The Wind Beneath My Wings'?"

" 'To Dream the Impossible Dream'?" I suggested. The Whiz grinned and Ruby shuddered. I turned to Sheila. "What's in the newspaper? One of my articles?"

A few months ago, Hark Hibler, the managing editor of the *Enterprise*, talked me into editing the paper's weekly Home and Garden page, which consists of a few recipes, some gardening tips, and an article or two. I certainly don't do it for the money, which is just about enough to pay for the Wednesday Special at Bean's Bar & Grill. But I figure that the publicity will bring customers into the shop and help to spread the word about our classes, which always helps to attract new people. And with the chain stores getting into herbs in a major way, Thyme and Seasons needs all the advertising it can get. I'm even thinking about putting up a Web site.

"Nope, it's not your article," Sheila said, and opened the paper. "Look at this." She pointed.

" 'Edgar Coleman Dead in Bloody Garage Murder,' " the Whiz read out loud. She looked questioningly at Sheila. "So who's Edgar Coleman?"

"Edgar Coleman," Ruby said, "is a local real estate shark." She glanced at the paper. "To tell the unvarnished truth, the only thing surprising about this murder is that it hasn't happened before now. Edgar definitely had a karma problem."

"Ruby," I *tch-tch*ed, "how you talk."

She tossed her head. "Well, it's true. He's made hundreds of enemies over that annexation proposal. Read the Letters to the Editor, if you want to know how people feel about him."

"Annexation proposal?" the Whiz asked.

"Blessing Ranch," Sheila told her. "Five hundred acres west of town. A classic example of bad development. Coleman carved it up into five-acre parcels, stuck big, fancy houses on the land, and promised roads and a water system. But he didn't make good on his promises. Instead, he's been pushing the Council to annex the development as part of Pecan Springs's extraterritorial jurisdiction, and he's sweetened the pot by offering to throw in some choice land along Pecan Creek, right next to the city park. But the deal is highly controversial. The Blessing Ranch residents want a reliable water supply and paved roads, but they don't want to pay city taxes. The Council wants to expand the tax base and there are a couple of prime commercial properties involved. But Pecan Springs doesn't have the money to extend water and sewer lines to all those residents. And while lots of people want to see Pecan Park expanded, they know that annexing the Blessing Ranch subdivision won't bring in enough taxes to pay for the utilities."

"That land should never have been developed in the first place," I said, "at least, not the way Coleman did it. That's fragile land out there, and he pretty well ruined the wildlife habitat. Not to mention that he cleared off several large building sites on the slope of Lookout Mountain without paying any attention to erosion control. He hasn't sold the lots yet, and every time it rains, another piece of the hillside slides down."

"Ah," the Whiz said wisely. "So it was the Sierra Club that offed him."

"Or Greenpeace," Ruby said in a serious tone. "If you ask me, somebody took out a contract on him." At my skeptical look, she added, heatedly, "Well, it happens. People hire hit men all the time. And don't tell me I ought to feel sorry for that jerk. I don't, not one bit."

"Letty Coleman is the one I feel sorry for," I said. "She's nothing like her husband." I turned to Sheila. "McQuaid didn't know about Coleman's murder when he went to work this morning, so it must have just happened. I wonder how Hark got it into the paper so fast — and how he got that headline past Arlene and her red pencil."

The Whiz looked at the headline. "What's wrong with it?"

Ruby laughed. "Three things. 'Dead,' 'bloody,' and 'murder.' Arlene wouldn't approve."

"That's the old Arlene," I said. "Now that it's her turn to worry about the bottom line, it's a different newspaper."

When Arlene Seidensticker took over the weekly *Enterprise* from her father, Arnold, she turned it into a daily. Arnold's idea of hard copy was the police blotter at the bottom of page 20, which reported such criminal events as old Mr. Spitzer getting picked up for drunk and disorderly again, or Mrs. Sampson's goats jumping their fence and terrorizing the neighborhood. If you wanted the nitty-gritty details of the $200,000 embezzlement in the Adams County Hospital accounting office or the assault on the ten-year-old girl who was on her way home from choir practice, you had to catch it on the local grapevine. It wasn't that we didn't have crime in Pecan Springs — it was just that Arnold Seidensticker didn't believe in telling anybody about it. Traditionally, Pecan Springs washed its dirty laundry in secret, and it was clean and sweet-smelling by the time the *Enterprise* hung it out to dry. The times are changing, though. For better or worse, Arlene's daily is tougher, grittier, and does a better job of covering the news than her father's old weekly.

"Coleman's wife found the body about

seven this morning," Sheila said. "Hark was driving past the house when the first police car showed up. He got to see the crime scene before they closed it off."

Hark Hibler is the latest in Ruby's long string of boyfriends. I like him very much, although I'm not sure the two of them are a good match. Ruby is wonderfully wild and exotic, like eating mango ice cream naked between satin sheets. Hark is down-home Texas, chicken fried steak with mashed potatoes and canned green beans. Separately, they're fine. Together . . . well, it's a weird combination.

The Whiz took her feet off the porch rail. "Who dunnit?" she asked. "Any arrests yet?"

"I have no idea," Sheila said. "China will have to ask McQuaid."

"Sure," I said amiably. "I'll snoop around and get the lowdown for you. Then the next time you run into a Council member, you can casually toss out some of the details of the investigation, thereby appearing to have an inside track and enhancing your chances of —"

Sheila bopped my shoulder with her fist. She does weight training, and her bop was not gentle.

"Okay." I rubbed my shoulder. "You can

appear ignorant and uninformed and blow your chance at the job. But Howard Cosell will still love you."

"Personally, I like the idea, Sheila." Ruby began to braid another lavender heart. "Why don't you volunteer to help with the investigation? The Council will see what you can do, and the turkeys who keep saying women don't have what it takes will have to eat shit and die."

"Absolutely not," Sheila said firmly. "This is McQuaid's case, and he won't welcome any help." She patted my arm. "I hope I didn't hurt you, China. Sometimes I don't know my own strength."

McQuaid's case, huh? I didn't like the sound of that. To comfort myself, I reached for another cookie.

"There's a bright side to this," Ruby observed thoughtfully, adding a white bow to her lavender heart. "With Coleman dead, the Council can stop arguing about the annexation proposal, at least for now. They can get busy and hire a chief of police."

"Don't count on it," Sheila said. "Anyway," she added glumly, "I'm not sure I want the job."

"Oh, yeah?" The Whiz was curious. "How come? Is the university upping the ante?" Central Texas State was not happy when they heard that their female chief of security was on the Council's short list. I wouldn't be surprised if they offered her a nice raise.

"Not yet," Sheila said. She made a face. "It's Blackie. He doesn't think I ought to take it."

Ruby scowled. "Well, you can inform Sheriff Blackwell that he has *no* right to tell you what to do. You're not married to him. And even if you were, he still wouldn't have any right."

Sheila was quiet for a moment. "If I take that job," she said at last, "we probably won't be married."

"That," I said sympathetically, "would be too bad."

Blackie Blackwell is a third-generation lawman who inherited his father's job as sheriff of Adams County. He and McQuaid were friends at Sam Houston State and have graduated to become fishing and poker buddies, so I see quite a bit of him. McQuaid says Blackie is the best lawman he knows, and has asked him to be best man at our wedding.

"He doesn't like the idea of having two law enforcement officers in one family," Sheila said.

Ruby hooted. "What does he think you are now? The campus mascot? For Peter's sake, Sheila, you've been a cop your whole adult life!"

"He says my university job is mostly administrative, and I have to agree with him." Sheila's eyes were dark. "It's been a while since I've done any real police work."

"I perceive a certain professional conflict of interest," the Whiz remarked, "not to mention an undesirable degree of geographical proximity and political entanglement. Sheriff Blackwell is the elected county sheriff. *Chief* Blackwell would be the chief of police in the largest town in his county." She pushed her lips in and out. "If you step on the wrong toes, Sheila, Blackie might not be reelected. If you pull the right strings, he could be a winner. Either way, he may feel that you are capable of exercising a potentially dangerous control over his career."

Ruby frowned. I stared. Howard Cosell dropped his jowled muzzle onto Sheila's foot and gave a ponderous sigh. There was a long silence. Sheila was the first to speak.

"Omigod," she said. "I hadn't thought of it *that* way."

I shook my head. "Justine is being very legalistic, not to mention pompous and bombastic. I'm sure you and Blackie can work it out."

"I don't mean to be disheartening," the Whiz said apologetically. "I felt it might be useful for us to analyze the relationship from a political, rather than a personal, point of view. Romance often blinds us to the disturbing and even ugly realities of our everyday lives."

"I can't wait for *you* to fall in love, Justine," Ruby said fiercely.

"Love is all well and good," the Whiz replied in a defensive tone, "but marriage exists in political, economic, familial, and social environments. Take our China, for example." She waved her hand in my direction. "She and McQuaid must deal with the impact of the recent unfortunate events on their relationship. It is likely that not all of the expenses are covered by insurance, and that there are serious financial implications. Indeed, in the many divorce cases I have handled over the years, I have learned that what appears to be a purely personal difficulty between two partners often has its roots in the —"

She broke off as Ruby rose from her chair, drawing herself up to her full height, putting her fists on her hips and scattering lavender stems on the floor. Howard Cosell looked up in alarm.

"Justine Ayn Rand Wyzinski," Ruby hissed, "you are without a doubt the most cold-blooded, hardhearted, fundamentally *insensitive* woman I have ever met. Why don't you just whiz on back to San Antonio and abandon us to our pursuit of romance — blind as we are, of course, to the ugly political, social, familial, and economic realities of our everyday lives."

The Whiz was pained. "I just think that this is a good time for China and Sheila to step back and —"

"Ouch!" I said loudly, and put my hand to my cheek. "Oh, *rats!*"

"What's the matter?" Sheila asked.

"I just bit down on something and my temporary crown came out." The week before, I had lost a crown on my left molar and the dentist glued in a temporary as an interim measure while the lab made a new one. I explored with my tongue. There was a crater the size of the Gulf of Mexico on the left side of my mouth.

"You bit down on a splinter of mace," the Whiz said in an effort to be funny.

"A piece of pecan shell," I said crossly. "I should have been more careful when I shelled those nuts. Now I'll have to stop by the clinic in the morning and see if the dentist can fix it."

"The price of crowns is above rubies," the Whiz remarked in a ruminating tone. "I trust that you have dental insurance."

I gave a short laugh. "You forget, Justine, that I no longer charge people out the whazoo for a few words of legal wisdom, like some of my friends. No, I don't have dental insurance. I had to choose between replacing my crown and replacing the rear tires on my car."

Sheila patted me on the shoulder. "Bear up," she said. "At least you don't have to choose between McQuaid and your career."

Chapter Two

Lavender's blue, dilly dilly,
Lavender's green.
When I am queen, dilly dilly,
You shall be king.

"Lavender's Blue"
Early 19th-century song

In one of the apocryphal books of the Bible,
Judith annointed herself with perfumes, in-
cluding lavender, before seducing Holo-
fernes, the enemy commander. Once he was
under her heavenly scented influence, she
murdered him. . . .

Lavender
Tessa Evelegh

For the past fifteen months, McQuaid and I have leased a white-painted five-bedroom Victorian situated on three acres of Texas Hill Country. It is a truly splendid house. The kitchen windows open east into the sunrise, and the master bedroom looks out across green hills toward the sunset. There is a turreted room with windows on three sides for my library of herb books, a large garage workshop for McQuaid, and sunny limestone ledges where Brian collects the snakes and lizards who share his bedroom. As if this weren't enough, there is a garden, several two-hundred-year-old live oak trees, and a sparkling creek with a mossy waterfall draped with maidenhair ferns. The downside to this near-idyllic situation is that the roof leaks, the kitchen foundation needs some urgent attention, and — the worst part — the house isn't ours. It belongs to an English professor and his wife, who packed up their three kids and went off to spend an eighteen-month sabbatical in Italy and France. Unfortunately, they are due back the first of January, which means that we will be dispossessed in a little over three months. Every now and then I experience moments of sheer terror as I try to calculate how we'll fit ourselves, our hobbies, and our expectations into an ordinary house. Normally, I'm as courageous as the next person, but I'd rather face lions than look for a new house.

McQuaid was an hour late getting home from work. We avoided any mention of Edgar Coleman at supper, on the theory that Brian, who is now thirteen, has already seen his share of violence on television and doesn't need the gory details of a murder dished up with his spaghetti. So we saved that until later and talked instead about the science project that Brian is working on with Melissa, his twelve-year-old girlfriend. This requires extended closed-door observation of Brian's terrarium by both young scientists and detailed computer records of reptilian diets, down to the last mealworm. (If you ask me, this is a ploy to get his own computer, which will no doubt come loaded with games and equipped with the latest electronic joystick. Bribes have gone way up since I was a kid.) We discussed the dietary preferences of reptiles and segued into the topic of clothing for the Big Event.

"I don't have to get dressed up for your wedding, do I?" Brian asked defensively.

McQuaid leaned over to gaze at his son's unlaced Reeboks, ragged cutoffs, and knee-length T-shirt. "In a word," he said, "yes. You will be wearing shirt, tie, slacks, blazer, and shoes. *Real* shoes. You're going to look respectable if it kills you. Or us."

Brian flopped his head onto the table as if he had died of a sudden heart attack, narrowly missing his plate of spaghetti. After a moment he straightened up and brightened. "I don't have no *real* shoes."

"*Any*," I said automatically. I put a heaping spoonful of pesto on my spaghetti and added some grated Parmesan, taking an appreciative sniff of the pesto. "You don't have *any* real shoes."

"Right. I don't have none." He stuck out an unspeakably filthy Reebok and gazed at it fondly. "Guess I can't go, huh?"

"No such luck," I replied, thinking that I'd better snip all the basil tonight, before it got dark, and put it into the freezer. If October was hot, as it often is, there'd be time for one more crop. I'm one of those who believe a bag of basil in the freezer is a marvelous thing to happen upon in the chilly depths of midwinter. "Your grand-mother is coming up from Kerrville to take you shopping," I added. "She's in charge of your wedding costume."

Leatha, my mother, is good at clothes. When I was a kid, that was one of the few things I could count on: having the right outfits in my closet for school programs, dance recitals, tennis matches, and so on. I could also count on Leatha to show up at these events with whiskey on her breath — and my father to be too busy with his legal practice to show up at all. Back then, I thought it was her drinking that drove him away. Now, I suspect that his abandonment was responsible for her drinking. It's a little late to point fingers, though. He's dead and she, at long last, is sober, remarried, and reasonably happy.

"Costume?" Frowning, Brian spooned my homemade tomato sauce onto his spaghetti, then buried it in tomato catsup, which he liberally applies to everything except cake and ice cream. "What's this about a costume?"

"Think of the wedding as Halloween," I said, "without a mask."

McQuaid looked up from his plate. "What am I wearing? Not a tux, I hope." He narrowed his eyes. "Tell me I'm not wearing a tux."

"If you were wearing a tux," I said, passing the Parmesan, "you'd have heard about it long before this. You're wearing a Mexican wedding shirt."

"What's that?" Brian asked, swinging his foot against the leg of the table.

"Please don't kick the table," I said. "A Mexican wedding shirt is a loose short-sleeved white cotton shirt decorated with floral embroidery and lace. It's traditional."

"Lace!" McQuaid yelped. "Flowers!"

"Think of it as Halloween, Dad," Brian advised.

"Plus your black dress-up jeans and cowboy boots," I added. I'd had to compromise on a lot of things, but I'd gotten my way on our no-fuss wedding outfits. McQuaid's shirt was borrowed from Leatha's husband, Sam, who owns a ranch near Kerrville. I was wearing an ivory cotton dress with broomstick pleats and a handmade lace yoke that I found several years ago at a border market in Matamoros, and white sandals. Ruby, my matron of honor, was wearing — well, I didn't actually know. She had promised to tell me as soon as she figured it out. She had also promised that it wouldn't be so outrageous that it would upstage the rest of the party.

Brian jerked his head in McQuaid's direction. "If he gets to wear jeans, how come I gotta wear shoes and a tie?"

"*I* don't know," I said, and put a hand on his knee to remind him about the table leg. "Ask your father."

McQuaid pulled off another hunk of garlic bread. "We'll discuss it later," he said.

Brian dropped a piece of garlic bread in front of Howard Cosell's nose. "Whenever she says to ask him," he remarked to the dog, "he says we'll discuss it later. I wonder how come."

I snatched up the garlic bread.

"Because we can't think of anything else to say," McQuaid told him. He looked across the table at me. "You're not kidding about the jeans and boots?"

"Nope," I said. "But you can't wear your cowboy hat. We have to draw the line somewhere." I shifted my mouthful of spaghetti to the other side. I'd already called the dentist and managed to get an appointment for early the next morning. Until then, I'd just have to be careful not to break off what was left of my tooth.

"Jeans and boots," McQuaid said happily. "What a woman." He grinned at Brian. "Hey, do I know how to pick 'em, or what?"

Brian shrugged. "She's okay. But I'm not gonna get married till I find somebody who'll let me wear Reeboks."

After dinner, Brian went upstairs to do his homework and consult with Melissa on the phone about their project. When he had gone, McQuaid helped me with the dishes and cleared up some of the mystery about Edgar Coleman's murder — not much, but some.

"The autopsy report won't be back until tomorrow," he said, rinsing a plate and loading it into the dishwasher, "so we don't have an official time of death yet, but it's a pretty good guess that it happened between six and midnight. Coleman's wife thought he was supposed to spend the night in Houston. Anyway, he wasn't home when she went out, and if he'd been shot after she got home at midnight, she would've heard it. The bedroom is behind the garage, and the windows were open. She found the body early this morning." He bent over and set the spaghetti dish on the floor, and Howard Cosell undertook his part of the cleanup chores with much enthusiastic tail-wagging. When you move in with a man, his son, and his dog, there are some things you have to accept whether you approve of them or not. At least there wasn't enough spaghetti sauce to do any further damage to Howard's liver.

"Poor Letty," I said. "This is going to be hard on her."

"Oh, you know her?" McQuaid took the dish away from Howard, rinsed it off, and put it into the dishwasher. Personally, I find McQuaid very handsome, in a rough-cut way. Very rough. His nose was broken by an Aggie right tackle about twenty years ago, his forehead was slashed by a knife-wielding crack dealer in a Houston parking lot, and the bullet that did a job on his spine also left a sizable white scar on his neck. He looks a little the worse for wear.

"Not very well." I shook out the place mats. "She drops in at the shop a couple of times a month. She and her husband have always struck me as an odd match," I added, thinking of the timid, uncommunicative woman who buys several bottles of kava and St. John's wort every few weeks. Kava helps to relieve anxiety and St. John's wort is the herb of choice for the treatment of depression. People who purchase that much, that often, are probably using the herbs instead of Prozac.

McQuaid stuck a handful of forks into the silverware basket. "She's what — a dozen years older than Coleman? Not that I have anything against younger men marrying older women, of course," he added with a grin. McQuaid is eight years younger than I am. "I heard, though, that he married her for her money. He bought the Blessing property right after they got married seven or eight years ago."

"Her first husband died and left her a nice stash," I said. "He made his money in gas and oil." I paused. "I wonder what Letty was doing out so late on a Sunday night in Pecan Springs." At that hour, the only thing open are the all-night convenience stores.

McQuaid dried his hands on a towel. "She was visiting her sister in New Braunfels. She left at ten-thirty and had a flat tire on the way home. Most of her story checks out," he added. "She changed the tire herself, but the emergency spare was still on the car, and the flat tire was in the trunk. The sister corroborates her claim about the time."

"But if Edgar was lying dead in the garage, why didn't Letty find him when she came home?"

"Because the batteries in her garage-door opener were out of juice. She parked in the drive and went straight to bed, thinking he was in Houston on business." He filled the dishwasher with soap, shut the door, and turned it on.

"More shady dealings, no doubt," I said wryly. "That guy seems to have played every angle in the book. The neighbors didn't hear anything, I take it." I put the milk back in the refrigerator, carefully ignoring a saucer containing three dead frogs, a gift from Melissa to Brian. When I was Melissa's age, girls baked peanut butter cookies for their boyfriends. Dead

47

frogs may signal a new and welcome phase in female-male relationships. "What kind of gun was it?"

"There was a cartridge on the floor near the body," McQuaid said. "Thirty-two automatic. And the nearest neighbor is about a hundred yards away."

A mouse gun, only slightly louder than a Roy Rogers cap gun. "Any suspects?"

"Suspects?" With a short laugh, McQuaid grabbed his canes and made his way to a chair. "How many would you like? Coleman was having an affair with his secretary, a feud with his neighbor, and a fight with the City Council. And of course, there's always the wife. Her alibi isn't unimpeachable." He sat down heavily and stretched his braced leg out in front of him.

An affair? Knowing Edgar's reputation as a con man, I wasn't surprised. I was troubled on Letty's account, though. It's bad enough to have your husband blown away in the garage without having to face the distressing fact that he was unfaithful — and that you're a suspect in his murder. But there was another potentially troublesome aspect to this business, quite a bit closer to home.

I poured a cup of decaf and set it in

front of McQuaid. "I hope you're remembering what day this is."

He picked up his cup. "Monday, the last time I looked."

"Which means that there are only five days left until Sunday." I sat down opposite him. "You *are* planning to wind up this murder investigation before our wedding, I trust — no matter how many dozens of suspects you have lined up."

"Hey, wait." He put the cup down. "You're telling me it's *this* weekend?"

"Uh-huh." I ticked the days off. "Tuesday, Wednesday, Thursday, Friday, Saturday. Then comes Sunday and the wedding, immediately following which we are scheduled to hop a plane for a one-week Hawaiian honeymoon." I gave him a meaningful look. "With nonrefundable tickets, dear heart, meaning that we pay even if we don't go."

"I can't believe this," he muttered, his face pained. "I somehow got it into my head that the wedding was next week." He paused. "Listen, China, this is a big investigation. I mean, there are a lot of angles to cover and a long list of suspects to —"

"McQuaid, my love," I said softly, "I am not disparaging your competence in conducting a homicide investigation, but I do hope you haven't forgotten that you are an *interim* police chief."

His face tightened. "Yes, I know, but things have been quiet all summer, China. All I've done is shuffle paper and keep the staff morale up. And whether you like Coleman or not, he was a big player in this town. I can't just walk out on —"

"Of course you can," I said reasonably. "Appoint a backup who can take over if you haven't collared the killer by Sunday afternoon. And don't forget the party on Saturday night."

"A backup?" He snorted. "Like who, for instance? You know the situation in that department. With Bubba gone, there's not a trained homicide man in the lot. That's one of the problems with this dinky little police force. They need new blood. They need somebody who can —" He stopped, pulling his black brows together. "What party?"

"The dinner your parents are giving for us at the Pack Saddle Inn. Your mother has reserved tables for thirty, hired a mariachi band, and conned her bridge club into making crepe-paper palm trees. Shall I tell her that the groom may be off playing Columbo?"

He growled something indistinguishable.

50

"Okay, I apologize. That was tacky," I said. "Well, if there's nobody on the force who can help, how about asking Bubba to back you up? He may be mad at the City Council, but he's not mad at you." Bubba Harris, who had been Pecan Springs's police chief for nearly thirty years, had quit in a huff over the sensitivity training the Council mandated for the police force.

McQuaid shook his head. "Bubba and his wife got a new RV and went to California to see their grandkids."

"Then ask Blackie. He's the county sheriff."

Another shake. "Pecan Springs isn't Blackie's turf. Anyway, he's in the wedding, too. He's my best man."

"Yes, but he's not going on our honeymoon." I scowled. "Well, I suppose you can always call in the Rangers." The Texas Rangers are available to lend a hand when the local police don't have the resources to handle a case.

McQuaid looked at me. "What would you think about possibly postponing —"

It was a very, *very* good thing that Pauline Perkins chose that moment to knock at the kitchen door. Otherwise, there might not have been a wedding. Pauline, who works as hard for Pecan Springs as if she

51

were working for real money, is the town's four-term mayor. She was still wearing her mayor's uniform, a tailored navy suit with a yellow jewel-neck blouse, pearl choker and earrings, and sensible navy shoes. She also wears about thirty extra pounds, including a spare chin and a pair of love handles. In spite of this tendency to chubbiness, she is usually briskly confident and brimming with mayoral authority and civic pride. Not tonight, however. Tonight, she looked as if she'd just lost the primary.

"Is Mike here?" she asked. "I need to see him about a . . ." She swallowed and tried again. "A personal matter."

I generally think it's a good idea to stay on cordial terms with your boss. As mayor and head of the City Council, Pauline is McQuaid's boss. And I like her, although she's sometimes a teapot tyrant. "Of course, Pauline," I said warmly. "Come in and have a cup of coffee."

While McQuaid greeted her, I poured coffee. "I'll leave you two," I said, picking up my kitchen shears and a basket and heading for the door. "I want to cut the basil while it's still light enough to see."

Pauline put out her hand. It was trembling. "No, stay, China, please. You're awfully good at solving . . . well, problems.

Maybe you can help."

McQuaid nodded and I sat down. But while Pauline obviously had something urgent on her mind, we had to wait while she fumbled incoherently through several false starts, trying to decide what part and how much of it she was going to tell.

Finally, McQuaid leaned forward and said, "Does this have anything to do with what happened this morning, Pauline?"

Pauline set her cup down hard enough to slosh coffee into the saucer. "Well, yes," she managed.

McQuaid's face was very serious. "Do you know something about Coleman's murder?"

Pauline jumped as if somebody had dropped a firecracker down the back of her yellow blouse. "No!" she cried. "Whatever makes you think I —"

"Well, then, what is it?"

"I . . . well, you see —" She swallowed, bit her lip, and finally got it out. "Well, to put it bluntly, Edgar Coleman was threatening me. He said that if I didn't do what he wanted, he would —" She stopped, gnawing on her lower lip. "He said he would tell —" She stopped again, stuck.

If somebody didn't prod her, we might be here all night. "Threatening you?" I asked gently. "You mean, he was black-mailing you?"

She flinched at the word, but it brought her around. "Well, yes, I suppose you could call it that. Only he wasn't after money. It was 'teamwork' he wanted." Her round cheeks were bright as fire and her chins trembled. "That was his word. 'Teamwork.'"

"He was after your vote on that annexation project?" McQuaid asked.

"I . . . suppose," Pauline said. Her voice dropped to just above a whisper. "Actually, he hadn't yet told me what he wanted. That was Edgar's way, you know. He'd never come straight out with anything. He was always so devious. He'd hint and insinuate and promise and . . . and —" Her bosom began to heave and her words dissolved in huge, gulping wails. "Oh, what a fool I've been," she sobbed, pulling out a yellow hanky. "What a stupid, idiotic, romantic *fool!*"

McQuaid made a high sign. I got up, took a bottle of brandy and three small snifters from the cupboard, and poured. Pauline snatched hers and tossed it down. I poured again, and after a moment she was calmer.

"I'm sorry," she said. "I've had this on

my mind for an entire week, you see, ever since he phoned me and told me what he would do if I didn't —" She shook her head heavily, her pearl tear-drop earrings swinging against her mottled cheeks. "Then when I heard he was dead — well, I know it's not Christian of me, but I was actually relieved. The longer I thought about it, though, the more nervous I got, so I decided I had to tell you." She drew a deep breath, tanking up for a long confession. "You see, it all began when —"

McQuaid held up his hand. "Wait a minute, Pauline. Before you say anything else, we'd better call Charlie."

She looked at him blankly. "Charlie? Charlie Lipman?"

"He's your attorney, isn't he?" McQuaid asked.

Pauline stiffened her spine. "Of course he is. That is, he's Darryl's lawyer." Darryl Perkins is Pauline's husband. "But I don't need to pay Charlie Lipman good money to listen to —" Then it dawned on her. Her eyes grew as round as daisies and her voice was freighted with offended dignity. "You can't mean that I . . . that you suspect me of . . . Why, I'm the *mayor* of this town! I would never stoop so low —"

McQuaid looked at me. "Maybe you'd

better tell her, China." He reached for his canes and hoisted himself to his feet. "I think Brian needs some help with his homework."

"Homework!" Pauline smacked the table furiously. "You just sit your fanny right back down in that chair and listen to me, Mr. Michael Acting Police Chief McQuaid. I'm going to get this Coleman nonsense off my chest tonight, and you're going to hear me out." The two large red spots on her cheeks made her look like a belligerent clown. "That's an order, do you hear? An order!"

But Pauline was talking to McQuaid's retreating back. As he stumped out of the room, she turned to me. "I could fire him for failure to follow a direct order," she snapped. She narrowed her eyes, liking the idea. "And by golly darn, that's exactly what I'm going to do! He doesn't need to think he can get away with flouting my authority. First thing in the morning, I'm calling an emergency meeting of the Council. We'll just see who's the boss in this town."

"I wouldn't do that if I were you, Pauline," I said quietly.

She straightened her shoulders and shot me a look like the one Harry Truman must have worn when he signed General Mac-Arthur's walking papers. "And why not? If there's anything I hate, it's insubordination."

Pauline isn't dumb, but sometimes she's like the old Texas mule — it's next to impossible to get her attention. "McQuaid isn't being insubordinate," I said. "He's being careful. Don't you *get* it, Pauline? Coleman's attempt to blackmail you has given you a motive for murder."

She stared at me as if I'd whacked her with a two-by-four. "A motive!" she gasped. "But I had nothing whatever to do with —"

I checked her denials. "Now that he's heard about the blackmail, McQuaid has no choice. Like it or not, he has to treat you as a suspect, which means advising you of your right to legal representation before saying anything — *anything* at all, Pauline — that might relate to the crime."

"He has to —" She stared at me for a long moment. "Oh, God," she whispered.

"God won't be much help, I'm afraid," I said ruefully. "If I were in your shoes, I'd call Charlie Lipman instead. And I'd do it tonight."

Her lower lip was trembling and her eyes were beginning to fill with tears. "But I . . .

I can't tell Charlie. Darryl might find out."
She gave me a pleading look. "You're a
lawyer, China. Couldn't you —"

Darryl? What did Darryl have to do with
this? "Sorry," I said. "I sleep with the
enemy."

She frowned. "I don't — Oh, yes, I see."
She sighed. "Well, in that case, I suppose
I'd better . . ."

She stood and picked up her purse, her
face drawn and sagging. Pauline has so
much stamina and energy that I'd never
thought of her as being any age at all. Now,
I realized that she was probably closer to
sixty than to fifty and was feeling every
year of it. I put my hand on her shoulder.

"Tonight," I repeated urgently. "Call
Charlie tonight. You'll probably be hearing
from McQuaid first thing in the morning."

"All right," she said numbly. She turned
toward the door. "Oh, God," she whispered. "What have I done? What have I
done?"

Chapter Three

Farther south around Arkansas and Texas a prickly ash grows that was more familiarly known as the toothache tree, Zanthoxylum clavaherculis. The bumpy bark is hot to taste and will help a toothache. So deeply entrenched in the affections of the people has this weird tree become that it has accumulated several other names, including the sting tongue, the tear blanket, and pepperwood. For a toothache, dry the inner bark, powder it, and apply in the aching tooth cavity.

Plant Medicine and Folklore
Mildred Fielder

I don't know about you, but going to the dentist ranks at the bottom of my list of preferred activities, right along with doing my income tax return and getting my tonsils out. For a long time, I put off even the most necessary dental work until there was absolutely no escape. My attitude improved, however, when Dr. Carl Jackson moved here a year or so ago and took over old Dr. Smelser's practice. Dr. Jackson is the only dentist I know who has mastered the technique of administering Novacain so painlessly that you never even feel the needle. And while you're waiting to get numb, he hands you a headset and points to a rack of cassettes. You choose the music and when he starts to drill, you turn up the volume to drown out the noise. I usually pick Wagner, because he's so loud — *The Ride of the Valkyries* is good. The Valkyries thunder around the heavens while Dr. Jackson messes around in my mouth.

I showed up in the clinic's waiting room before nine, as I had been instructed, but I was not Dr. Jackson's first appointment. That honor belonged to Melissa, who in addition to being Brian's girlfriend, is my dentist's daughter. She had come in early to get her braces checked.

If I were choosing a girlfriend for Brian — or a daughter for myself — Melissa would be high on my list. She's not a cute kid. Her nose is too chunky for prettiness, her face is splattered with freckles, and her hair is a bright orange — brighter, even, than Ruby's. And there are, of course, the braces. But she's smart and unselfconscious and independent and seems to have resisted (so far, anyway) our culture's efforts to convince her that life's most important decision is choosing the right Barbie doll. I also appreciate the matter-of-fact way she relates to Brian as a buddy, rather than as a boyfriend. She says she wants to be a botanist when she grows up, and a while back asked if she could get some practice by working in the Thyme and Seasons garden. I said an enthusiastic yes, and she showed up last weekend. She has a stout back, exactly as many hands as someone twice her age, and an admirable willingness. What's more, she brought Brian, who is more interested in lizards than lavender and isn't quite so willing. Between the two of them, they pulled several bushels of weeds, harvested the yarrow, and deadheaded the echinacea. At the end of the day, she announced that this was even more fun than going camping, and she'd love to come back and help some more.

"Hey," she said when I walked into the clinic. "Hi, China."

"Hi, Melissa," I said, and gave her a quick, affectionate hug. Unlike Brian, who believes he is too old for such things, Melissa hugged me back. I held her at arm's length so I could look at her. "Hey, that's a cool shirt."

She stuck out her chest. Her green T-shirt said *Trees Come First. People Came Later.* "Yeah," she said. "It's my birthday present from my dad. Yesterday was my birthday. I'm twelve now."

"Happy belated birthday," I said. "Twelve is a big year." At twelve, I got my first period and my first boyfriend, who turned out to be a total jerk. He threw me over for Gloria Gaye, who had curly blond hair and 32-B boobs.

"Thank you." She bent over to rebuckle the tab of her leather sandal. She straightened up, flipped her hair back, and said, "Listen, if I bring my mom to your shop, will you help her pick out some herbs? I'm digging her a garden in our backyard. It's a present for her," she added.

"A good one, too," I said. I don't know many young girls who would be willing to do the spade work.

"I like that stuff that's growing beside the patio at the back of the shop," she said. "It smells good."

"That would be rosemary," I said. "Your mother will enjoy that."

"Actually, she's my stepmom," Melissa confided. "But it's a pain to keep calling her that, so I don't bother. How about sage? It'll grow big enough to have some for Thanksgiving, won't it?"

"Sure thing. Why don't you draw a diagram of the garden you're making, with the dimensions, and we'll see what we can fit into it. My treat."

"Cool," she said. "Hey, about those frogs."

"Frogs? Frogs? What frogs?" I frowned, pretending to think. Then I snapped my fingers. "Oh, sure — you're talking about the plate of refrigerated frogs I found between the pickles and the marmalade."

She giggled. "Yeah. I hope they didn't gross you out. I was going to put a lid on them but I couldn't find one."

"After living with Brian," I said, "I think I'm gross-proof." I looked up as the clinic door opened and a petite, pretty woman came in, dressed in a stylish belted shirtwaist that matched her blue eyes. Her ash-blond hair was attractively waved but stiff with spray, like a doll's hair, and her brows and lashes had the same quality of careful artifice. I shifted, feeling uncomfortably that my jeans and plaid shirt — perfectly fine for the shop and gardens — were out of place in Mrs. Jackson's company.

She smiled at Melissa. "All finished, my dear? We'd better get you to school before you're late." Her voice was soft and cultured.

Melissa made a face. "I'd just as soon be late. It's English, and Mrs. Carlisle is a bummer." With aplomb, she swung into introductions. "Jennie, this is Brian's mom. Her name is China."

"Oh, so *you're* the one I've been hearing about." The woman gave a light laugh and extended a hand, her slim wrist decorated with bangle bracelets. "I do hope that Melissa isn't making a nuisance of herself. She told me about leaving those awful frogs in your fridge."

"That's perfectly all right," I said, trading a brief handshake. Mrs. Jackson's fingers were cool and delicate and her manicure impeccable — hardly the hand of a gardener. I wondered whether she would appreciate her stepdaughter's present. "Melissa is a girl after my own heart," I added. "Frogs and all."

Mrs. Jackson shuddered. "When I was her age, my friends and I were putting on lipstick and perfume and going to sock hops with our boyfriends — not grubbing around in the mud and weeds, looking for lizards." She gave Melissa a reproving look. "I'm not asking her to wear dresses or play with dolls — just to learn a few feminine graces. I'm afraid that most of the men in her life won't be terribly interested in lizards."

"They will be if she studies herpatology," I said. Melissa giggled. Mrs. Jackson's face tightened. The situation was saved by the appearance of Dr. Jackson, a man in his mid-fifties, tanned and slim and as youthful-looking as his wife, with wavy brown hair touched with gray.

"I thought you were off to school, Melissa." He spoke severely, but with a smile. "Aren't you going to be late?"

Melissa blew him a kiss. "We're just leaving, Pops. 'Bye." She headed for the door.

Mrs. Jackson stepped close to her husband, and put her cheek to his. Their heights matched, their bodies fitted together — a romantic, picture-book couple. He held her affectionately, his arm circling her waist. "I hope you have a good day, my dear."

She put her hand possessively on his cheek. "I shall," she said, with something like determination. Her eyes were on his. "Don't fret, Carl."

He seemed to sigh, and I noticed that he wore a worried look. "No, of course not, Jen."

Mrs. Jackson turned to me. "I enjoyed meeting you, Ms. Bayles," she said formally. "Perhaps you and Mr. Bayles might come to dinner one evening."

"That would be fun," I replied with a straight face. Actually, I wondered just what Mrs. Jackson did for fun — and I much preferred Melissa's approach to growing up female. When they had gone, I turned to Dr. Jackson. "Your daughter is very special. We enjoy having her around our house. Please let her come as often as she likes."

"Thank you," Dr. Jackson said. "As long as she isn't a pest." We went to the window and watched through the blind while Melissa climbed into Mrs. Jackson's blue Taurus. "I would do anything for that child," he said intently. "Anything in the world." He watched for a moment longer, then turned back to me. "So, China, I understand you lost that temporary we put on last week. Shall we see what we can do about it?"

Refitting the temporary required no needles, no drilling, and no Valkyries. I reconfirmed Friday's appointment to get the permanent crown installed and headed for the shop, relieved to have survived another dental ordeal.

Thyme and Seasons is located on Crockett Street, a couple of blocks from the town's main square, in a century-old building with foot-thick walls constructed of hand-cut limestone from a nearby quarry and pine floors milled from old-growth trees in East Texas. There are two retail shops in front, mine and Ruby's, and what used to be a similar-sized residential space in back, where I lived until I moved in with McQuaid. That's the space Ruby and I are converting into our tearoom. But this morning, the conversion seemed to have hit a snag.

"Look what they've done!" Ruby pointed to the newly painted beadboard wainscoting that extends partway up the stone wall in the new dining area. "It's the *wrong* green! It's hunter green, when it was supposed to be chrome green."

I bent over to inspect the paint job. "It looks fine to me, Ruby." I turned around. "If you ask me, the place looks pretty darn good."

I wasn't just saying that to calm Ruby down. The green of the wainscoting was echoed in the chintz chair seats and place mats, baskets of ivy and philodendron hung from the old cypress ceiling beams, and through the door I could see the gleam of the new stainless-steel kitchen. The *expensive* kitchen that the inspector from the Texas Department of Public Health would soon pronounce kosher. At least he ought to, seeing how many dollars we had poured into it.

"Do you really think so?" Ruby asked uncertainly. She was dressed for her tea-room-hostess role in a long blue-denim jumper, flowered print top, white stockings, and white Alice-in-Wonderland shoes, and her red hair was a mass of artfully frizzed tangles. "You don't think it's the wrong green?"

"I think it is absolutely the right green, Ruby. When's the inspector coming?" As far as I knew, we were ready — unless we had overlooked some important but obscure requirement, like a drain in the floor, or an exhaust fan. I'd gone over everything carefully, but you never know.

"The plumber has to hook us up to the water main and the sewer before the inspector comes," Ruby said. She frowned at the offending wainscoting. "Really, China, I can make them repaint it if you think —"

"For Pete's sake, leave it the way it is," I said. I looked at my watch and saw that it was after ten. "Oops! I'd better open up."

"Isn't Laurel coming today?" Ruby asked.

"At eleven." Laurel Wiley works full time in the shop, which gives me more time for the gardens. I've also started letting people know that I'm available for garden design work, to add to the income from the shop and the herb cooking and crafting classes I teach. When you're in business for yourself, you've got to find creative ways to make more out of what you already have.

Ruby followed me through the newly installed French doors that open into Thyme and Seasons. A matching pair opens from the other end of the dining area into the Crystal Cave. Our plan, you see, is to attract tourists to drop in for a cup of herb tea and a few savories and sweets and then lure them into our shops, where they will discover many fascinating items on which to spend whatever money they have left after tea-and-something. Or conversely, to attract them to the shops and then entice them into the tearoom. That's the theory, anyway.

I tied my khaki Thyme and Seasons apron over my jeans, took the cash drawer out of its hiding place under the dust rags, and put it into the antique cash register. I unlocked the front door and propped it open with a ceramic chicken planter filled with hen-and-chicks, letting in the morning sunshine and fresh air. Thyme and

Seasons is a small shop, and I use every square inch of it. Herbal soaps and cosmetics, bottles of vinegar, packages of tea, and tiny bottles of essential oils and baskets of potpourri and other herbal products, many of them handmade, fill the wooden shelves that are fitted along the walls. A rack of herb books and garden magazines occupies the space beside one of the windows, and dried herb-and-flower wreaths, red pepper *ristras*, and garlic braids hang from the ceiling. On the floor stand baskets of blood-red celosia and love-lies-bleeding, bright yellow yarrow and tansy, and silvery artemisia and baby's breath. Outside the open door a lush, fragrant rosemary tumbles onto the flagstone path that leads to the rose arbor and fountain McQuaid built a couple of years ago. That's where we would be married on Sunday — if all went according to plan. After discovering that the groom had the wrong weekend in mind, I wasn't sure just what lay ahead.

Ruby seemed calmer, now that the green-paint dilemma had been resolved. "I guess I'd better open up too," she said. "But there are still a few things to decide about the wedding. Have we agreed on Pachelbel's *Canon* for your entrance?"

"How about 'Oh, Pretty Woman'?"

Ruby's look was reproving. "If you don't get serious about this, you're not going to have any music."

"That wouldn't hurt my feelings," I said. "Anyway, I have to ask McQuaid what he thinks. It's his wedding too, you know."

"Okay," Ruby said, "but you'd better do it today. It might take a little while to find the CD you want. Also, we need to locate another punch bowl. We're having two different punches. One of them is a great lavender-mint punch, the other is spiked."

I knew which kind I'd be drinking. "The punch bowl is easy," I said. "Call Fannie Couch." Fannie is the oracle of Pecan Springs, a seventy-something lady with a daily two-hour radio talk show and a large group of dedicated fans. If she didn't have a punch bowl herself, she'd tell her listeners about it and that would take care of the problem. Last year, when the Pecan Springs Free Library was collecting books for a book-sale fund-raiser, Fannie put out the word and the books rolled in by the truckload.

"Good idea," Ruby said. "I'll call her." Reaching into the pocket of her jumper, she pulled out an envelope with about thirty items written on it. She scanned the list.

"Oh, yes. Rice. I'd like to dye it blue, for loyalty and devotion, and put it in pretty tulle bags tied with lavender ribbons. We could even have little paper hearts with China and Mike written on them, and the date. Wouldn't that be romantic?"

"No rice," I said firmly. "Birdseed. And how about putting it in Baggies instead?" I had just about reached my limit on organdy and lavender ribbons, not to mention romance.

"But birdseed has no symbolism!" Ruby waved her hands. "Rice represents fertility. It makes a lovely tribute to the goddess."

"It also makes a mess," I said, checking the answering machine for messages, "while birds go cuckoo over birdseed. And I seriously doubt that a little symbolic rice will have any effect on my reproductive system. The hands on my biological clock have just about reached midnight." I paused to answer the phone and write down the number of a customer who wanted to know whether I had any fennel plants. "I vote for Baggies of birdseed," I resumed. "If it's symbolism you're after, we can stir in some dried rosemary for remembrance and rose petals for love."

"There's an idea," Ruby said, scribbling it down. "Now, for guest favors —"

She was interrupted by the day's first customer — Phyllis Garza, a small, pretty blonde with a quick smile, who owns a day-care center. I met her a few years ago when she called to ask for some legal advice about a program that she and her husband, Jorge, had established at the church where he was the assistant minister. They were helping resident aliens qualify for American citizenship — a worthy project, if a risky one. Some of their clients had probably slipped across the Rio Grande without bothering to stop and say hello to Immigration. The project is still alive and both continue to be involved, although Jorge has left the ministry for a job as a social worker for a state agency.

Phyllis said an unsmiling hello to both of us and added, "If you've got a minute, China, I need some advice."

"Time for me to open up," Ruby said tactfully, and headed for her shop, closing the door behind her. The instant she disappeared, Phyllis pushed a business-sized envelope across the counter. "This came in the mail. Please read it and tell me what you think."

The envelope had been neatly slitted. Something in Phyllis's face told me that it would be a good idea to open it carefully and hold it by the edges. I took out a plain white sheet of paper. It bore a brief message, typed and unsigned.

Dear Mr. and Mrs. Garza,

I have evidence that you have been providing forged documents to illegal aliens. If I show it to the authorities, both of you will go to jail. I'll trade my evidence for a little teamwork. I'll be in touch with instructions.

I whistled softly. "What do I think? I think this is bad news. When did it show up?"

"One day last week," Phyllis said, "I don't know exactly when. Jorge didn't tell me about it until yesterday, and then he made me promise to keep it a secret." She leaned forward. "You know how Jorge is, China. Please don't tell him we've talked. He'd be furious with me."

I nodded. Jorge does not handle stress well, to put it mildly. I've often wondered how he got into the ministry, and more recently, into social work. I turned the envelope over. It was addressed to Mr. and Mrs. Jorge Garza and bore a San Antonio postmark. "Any idea who sent it?"

She shook her head. "You know how it is

with a project like this. You make enemies. And Jorge makes things tough. He can't seem to —" She stopped. "Lots of people might be angry with us," she finished, almost lamely.

"Is the charge true?" I raised my hand, thinking better of the question. "No, don't answer that, Phyllis. I don't need to —"

"But I *want* to answer you." Phyllis pulled herself up. "Of course it isn't true. A few immigrants might've tried to deceive us about their status, but Jorge and I have been careful to stay within the law. As for illegal papers, we'd never do anything like that. There's too much at stake. That's why I don't understand this thing about evidence. There can't *be* any evidence! It's impossible."

I shook my head. "Sorry, Phyllis, but I'm afraid it *is* possible — which has nothing to do with its being true. Imagine me as one of the enemies you mentioned. If I wanted to set you and Jorge up, all I'd have to do is forge a set of fraudulent papers in your names, then hand them over to Immigration. There's your evidence."

She stared at me. "You're kidding."

"Think about it," I said. "Has Jorge received any instructions yet on how to respond?"

"No, nothing," she said bleakly. She was silent for a moment, then burst out, "I can't believe the blackmailer wants money. Jorge's salary is better than what he used to get at the church, but it doesn't go very far. I started the day-care center last year, and it's still struggling. Where would we get money?"

That opened up a new puzzle. I glanced back at the note. "The writer says he — or she — wants 'teamwork.' What do you think that means?"

Phyllis shrugged wordlessly.

Teamwork. Where had I heard that word recently? I remembered suddenly, and things began to make sense. "You're on the City Council, aren't you, Phyllis?"

"Yes," she said, "since early this year." She managed a smile. "I'm not Hispanic, but I work in the Latino community. A group of women got together and helped me get elected, which makes me very proud. I consider myself their representative." She paused and added quietly, "The Council meetings haven't been pleasant lately. There's too much wrangling."

I knew what they'd been wrangling over. "Is it possible that Edgar Coleman sent this note?"

She pulled back, startled. "Edgar Coleman? But why would he — ?"

"Because he wanted your vote on the annexation project."

She was silent for a moment, considering. "Well, I suppose," she said, and then added bitterly, "Maybe I shouldn't say this, but Coleman is such a crook himself that he might figure he could make a crook out of me."

"Well, if Edgar Coleman wrote this blackmail letter, you won't be getting any instructions from him."

She reached for the envelope. "What do you mean?"

I put my hand over hers. "You don't know?" I asked, surprised. "You haven't read yesterday's newspaper?"

"No, I've been too busy. One of my teachers has been sick, and I've been with the children. Why? What's happened?"

"Coleman was shot to death on Sunday night."

She gave a visible start and the breath escaped from her lips. "I won't waste any pity on him," she said after a moment, "but I feel sorry for his wife. Letty is kind. She volunteers to take the older day-care children on field trips."

I let go of her hand. "You're *sure* there's

been no further communication from the blackmailer?"

"If so, Jorge didn't tell me." Phyllis frowned. "But he's been very . . . upset. He might not have told me everything." She lifted her head and smiled tightly. "And you are certainly right, China. If it *was* Edgar Coleman who wrote this letter, we have nothing to be afraid of."

"Not exactly," I said regretfully.

It would take a good homicide detective about thirty seconds to conclude that Jorge Garza belonged on the list of suspects for the murder of Edgar Coleman. And I happened to know that the man who was in charge of the investigation was a very good homicide detective indeed.

I sighed. I hated to put Phyllis on the spot because I knew that Jorge would make it rough on her. But a man was dead, and there was something she had to do, like it or not.

McQuaid certainly couldn't want the police chief's job for the glamour and excitement of the office. The Pecan Springs Police Department is located on one corner of the town square, in the basement of an old brick building that also houses the town's Parks and Utilities Department, the Tourist and Information Center, and a sizable colony of Mexican free-tailed bats that swarm out at sunset on mosquito patrol. Dorrie Hull, the receptionist and day-shift dispatcher, sat behind a wooden counter in blue jeans and a fringed Western shirt, pasting glittery gold hearts on her green-painted nails, occasionally speaking into the dispatcher's mike, and listening to a radio that sat on one corner of her desk. On top of the radio was a silver-framed photo of Buddy Holly. Smoke drifted languidly from a cigarette propped in a green ceramic ashtray shaped like a saguaro cactus.

"Oh, hi, Miz Bayles," she said, looking up. She turned down the volume on the radio. "What a coinkidinks. I just heard Fannie Couch say y'all need a coupla extra punch balls for your weddin' reception. Barbara — she's my sister — got one in her bridal show'r and she'd be pleased as punch to loan it to you." She chuckled. "D'ja get that?" She added another gold heart and lifted her fingers, admiring her art work. "Pleased as punch."

"Pleased as punch," I said. "Very clever. Tell Barbara we'd love to borrow her punch ball. She can leave it at the shop."

"Sure thing," Dorrie said gaily. She

picked up her cigarette, inhaled deeply, and waved it in the direction of McQuaid's office. "The boss is in there, but he's got the mayor and Charlie Lipman with him." She glanced at the clock. "They oughta be 'bout done, though. They been at it for the most part of an hour. Take a chair."

"I think I'll wait in the car," I said. Dorrie is a chain smoker, and the basement waiting room has no windows.

"Yeah," Dorrie said, her voice sympathetic. "I keep tellin' the chief them plastic chairs is hard on folks' tailbones. But he says chairs gotta wait till the new chief gets here." She leaned back, took another pull on her cigarette, and breathed out a cloud of smoke. "You know, some things don't make no sense to me. Like how the Council can lay out good money for sensitivity training but no money for chairs." She shook her head. "Go figger."

"It's a mystery," I remarked, and went back to my blue Datsun, parked diagonally out front. I rolled down the windows and settled back to wait. A minute later, MaeBelle Battersby strolled past in her spiffy blue polyester meter maid's uniform, buttoned up to the chin like a British bobby and proudly pushing her wheeled coin collector in front of her. MaeBelle declares that the day she put on her uniform was one of the happiest days of her life, second only to the moment she opened her first meter and heard the coins cascading like pennies from heaven into her coin collector. MaeBelle takes pride in her work.

Five minutes later, Pauline Perkins came out and strode angrily up the street in the direction of City Hall. You could almost see the steam puffing out of her ears and nostrils. Two minutes after that, Charlie Lipman emerged, tight-mouthed and grim-faced. I got out of my car.

"Good morning, Charlie," I said brightly. "How's life?" It was a rhetorical question. From the look on his face, life was not good.

" 'Mornin', China," Charlie growled. Charlie is another of McQuaid's poker pals, but my acquaintance with him goes further back, to the days when we were both *Law Review* at the University of Texas. Charlie was an energetic, competitive student with a cheerful grin and a quick comeback, but the day-in day-out grittiness of the legal business has worn off his cheeriness and given him a cynical edge.

I gave his arm a sympathetic pat. "You don't look like the sun's shining for you this morning. Something on your mind?"

Gloomily, Charlie shrugged out of his brown suit coat and slung it over his shoulder, hooking it with one finger. "Nothin' thet a good two-week border drunk wouldn't cure. I feel like I bin chewed up, spit out, an' stepped on."

Charlie does not talk like this all the time. He grew up in a wealthy suburb of Dallas, acquired a first-class education, and is perfectly capable of addressing the bench, the legislature, or a New York City client in Standard English. The rest of the time, he talks like a good old boy.

"The mayor looked a little hot under the collar," I agreed, suspecting that Pauline had done most of the chewing and spitting.

He sighed. "Hot as a ten-dollar whore on the Fourth of July."

"Is she mad at you or at McQuaid?"

"Both. You know Her Honor. You cain't tell that woman a thing she don't already know." He eyed me warily. "She said you and she had a talk last night, so I s'pose you know about this Coleman bidness."

"Some of it," I said. "Enough to make me hope Pauline has an alibi for Sunday night."

With a heavy sigh, Charlie loosened the

knot of his tie. "Pauline was howlin' like a stuck hog. Dorrie musta heard ever' word she said, which means it'll be all over the whole damn town by suppertime."

"Dorrie was dispatching, listening to Fannie, smoking a cigarette, and doing her nails, all at the same time," I said. "She might not have heard." I gave him a slant-wise look. "You're saying that Pauline *doesn't* have an alibi?"

Charlie unbuttoned his shirt collar, pulled out his handkerchief, and mopped his face. "Damn that bastard Coleman," he growled. "I cannot for the life of me figger how a woman smart enough to get herself elected mayor four times would fall into bed with a sorry sonofabitch that ain't worth spit."

I thought about Pauline, sobbing into her hanky. *Oh, what a fool I've been. What a stupid, idiotic, romantic fool.* No wonder she was worried about Charlie spilling the beans to her husband. Darryl Perkins is a kind, mild-mannered man who owns the Do-Right Used Car dealership and does right, generally speaking, by everybody. He is, however, notoriously and publicly jealous, much to Pauline's embarrassment.

"Women do inexplicable things in the name of love," I said. "How about Darryl?

83

How much does he know?"

"Love!" Charlie snorted. "Is that whut it is?" He stuffed his handkerchief into his pocket with the sad, sour look of a man who has lost whatever illusions he once had. "I sure am glad *I* never bin tempted to git married," he said gloomily. "Sure as shootin' I'd pick somebody who'd make a fool of me. I'd end up in the same perdicament as Darryl Perkins. Forced to defend my marriage when I heard my wife was in the sack with somebody else."

Aha. "Does Darryl have an alibi?"

Charlie's shoulders slumped as if the sins of the world had suddenly settled on them. "Goddamn that Coleman," he repeated softly. "Goddamn him to hell."

"I really appreciate your direct, forthcoming answers," I said. "You could've told me that this was none of my business."

He looked at me innocently. "Hell, China, you know I cain't go talkin' 'bout this case. That'ud be unethical." He paused. "Speakin' of gittin' married, ain't you 'n' McQuaid tyin' the knot on Saturday? Seems like I got an invitation on my desk somewhere."

"Sunday," I said. "Four o'clock, in the garden at the shop. We're having a reception afterward. You'll be there, won't you?"

"I ain't too crazy about weddings," he replied, "but I guess I'll make an exception in this case." He frowned. "I sure do hope you know what you're doin'. I bin in the divorce bidness long enough to know that marriage ruins a whole lotta good sex. But I'm lookin' forward to kissin' the bride." And on that happy note, he walked off.

McQuaid put down the telephone and pushed his chair around to face me. Since he had signed on for only a month or two, he'd decided not to bother with a uniform. He was wearing jeans, a plaid cotton shirt with the sleeves rolled to the elbows, a denim vest, and a silver star. He looked like Wyatt Earp.

"Early for lunch, aren't you?" he asked. "It's not even eleven-thirty. I still have three more phone calls to make before I can knock off."

"A lovely morning to you too, cupcake," I replied sweetly.

"Sorry." He relaxed and leaned back in his chair, brushing his dark hair out of his eyes. "I've been here since seven and it's been a roaring bitch the whole way."

"I know. I saw Pauline sailing down the

street with her war flags flying. After that, I ran into Charlie, who told me that neither Pauline nor Darryl have alibis for Sunday night and that Darryl knew that Coleman was blackmailing Pauline. He was gloomier than usual."

McQuaid reached for his canes and stood. "Charlie told you all that?" he asked, sounding slightly amazed.

"Well, not in so many words," I admitted. I took his cowboy hat from the deer-antler rack on the wall and held it out to him. "Did you remember that today is the day we're getting our marriage license?"

"Of course I remembered," he lied. He reached for his hat, then for me, his mouth coming down on mine. After a moment, his lips against my hair, he murmured, "Just like in the movies. Boy meets girl. Boy gets girl. Boy and girl get married and live happily ever after."

"Boy and girl get married *this* Sunday," I said, and kissed him again. There was a brief interlude that Sheila (who devours romance novels) would have called "steamy." After a moment, I murmured, "Who's your backup? Just in case you haven't made an arrest by the time we have to catch our plane."

He gave me a final husbandly peck and dropped his arms. "I took your advice. I called Ranger headquarters. They're sending somebody."

"Wonderful! That's the best news I've had all morning."

"Yeah," he said gruffly. "The more I think about this case, the more it feels like a nest of ornery rattlesnakes. Not just murder, but a mayoral sex scandal and the attempted bribery of a public official."

"Have you interviewed any of the other members of the Council?"

"Not yet," he said. He gave me a narrow look. "Why?"

"Because the mayor's vote might not have been the only one Coleman was trying to buy. Would you prefer to hear the details now or over lunch?"

He jammed his hat on his head and reached for the pair of aluminum canes that are a legacy of the shooting. "Over lunch," he growled. "I don't think I can handle any more good news on an empty stomach. But it'll have to be a quickie. I've got a hell of a lot to do."

"A quickie," I said. "The story of my life. What did you have in mind? Taco Bell?"

Instead of Taco Bell, McQuaid took me

to Bean's Bar & Grill, which is only slightly more romantic and not nearly as clean and well-lit. Located between Purley's Tire Company and the Missouri-Pacific railroad tracks, Bean's is owned and operated by Bob Godwin, who bought it a few years ago with the cash settlement from a motorcycle accident. The place looks like a Texas roadhouse, with the food up front, the fun — pool tables, dart boards, and pinball machines — in the back, and a mirrored walnut bar down one long side. It's a good place to go if you're in the mood for chicken-fried steak or barbecue. It's a bad place to go if you're counting fat grams. There is no such thing as chicken-fried lite. However, when Bob's current girlfriend, Maria Sanchez, is cooking, she makes a fine black bean soup, which I highly recommend, and her German coleslaw is crunchy and perfectly sweet-sour, with just the right amount of caraway and celery seed. Unfortunately, she doesn't cook for Bob all the time, so you take your chances.

When I had ordered, Bob leaned over and whispered, with a sly grin, "Cuttin' calories so you can get into that weddin' dress?" There's not much of Bob's gingery hair left on his head — it's all migrated to his eyebrows — and he carries a heavy paunch under his apron.

McQuaid lifted his Lone Star in salute. "You coming to the wedding, Bob?"

"Wouldn't miss it," Bob replied in his nasal East Texas twang. He poured my iced tea out of the side of the plastic pitcher, being generous with the ice. "Wanna see you make a honest woman outta this sweet li'l gal." He ran an approving eye over my plaid shirt, jeans, and tennis shoes. "She's cuter'n a speckled pup."

I must be getting used to it — I no longer bristle when Bob lavishes one of his infamous compliments on me. I smiled. "Getting married is a serious step. We didn't want to be hasty."

"Hasty?" He snorted. "Ya'll are about as hasty as a bullfrog stuck in the ice. However, I reckon it don't pay to tie the knot till you're sure. A bad marriage don't getcha nothin' but grief." He took a catsup bottle out of his apron pocket and exchanged it for the one on the table. "Take ol' Darryl, fer instance."

McQuaid became alert. He was wearing his cop face, intelligent, wary, with eyes that see everything and give nothing away. It's not a face I particularly like. "What about Darryl?"

"Why, din't you know?" Bob offered a heavy sigh. "Darryl went to Austin last week an' hired hisself a big-time divorce lawyer. Says he intends to keep Pauline from gittin' any part of Do-Right Used Cars, after whut she done." He leaned forward and added, in a stage whisper, "And with that skunk Coleman, to boot."

"Goodness gracious," I said helplessly.

"An' you know whut?" he went on. "I don't blame Darryl one li'l bit. Pauline was my wife, I'd be hoppin' mad too." He narrowed his eyes at me. "Let that be a lesson to you, young lady. You make your man jealous enough, he might just pick up a gun an' go horn-tossin' wild."

McQuaid gave him a hard look. "Are you saying that Darryl Perkins picked up a —"

"Ain't sayin' nothin'," Bob replied sternly. "You ain't gonna trip me up with them cop tricks of yers." He picked up the menus. "But I'll tell you one thing. No woman who'd shack up with a polecat like Coleman is gonna get *my* vote. And from whut I hear, ever' single man in this town feels the same damn way." And with that parting shot, off he marched.

"So it's all over town," I said. "Poor Pauline. She'll never live this down."

"Poor Pauline, my foot." McQuaid was scowling. "How come she didn't tell me that Darryl's already filed for divorce?"

"Because it might not be true," I said, stirring my iced tea. "Or maybe she doesn't know." If Bill Gates wants to improve the speed of his computer network, he should come and study our grapevine. It works so fast that half of Pecan Springs can know something before the people who are immediately involved have the slightest inkling of what has happened. "You haven't talked to Darryl yet?"

"He's in Fredericksburg, delivering a car. I've left a message for him to come in." He frowned. "But Darryl's pretty meek. Somehow, I can't picture him shooting somebody, even in a fit of temper."

"Not even in a fit of *jealous* temper? You don't remember the time he took out after that old boyfriend of Pauline's and all but chased him out of town?"

"Well, maybe." McQuaid dipped a nacho into a bowl of salsa, tasted it, and picked up a bottle of hot sauce that was sitting on the table. He likes his salsa so hot that it sears all the way down. "So. What do you know that I don't know?" He shook hot sauce into the salsa. "How come you think I have to interview all the other members of the Council?"

"Not all," I said. "Just some."

"Why not all?"

"Because two of the seven Council members voted for Coleman on the first reading of the annexation proposal. Right?"

"I guess so. I wasn't keeping score."

I wasn't either, but I'd called City Hall and gotten a secretary to tell me who had voted for and against. "Take my word for it," I said. "In order to get the development annexed, Coleman had to get a majority — four votes. He already had two in his pocket, so he needed two more, three to be on the safe side. If he got Pauline's vote, he was down to two. If he got Phyllis Garza, he'd need —"

McQuaid scowled. "What makes you think he went after Phyllis Garza?"

I opened my shoulder bag and took out the plastic folder containing the letter and envelope. "Phyllis brought this to me this morning. I had a tough time persuading her to turn loose of it, but I knew you'd need it — and if she took it back to Jorge, it might disappear." I laid it on the table. "It's been handled by both Phyllis and Jorge, so I doubt that you'll find any usable prints. But you might want to give it a try."

He grasped the significance of the letter on the first reading. "You think Coleman wrote this?"

"Last night, Pauline said that Coleman wanted 'teamwork' — the same word this writer uses. It seems like a pretty substantial coincidence." I paused. "Phyllis said at first that Jorge hadn't heard anything more from the blackmailer, but when I questioned her, she admitted she wasn't sure whether he had or not."

"I see," McQuaid said slowly. He looked at me sideways. "You know the Garzas pretty well, don't you?"

"I helped them get a few legal issues straightened out when they first started their alien assistance program. I know Phyllis better than Jorge."

"Does either of them have what it takes to kill somebody?"

"That's an unanswerable question," I said bleakly. "How can you know how far a person will go to protect somebody or something he — or she — loves?" There are human imponderables here that no forensic psychologist can unravel. People do things when their livelihoods or their loved ones are threatened that they couldn't imagine doing under other circumstances. "But if I'd killed Coleman, I sure as heck wouldn't volunteer this letter." I paused, thinking. "Of course, it was Phyllis who brought it in, not Jorge. I told her about Coleman's murder, and I swear it was a surprise to her."

McQuaid got my point. "What about Jorge? Could he have done something like this?"

I hate being a stoolie on my friends. "I suspect he isn't an easy man to live with," I said reluctantly. "Phyllis has told me enough, now and then, to give me the idea that they've had their share of marital problems. And there was that sad business about his leaving the ministry and getting a job as a social worker, which she never tried to explain." I met McQuaid's eyes. "I don't know for sure that there has been any domestic violence, but it's possible."

"Yeah," McQuaid said dryly. "Ministers and social workers are like cops. The last ones you'd suspect of beating their wives. But it happens."

"Do your best to protect Phyllis," I said, not liking to think what Jorge was going to say — or do — when he found out that the cops had possession of the letter. True, Phyllis knew what I intended to do with it when she gave it to me. But that didn't keep me from feeling as if I'd betrayed her.

"I'll try," he said. "But this is a murder investigation. If Garza had anything to do with Coleman's death, we'll find it out." He looked at me. "Do you happen to know which of the others Coleman might've tried to get to?"

I took out my notes and put them on the table. There were two names in the "for" column and five names in the "against" column, including Pauline's and Phyllis's.

McQuaid ran his finger down the "against" list. "Blast," he muttered. "Guess I'm going to have to talk to all of them." He looked at his watch. "Bob better get out here pretty quick. I've got to get back to the office."

"That's the trouble these days," Bob said, appearing with our plates. "Ever'-body's in too big of a hurry to chew right, an' when they get the bellyache, they blame the food." He looked at me. "Maria says to tell you that she dropped a punch bowl by your store a little while ago. She heard you needed one."

"Thanks," I said. To McQuaid's questioning look, I added, "For the reception. Which reminds me. We have to decide about music for the ceremony."

"How 'bout 'Boot Scootin' Boogie'?" Bob said. "That'ud gitcha down the aisle fast." He two-stepped off, singing it.

"I don't want to think about music," McQuaid said. "Whatever you decide will be okay with me."

"Ruby says it should be Pachelbel's *Canon*. Would you like that?"

McQuaid looked confused. "Isn't that the one with guns and bells?"

"You're probably thinking of the *1812 Overture*," I said tactfully. "That has cannons in it."

"Oh." He picked up his knife. "Well, that's how much I know about music. You choose. Come on, let's eat. I've got to get back to work."

"If I choose," I said, "it'll be something like 'Devil With a Blue Dress On.' "

"Great," he said, chewing fast. "That'll work. And listen, let's leave the license until tomorrow, okay? I probably should've let you go out to lunch by yourself and sent Dorrie across the street for a burger for me. This is a murder investigation. I haven't got time to be sociable."

"For the recessional," I said darkly, "we can play 'All My Exes Live in Texas.' "

Chapter Four

Lavender has been the royal herb of Europe. Charles VI of France (who was periodically convinced that he was made of glass) insisted on having cushions stuffed with lavender to sit on wherever he went. . . . Queen Elizabeth I of England commanded that the royal table never be without conserve of lavender . . . and is reputed to have been a great afficionado of lavender tea. This was used extensively for centuries to relieve headaches of nervous origin.

Lavender, Sweet Lavender
Judyth A. McLeod

Lavender has an especially good use for all griefes and paines of the head and brain.

Paradisi in Sole Paradisus Terrestris, 1609
John Parkinson

After lunch, Ruby and I left Laurel to keep an eye on both shops and adjourned to the

97

tearoom to make centerpieces — small pots of lavender and other herbs set into plastic containers wrapped with batting to make them look puffy, then covered with chintz in colors that coordinated with the tablecloths. They would do double duty for the reception and for the grand opening later.

"Eat your heart out, Martha Stewart," I said, tying a red ribbon around a puffy chintz-covered pot. In the background, providing an accompaniment to our work, was the hammering and muffled conversation of the two young men who were installing the pantry shelves. In the foreground sat Khat, the large and elegant seal-point Siamese that lives in the shop. I took him to live with me when McQuaid and I moved in together, but that didn't last very long. Khat and Howard Cosell are not a match made in heaven.

"What we need," Ruby said, "is to write the names of the herbs and their symbolism on little white cards. You know, sage for wisdom, mint for virtue, rosemary for fidelity, parsley for . . ." She frowned. "What does parsley represent?"

"The woman of the house is boss," I said. In one graceful motion, Khat sprang up on the table to see what we were doing.

"No, seriously."

"Yes, seriously. That's what it means. They used to say that about a lot of herbs, actually. 'Rosemary grows where the woman is master,' that sort of thing. Back when herbs were mostly used as medicinals, a woman who grew them knew her stuff, poison-wise. You probably didn't want to mess with her."

"Well, we certainly can't write that," Ruby said, moving her material aside so Khat would have a place to sit. "McQuaid wouldn't want people thinking you have the upper hand, even if it is just a joke."

"McQuaid is too busy with his murder investigation to think about anything else," I said. "Over lunch, he added more names to his suspect list. It now includes all but two members of the City Council." Purring throatily, Khat lay down, arranged his paws, and gave us a penetrating Siamese stare.

"The City Council!" Ruby looked baffled. "Why?"

"Because Coleman seems to have been applying a little covert leverage to get the votes he wanted." The minute the words were out of my mouth, I regretted them. Giving necessary information to an investigating officer is one thing. Gossip is another. I tucked some basil into a pot and added, to cover my blunder, "Basil means 'the enemy is near.' You could write that down."

"Ha ha," Ruby said. "Where do you get all this weird stuff?"

"That's not weird," I said, glad of a new subject. "The Victorians had all sorts of meanings for herbs and flowers. They made up floral dictionaries and —"

The French door flew open and Laurel Wiley staggered in with a tall stack of punch bowls. "Where do you want these?" she asked, holding the top one with her chin.

Ruby's lips moved as she counted. "*Six* punch bowls?"

"And that's not all," Laurel said as I took the bowls and put them on the floor. She straightened up and flipped her brown braid back over her shoulder. "There are five more in the shop, and more on the way. I just got another couple of phone calls."

"Well, for heaven's sake," Ruby said plaintively, "tell them we don't need any more! I hope these have names on them."

"Some do and some don't," I said, inspecting.

Ruby groaned.

"I'll tell them," Laurel said, and disappeared. Khat, imagining that she had gone to find him a treat, leaped off the table and went after her, his black tail in the air.

"I guess asking Fannie to find punch bowls wasn't a very good idea," Ruby said.

"It was *too* good an idea," I replied. I looked at the chintz-covered pots lined up on the table. "How many of these do we have to make?"

"A dozen." Ruby picked up another pot and began to work. "What's this about Coleman and the Council and leverage?"

Rats. I thought I'd successfully dodged that bullet. "I'm sorry, Ruby. I shouldn't have said anything."

"Actually, it's not a surprise." Ruby tied a green ribbon around a pot of sage. "I ran into Pauline when I went to lunch. She was sitting by herself on the patio at Dos Amigas, looking wretched. I sat down with her and two minutes later she whipped out her hanky and started to cry."

"And the more she cried," I guessed, "the more she talked."

"That's Pauline," Ruby said philosophically. "She's a very tough lady, but she's got no *give*. When something gets to her, she goes to pieces. She's afraid Darryl's in trouble. She wasn't clear about the details, but it has something to do with Coleman and the annexation proposal and her being a romantic fool. I got the impression that Darryl had a good reason to be jealous of Coleman." She looked at me. "McQuaid doesn't think *Darryl* did it, does he?"

"McQuaid doesn't think anything yet," I said. "The investigation is just getting underway."

She tucked tissue paper around the pot and gathered the chintz with her hands. "So what's this about a list of suspects?"

Since she already knew about Pauline and Darryl, it wouldn't hurt to tell her a little more of the story. "Well," I said cautiously, "it may be that Coleman was killed because he was attempting to blackmail somebody."

"Why am I not surprised?" Ruby murmured, looping the rim of the pot with a lavender ribbon. "Like, a Council member, maybe?"

"Possibly."

"Like Phyllis Garza? Was that why she was here this morning? I saw her when she left, and she looked pretty upset. What did he do, send her a letter? Call her on the phone?"

"Ruby," I said, "will you *stop?* I really don't think McQuaid would like it if I said anything else."

Ruby was silent for a minute, regarding her handiwork. "If you wanted me to," she said at last, "I could find out whether Coleman tried to get Darla McDaniels's vote. I went to school with her. We were both on the cheerleading squad our junior year and we had a crush on the quarterback." She giggled. "But *she* married the jerk."

"You were a cheerleader?"

"Sis boom bah."

"Knowing you, I find that hard to believe."

Ruby tossed her frizzed curls. "I don't see why. I mean, I was a perfectly normal Texas teenager."

"That's the part that's hard to believe," I said. "And Darla McDaniels was a cheerleader too? She must have . . . well, changed." Darla is on the high side of one-eighty.

"We've all changed," Ruby replied. "But we were good friends once. I'm sure she'll open up to me about Coleman. You should come too, though, and hear what she says."

"Actually," I said, "I'm not sure it's a good idea for us to talk to anybody. McQuaid won't want us messing around with his investigation."

Ruby frowned. "Maybe so. But if Mc-

Quaid asks Darla whether Coleman was blackmailing her, she'll say no. I mean, *I* would." At my questioning glance, she added, defensively, "Well, I would. If I said yes, I got a letter or a phone call or whatever from that turkey, McQuaid would put me on the suspect list immediately, which would mean that he'd want to interrogate me and check my alibi and all that police stuff. And if Coleman was blackmailing me, it means I've done something I don't want anybody to know about, so I wouldn't be anxious to tell the cops anything." She tossed her red curls, warming to her subject. "On the other hand, if I'd killed Coleman to keep him quiet, do you think I'd tell the police he was blackmailing me? Not on your life. That would be criminally stupid."

"Dang," I said. Sometimes Ruby's logic amazes me.

"In either case," she went on, "it would be a heck of a lot easier to deny everything and save myself a lot of grief, and maybe some public exposure I couldn't afford. Take it from me, China, McQuaid's investigation will still be at ground zero on Sunday afternoon. He'll probably show up for the wedding, but you can forget about the honeymoon. Unless *we* help."

"He's called the Rangers," I said. "They're sending an officer. That ought to be enough. 'One riot, one Ranger,' remember?"

"A Ranger?" Ruby gave me a scornful look. "That's not the kind of help he needs. Anyway, it's just another reason to worry. Have you ever heard of a police officer — especially an *interim* officer, taking off on his honeymoon and leaving a Ranger in charge of a big investigation? Why, it's against the code of honor, or whatever they call it."

I hated to admit it, but Ruby was probably right. McQuaid would leave only if he had a suspect in custody and either a viable confession or a strong evidence-based case that the county attorney could go to work on. And even then —

"Anyway, this isn't a case for the police, and you know it." Ruby looked at me. "Did you ever, in all the years you practiced as a criminal attorney, hear of a single living soul who actually volunteered to be a suspect in a murder investigation?" She answered her own question with an emphatic shake of her head. "Of course not. Phyllis would never in the world have gone to McQuaid on her own, or to *any* policeman. Darla isn't going to be any more forthcoming — to an official investigator, that is. But we are not officials. We are not investigators, public or private. We are sincere, helpful people who might be able to get our friends out of a jam. Do you see?"

"I do," I conceded, "although a sincere helpful person who rats to the cops is a pretty lousy friend. Anyway, I don't know where that leaves us, as far as the honeymoon is concerned. McQuaid still has to interrogate every single —"

"McQuaid can do anything he wants," Ruby said, "any time he wants. Meanwhile, we'll just poke around a little bit and see what we can find out that might expedite his investigation. There's no law against a private citizen asking a few questions of her friends, is there?" She had a gleam in her eye.

"Not as long as the private citizen doesn't obstruct justice," I said cautiously. "But on the whole, it's not a good idea to get in the way of an official —"

"Right. We won't stand in front of any police cars." Ruby pursed her lips. "Really, China, I should think you'd be anxious to get this case wrapped up so that you and McQuaid could get on with your lives."

"Well, I am. But —"

"Good." Ruby smiled. "The Council has seven members. Why are there only five on your list?"

I took out my two "fors" and five "againsts" and explained the arithmetic. "McQuaid is concentrating on Pauline and Phyllis," I said, ticking them off. "Which leaves three. Darla McDaniels, Winnie Hatcher, Wanda Rathbottom." I frowned, thinking that I knew all of these people, one way or another. Pecan Springs is a small town.

"Wait a minute," Ruby said. "Why couldn't one of the 'fors' have killed him? Maybe he laid a little blackmail on them before the first vote was taken."

"Why didn't I think of that?" I asked.

"Because you subconsciously wanted to keep the list as short as possible, hoping to speed things up." Ruby had shifted into her brisk, take-charge mode. "Who are they?"

"Ken Bowman," I said. "And Billie Jean Jones."

"Well, that's easy," Ruby said. "Ken Bowman lives just across the street from me. He can help me jump-start my car tomorrow morning."

"Your Toyota?" I asked, surprised. "It's almost new. What's wrong with it?"

"Whatever it is," Ruby said with a twinkle, "it will go wrong first thing in the morning, just as Ken is on his way to work. And Billie Jean works at the House of Beauty. You're going to get your hair done before the wedding, aren't you? Why don't you make an appointment with her?"

"I suppose I could, although I was thinking maybe I'd just shampoo it." I rubbed a strand of hair, thinking that it felt pretty dry. I've started to think about getting it frosted, to hide the streak of gray that runs down the left side, but I never manage to find the time.

"You will get a style cut," Ruby said emphatically, "*and* a manicure."

"A manicure! Not on your life."

"A style cut, a manicure, and a facial," Ruby said. "That should give you plenty of time to give Billie Jean the third degree." Pointing to Winnie Hatcher's name on the list, she ignored my strangled protest. "And don't forget that Winnie offered to give us roses for the wedding. So we've got a good excuse to go talk to her."

I shook my head. "If Winnie got mad enough, she wouldn't hesitate to bash Edgar Coleman with anything she could reach. But she wouldn't *shoot* him. She's led the anti-gun lobby at the legislature every session for the last ten." Not that it's made any difference. Texans would sooner give up their wives than their guns.

"I agree," Ruby said, "but Winnie is a very smart woman and knows everybody and his nephew, so we ought to start with her. And that just leaves Wanda Rathbottom." She gave me a meaningful look.

When Ruby revs into high gear, you either have to climb on her bandwagon or get out of the way before she careens over you. "I guess I can talk to Wanda," I said. "But we're not exactly bosom buddies. I doubt that I'll be able to get anything out of her." Wanda Rathbottom owns a nursery called Wanda's Wonderful Acres, which makes me her competitor — in her mind, anyway. We've never been very friendly. We've gotten even less so since I took over her job editing the Home and Garden page for the *Enterprise*. No matter that Hark fired her before he hired me. The way Wanda sees it, I'm the one who killed her promising career as a garden columnist.

"You'll just have to be creative," Ruby said. "If she acts nervous and suspicious, that tells us something."

"Tells us what? I might be nervous and suspicious if somebody came around asking me nosy questions about my private business. And Wanda is a nervous and suspicious woman by nature. She sees a bee in every blossom, and it's always about to sting her."

Ruby waved her hand. "You'll do fine. Just pretend she's a hostile witness, and you've got her on the stand in front of a judge and a jury. All your old grilling tricks will come back to you. Anyway, what we're trying to do is eliminate people. We'll let McQuaid worry about getting the confession." Ruby looked at her watch. "You call the House of Beauty and make an appointment with Billie Jean, and I'll give Winnie a buzz and see if we can drive over there this afternoon."

"You won't hear me objecting to a tour of Winnie's garden," I said, "but the wedding isn't until Sunday. We can't cut roses this early."

"We're not going to cut the roses *today*, silly. We're just taking a look. That way, we'll know how many and what colors Winnie has, and somebody can get them later. And while we're there, of course, we can discreetly find out what she knows about Edgar Coleman." She lined up the last chintz-covered pot. "There," she exclaimed. "All done! China, we make a great team. When we decide to do something, it gets done right, with no dawdling."

"I doubt that McQuaid will be so enthusiastic about our detective work," I said. "We'd better stop by the office and let him know what we're up to. We probably won't cause him any trouble, but I don't want to run the risk."

Ruby frowned. "Is that really necessary — before the fact, I mean? We're simply gathering information. If we find out anything, sure, we'll tell him. If we don't, what he doesn't know won't make him mad."

Ruby's response made a certain kind of sense. "Just the same," I said, "I'd feel better if I talked to him." I was betting that he'd say no, which would put an end to Ruby's nonsense. I could go back to getting ready for the wedding and leave the investigating to my future husband. Husband? I shivered. I was still having trouble getting used to the idea.

"Excuse me," Laurel said, opening the doors again. "I hate to keep interrupting you when you've got so much to do, but we're piling up punch bowls out here. At last count, there were eleven, plus a couple of sets of crystal cups with matching trays. Somebody even left a big bag of plastic tableware and a bunch of paper peonies sprinkled with glitter. Where do you want me to put this stuff?"

"Eleven!" Ruby cried. "Plus six — that makes seventeen punch bowls!" She shook her head. "It's out of control. I feel like the Sorcerer's Apprentice with his brooms and buckets."

"I thought you were going to tell people we don't need any more punch bowls," I said to Laurel. "This is a *pain*."

"I *am* telling them," Laurel replied earnestly. "But folks are leaving them outside the door and driving away. I guess I'd better put up a sign, huh? *No more punch bowls, please*."

"Definitely," I said. "Or hire a sorcerer to get rid of them."

Ruby drove her Toyota to the square and parked in front of the police station, next to a green pickup with two bales of hay in the back and a bumper sticker that declared "Oprah is the only mad cow in Texas." But Ruby was more interested in the car on the right.

"Isn't that a Ranger car?" she asked, pointing at the discreetly marked blue Ford.

"McQuaid's backup must have got here

already," I said, getting out. "Maybe there are some new developments." Maybe they had wrapped up the case already, and Ruby and I could go back to other important things.

"I'll wait," Ruby said. "I can read my book. Maybe I'll get some ideas for our investigation." She hauled out a copy of *N Is For Noose*. Kinsey Milhone is Ruby's favorite fictional character, which is probably why we embarked on this mission this afternoon. When Ruby grows up, she wants to be Kinsey and live in a remodeled garage and have alphabetical adventures. I tell her that she wouldn't like the life, but she doesn't believe me.

Dorrie was still smoking and playing the radio, but now she was reading as well. The cover of her book featured a beautiful young woman wearing a few tattered rags of leopard skin, clutched in the muscular grip of a Sylvester Stallone look-alike with a handsome black ponytail tied with a raven's feather. She glanced up long enough to see that it was me.

"He's in there," she said, tilting her head toward the chief's door. She turned a page. "Him an' the Ranger are talkin' about the Coleman case."

"I don't suppose he'd mind if I interrupted him for a minute. I need to ask him something."

Dorrie looked doubtful. "The *chief* wouldn't," she said. "The Ranger might. He looks like the kind who —"

But I was already on my way to the door. I rapped lightly and opened it.

McQuaid and the Ranger were seated at the conference table. McQuaid was in working clothes, a blue shirt, jeans, and scuffed boots. The Ranger looked as if he'd just come from dress parade, with creases down the front of his starched Western-style shirt; gray polyester Western pants, snug-fitting and also sharply creased; and a spit-and-polish finish on his shiny black boots. On the table in front of McQuaid was an untidy litter of handwritten notes on odd bits of paper, napkins, and the backs of matchbooks. Arranged with precision in front of the Ranger were two pencils, a yellow pad, a lap top computer, and his white Stetson.

"Oh, hi, China," McQuaid said. He leaned back with a slight grin. "Guess who."

The Ranger jumped up and stuck out his hand. "China Bayles! Hey, girl, you *are* a sight for sore eyes."

"Good to see you again, Marvin," I said.

There is something about Marvin Wallace's enthusiasm that always strikes me as phony, and I *detest* it when an ol' boy calls me a "girl." But I usually try to remind myself that this is just Marvin's style and I shouldn't take it personally. McQuaid and Marvin had served together on the Houston police force, before McQuaid left to get his criminology degree and Marvin became a Ranger. Marvin drops in at the house when he's in our area and spends a couple of hours nagging McQuaid about going back into law enforcement. I'm sure he was thrilled down to the toes of his polished boots when he heard that McQuaid had accepted a temporary assignment with the Rangers last February and was now serving as Pecan Springs' interim chief. It must have given him hope.

"China and I are getting married," McQuaid said, putting an arm around my shoulders.

"This weekend," I added.

Marvin was startled. His glance went from me to McQuaid and back again. "This . . . weekend?" His tone implied that I must be mistaken.

"Right," I said, pleasantly cheerful. "Sunday at four. Would you like to come?"

Marvin's eyes narrowed slightly. "Thanks,

but no thanks," he said stiffly. "I don't make personal plans when I'm on assignment. The case comes first."

"Well —" McQuaid said. He dropped his arm uncomfortably, looking as if he were being measured and found to be a half-inch too short. "I mean, sure it does. On the other hand —" He grinned, half-abashed. "I mean, a wedding's pretty important too."

I appreciated McQuaid's dilemma, trapped between his temporary allegiance to his badge and his long-term commitment to his soon-to-be-wife, but I also needed to be sure that Marvin knew exactly where things stood.

"Our wedding," I said firmly, "has been in the works for several months, long before Edgar Coleman got himself shot to death. The arrangements have been made, the food's planned, and friends are coming from out of town. Our honeymoon is finalized, too. We're flying to Hawaii early Monday morning." Marvin was looking grim, so I tried to ease the tension a little by fluttering my hands and swaying my hips in an imitation of the hula. "Aloha, blue Hawaii," I warbled.

Marvin was not amused. He turned to McQuaid. "Sounds like we've got somewhat of a problem."

You've got somewhat of a problem, Marvin, I thought darkly. But I put on a bantering smile. "Hey, come on. Where's the old confidence? Where's the Ranger spirit? There isn't a killer in Texas who can buffalo you two guys. This is only Tuesday, for Pete's sake. Sunday is five whole days away. By then, you'll have the perp in jail and the case on the county attorney's desk."

As a cheerleader, I thought I sounded pretty darn good, but Marvin was not moved.

"You can tell a professional lawman by his dedication to the case," he said. He gave McQuaid a tight smile. "I've always considered you a pro's pro. The best there is, in fact. But if a wedding is more important than bringing a killer to justice —" He shrugged. "Maybe it would be a good idea if I brought another man in from Austin. If China keeps insisting that you get off the case before it's wrapped up, I sure as hell don't want to be left shorthanded. Looks like it's shaping up to be an important investigation."

"Just a damn minute," I said hotly. "Who says I'm insisting that McQuaid get off the case? I didn't say —"

"China doesn't tell me what to do," McQuaid growled. He folded his arms with a stern look. "And it's *my* case, remember? If anybody else comes in from Austin, it'll be on my say-so, not yours."

"Okay, okay," Marvin said soothingly. He gave me a patronizing smile. "I'm sure you've got plenty of wedding details to keep you busy, China — dresses, flowers, food. All that great girl stuff." He glanced at his watch. "And we're wasting time, McQuaid. While we're talking, the killer could strike again."

"Oh, right," I said, sarcastic. "This killer had it in for Edgar Coleman. He's not interested in anybody else."

"China," McQuaid said warningly. He put his hand on my arm and lowered his voice. "You wanted to talk to me?"

"Yes," I said, also in a low tone. "It's about the case. I've been thinking that I ought to talk to —"

"Let's go over these suspects one more time." Marvin sat down in front of his computer and hit a key. The screen blinked into life. "I want to be sure I've got their backgrounds straight when I interview them."

I tried again. "I've made a list of the Council members who —"

McQuaid squeezed my arm. "Okay if we put it off until tonight?" His tone was apologetic, and his eyes asked me to understand.

"Glad I got to see you again, China," Marvin said, addressing his computer screen.

"Likewise, I'm sure," I said furiously.

I turned on my heel and walked smack into the half-open door.

"What did you do to your *nose?*" Ruby asked when I got into the car five minutes later.

"Nothing," I said in a muffled voice, and slammed the door so hard that the Toyota rocked.

Ruby tucked her book into her purse. "Then why are you holding those ice cubes to it? And what's with the door-slamming?"

"None of your beeswax," I said. The paper towel was starting to disintegrate and icy water was running down my forearm. When I had my accident in the barn earlier in the summer, I had banged up my nose — this felt like déjà vu. "Let's get the hell out of here. We're wasting time."

Ruby turned the key in the ignition. "So

McQuaid said yes, huh? He wants us to expedite this investigation?"

"Who cares what McQuaid wants," I muttered. "He can't tell me what to do. And Marvin doesn't need to patronize me."

"Marvin who?" Ruby asked.

"Marvin Spit-and-Polish Wallace," I said. "The Wonder Ranger." I leaned my head against the back of the seat, squeezing my eyelids shut to keep the tears from leaking. My nose was hot and throbbing, my face hurt, and I had one hell of a headache. I was going to walk down the aisle wearing an ivory dress and matching black and blue shiners.

"So what are we going to do?" Ruby asked.

"We're going to Winnie's house," I snarled. The ice cubes were melting all over my jeans. I opened the window and tossed them out. "Drive, damn it, and stop asking questions. We've got suspects to interview, and Sunday's getting closer by the minute."

Chapter Five

The god of silence is represented as a young man, half-naked, holding a finger to his lips and with a white rose in the other hand. A white rose used to be sculptured over the door of banqueting rooms to remind guests that they should never repeat outside the things they had heard in their festive moments. The same emblem was once carved on confessionals. Sometimes actual white roses were hung by a host over the tables where he entertained his guests — the origin of the phrase sub rosa, *"under the rose." The phrase goes back in English at least until the time of Henry VII.*

The Meaning of Flowers
Claire Powell

Winnie Hatcher was one of the first people I met when I came to Pecan Springs. She dropped in at the shop on the day I opened and offered to introduce me at the next meeting of the Myra Merryweather Herb

Guild. We're not friends, exactly — more like friendly acquaintances. Winnie is involved in so many activities — the City Council, the local environmental group, the anti-gun lobby, her garden — that she doesn't have a lot of time for friends.

Winnie lives in an older neighborhood, not far from CTSU, on a street shaded by massive pecan trees and wide-spreading live oaks, heavily populated by squirrels and boisterous grackles. Driving past, you probably wouldn't give her house a second glance. It's a small cottage fronted by a patch of close-clipped grass about the size of a green potholder, bordered by a ragged fringe of bright yellow day lilies. The house itself is weathered gray, with red shutters that could use a coat of paint and a green screen door with the bottom cut out so Winnie's multitudinous cats can come and go. What is special and different about Winnie is hidden behind the house, where it can't be seen from the street.

Ruby knocked at the front door, waited a few minutes, then opened it and called. "Yoo-hoo. Anybody home?" When no one answered, we went around to the picket fence at the side and Ruby called again. "Winnie, we're here."

"Come on in," a deep, almost masculine

voice boomed out. "And mind you latch the gate. I haven't got around to fixing the hinge."

Winnie has been meaning to fix that hinge for years. But a sagging gate doesn't detract from the beauty of the rose bower overhead, covered by delicate butter-cream blossoms brushed with apricot, and beyond that, a garden glowing with the pale, muted pastels of old roses, blended with the abundant soft blues and greens of Winnie's carefully tended perennial borders. It's like stepping into a jewel box heaped with magnificent opals and pearls and topazes.

"Oh, lovely!" Ruby exclaimed, gazing up at the rose-covered arch. She took a deep breath. "And what a wonderful scent!"

"Fine, isn't it?" Winnie said happily, coming toward us down the gravel path with a basket of spent blooms in one hand and clippers in the other, trailed by a black cat and three black-and-white kittens. She was dressed in baggy khaki pants and a faded green shirt with one sleeve ripped at the elbow. Her straggly gray hair was half-covered with a red bandanna, and she wore another one, loose and damp with sweat, looped around her neck. Her face was sun-browned and freckled, and her skin was almost as weathered as the shingles on her house. Winnie pays more attention to her plants than to herself, but beneath that seasoned exterior is a sharply tenacious intellect. I didn't think Coleman would have been dumb enough to have tried for her vote, but she might know something that would help us.

I sniffed at one of the climber's musky blossoms. "I'd love to have a few of these for my bouquet, Winnie." I spotted some lavender and picked several stems. Sniffing it can sometimes help a headache.

"Take all you like. It blooms like a sonofagun right up to frost." She reached up to clip a couple of spent flowers and dropped them into her basket. "It came from my granny's garden in South Carolina. Dates back to before the Civil War. It's a Juane Desprez." Winnie pronounced it Zhohn day-*pray.*

"Amazing." Ruby's eyes widened in surprise. "It looks awfully healthy to be almost a hundred and fifty years old!"

"Not *this* plant, Ruby." Winnie grinned, showing a chipped front tooth. "Although this one is no spring chicken either." She stripped off her gloves and dropped them into the basket. "My momma brought it back as a cutting from Charleston after

Pearl Harbor, when she went East to see my daddy off to war." She glanced at me and frowned. "What'd you do to your nose, China?"

"I walked into a door," I said briefly.

She came closer, squinting at my face. "People'll think somebody socked you a good one."

"That's their problem," I said.

"Oh, yeah? Could be yours. Well, are we going to stand out here in the sun, or are we going to sit on the porch and have a cup of tea like civilized folks?" She brushed a bee aside. "I can give you some rose petal jam cakes. I made them for tomorrow's herb guild meeting."

"Jam cakes?" Ruby said quickly. "Terrific!" Winnie's rose petal jam cakes are unique. She swears she'll die clutching the recipe, and the only way anybody will get it is to pry it out of her dead fingers.

"Good," Winnie said and added, with a glance at me, "And maybe we can fix it so you can stand up in front of Maude Porterfield and say 'I do' without looking like a victim of domestic violence. Wouldn't be good for the groom's reputation. Yours either."

"You know," Ruby said, "I never thought about plants having birthdays." She gave a rueful laugh. "Most of mine don't make it out of their babyhood, poor things. My thumbs are both purple, not green."

"Winnie's roses are antiques," I said. "They've had a lot of birthdays." I was grateful to Ruby for changing the subject. The less said about my nose, the better. At Ruby's questioning glance, I added, "Technically, a rose is antique if it was introduced before the Civil War."

Winnie pulled off her red neckerchief and mopped her face with it. "I've got some that are older than that." She pointed to an erect, bushy shrub with dark gray-green foliage, covered with bright red hips — the small, flask-shaped fruit that some roses produce. "That *gallica,* for instance. The Apothecary Rose. Been around since the Middle Ages."

Ruby looked at the bush with respect. "Is this what Brother Cadfael would have grown in his garden?"

"Brother Cadfael?" Winnie asked. "Never heard of him." She bent over to pick a yellow leaf and held it up critically, examining it. "Damned black spot," she muttered. "One whiff of my baking soda spray, and you're history."

"Brother Cadfael was invented by Ellis Peters," I explained. "He's a fictional twelfth-century monk who grows herbs and solves murders."

Winnie headed toward a ramshackle back porch, its screen door canopied by fat pink cabbage roses. "I never read murder mysteries." She opened the door and set her basket on a bench. "Real ones are hard enough to stomach."

"Oh, right," Ruby said. "Even when it's somebody like Coleman."

Winnie made a face. "We won't talk about him. Good riddance to bad rubbish, as my momma used to say."

Ruby laughed a little. "Yes, the way I hear it, he was asking for trouble. I guess you know him from his Council appearances, huh?"

Winnie acted as if she hadn't heard. "If your Brother Cadfael grows roses," she said to me, "I might be interested in reading about him. Back in the Middle Ages, roses were medicine, you know." She pulled the bandanna off her head and ran her hands through her hair so that it stood up in damp gray spikes, giving her the look of an overage punk rocker. "*Good* medicine, too. If somebody had a heart problem, or a stomach ailment or a fever or trouble with his liver, he'd be treated with roses." She gestured toward a table at the far end of the screened porch, centered with a glass bowl weighted with crystal marbles and filled with large floppy white roses. "You girls sit there and look out over the garden and decide what you'd like to cut for the wedding. I'll be right back with the jam cakes and tea."

We settled ourselves in the wicker chairs, and I glanced around. The porch might have been a set for a 1930's movie, with an old oak icebox standing against one wall and a bench with a white enameled bucket and wash basin on the other, an embroidered hopsacking towel hanging above it. The painted floor was covered with a worn braided rug, on which lay several napping cats, like orange and white and gray dust mops. Somebody had told me that Winnie had inherited a great deal of money from her parents when they died ten years ago, but it didn't show in the modest way she lived.

" 'Treated with roses'?" Ruby asked, after we sat down. She leaned forward and sniffed deeply at the bouquet of white roses. "How do you treat somebody with roses?"

"With a tea made from the petals," I said. "Or with rose honey or rose syrup. Or rose vinegar, or oil of roses, or rosewater.

Or you could make rosehips into jam, or brew them as tea, or powder them to be added to wine. The hips are loaded with vitamin C and some P and K — although of course people didn't know that back then. They just knew it worked." I inhaled the fragrance of the roses. "The scent was thought to relieve headaches and encourage sleep, too. Early aromatherapy. And it still works."

With a glance over her shoulder, Ruby lowered her voice. "Did you notice the way Winnie avoided my question about Coleman? She must know something."

"If she does, I doubt if Marvin Wallace could get it out of her," I said, with a certain satisfaction.

Ruby nodded. "No matter how much Council members may know about Coleman, they aren't going to tell a Ranger." She looked up as Winnie came toward us. "Oh, goodie! Jam cakes!"

Winnie put the tray on the table and handed me a damp cheesecloth pad, folded into a poultice. "Hold this across your nose and under your eyes," she instructed.

"Rose petals?" I asked, taking it.

"Right." Winnie set three glasses and a pitcher on the table, followed by a plate of jam cakes decorated with fresh mint leaves and a single white rose. "In India, they use roses to treat abrasions and inflammations." She grinned. "I'd say you've got one hell of an inflamed nose, China. Comes from sticking it into somebody's business, I don't doubt."

"Thanks," I said wryly, pasting the damp, cool poultice to my face. "You sure know how to make a person feel better."

"I'd make you lie down with it," Winnie replied, "but you need to eat some of that jam cake. More good medicine. It'll make you feel even better."

It did, too. The poultice was awkward but cooling and the rosehip tea was iced and tasty, with the zing of ginger and a hint of anise. The jam cakes were light and luscious, and Winnie's rose jam, hidden inside, was the color of rubies. We said little as we ate. The taste was too good to spoil with the rattle of words.

After a few moments, Winnie refilled all three glasses from the frosty pitcher, sat back in her chair and said casually, "When I came in with the tray, you were talking about Edgar Coleman." She looked at me. "Has Mike got a line on the killer yet?"

With a start, I realized that Winnie, by virtue of her seat on the Council, was also one of McQuaid's bosses. "Not yet," I replied. "It looks like the investigation might drag on for a while."

"Which is why we're here, Winnie," Ruby said, getting to the point. "The wedding is Sunday, you know."

Winnie looked at me. "Well, sure. But what's that got to do with —" Then she snapped her fingers. "Oh, I get it. If Mike doesn't wrap up his investigation by Sunday, you're afraid he'll stand you up."

I winced. I turned the compress over to the cool side and held it over my nose, which was beginning to feel better. "I'm sure he won't miss the wedding," I said in a muffled voice, "but it might not have his full attention." I didn't want to think of McQuaid standing beside me, wearing his cop face and mentally sifting murder clues while Maude Porterfield joined us in holy matrimony. He might just mutter, "I don't know," instead of "I do."

"Their honeymoon might have to be postponed, too," Ruby said, looking mournful. "You can see why we're anxious to find out what happened. And we're not sure that everybody will come clean to the police." She paused. "Everybody on the Council, that is," she added, in a silky tone.

Winnie sat still for a moment, turning the matter over in her mind. "Well, you're right on that score," she said finally. "Most of the Council members wouldn't tell you the time of day unless it was in their best interest." She frowned. "But how come you're asking about the Council? Coleman had enemies all over town — across the state, for that matter. He was not what you would call a popular person."

Instead of answering, Ruby said, "You voted against the annexation proposal, I understand."

"You bet I did." Winnie thumped her glass on the table, and one of the white roses, jarred, dropped its petals in a soft heap. "What Coleman did out there at Blessing Ranch is just plain criminal. If I weren't a lady, I might've killed him myself." She paused and added, cautiously, "You didn't hear me say that. I was here by myself Sunday night, so I don't have a very good watchamacallit — alibi. But people in this town have been listening to my anti-gun speeches for years, so I doubt that anybody would seriously believe that I'd use one. Even on a rattlesnake like Coleman."

I sat forward. "We think Coleman tried to influence the vote on the annexation proposal, Winnie. One of the other Council members has shown us evidence that he was trying to blackmail her and her husband."

If Winnie was surprised by that information, or curious about who it was, she didn't let on. Absently, she pulled the fallen white petals toward her, pushing them into a circle on the table with her finger. "Blackmail, huh?" she said at last, not looking up. "So you think somebody decided to kill him rather than pay to shut him up?"

"Coleman dead is a lot more likely to keep his mouth closed than Coleman alive," Ruby said reasonably. "The trouble is that a blackmail victim isn't going to volunteer anything that might make them look like a murder suspect. We thought maybe you'd have some information that might move the investigation along. Can you help us?"

Winnie studied the rose petals as if they were tea leaves and she was looking for an answer to Ruby's question. After a moment, she said, slowly, "I was going to keep this to myself because I couldn't see that it mattered to anybody but me. But I guess maybe it's time to speak up." She glanced at me. "Are you going to tell Mike what you find out?" She rubbed her hand across her face. "Scratch that. Of course you will."

"If it's relevant," I said. "If it isn't . . ." I shrugged. I didn't want to get into the question of who was going to decide what was relevant and what wasn't. Strictly speaking, that was the investigating officer's job. Strictly speaking, Ruby and I should butt out, right now, before we got ourselves in trouble with the law. But there was Wallace, damn it, acting like he was the only one with enough brains to find a killer. And something about the way Winnie was responding made me want to hear what she had to say. Her next words decided me.

"To be honest, I'd rather tell you," Winnie said. "Telling Mike, I'm on the record, and he's got to act on what I say. Talking to you, I'm just having a conversation with a couple of friends. What you do with the information is up to you."

Ruby nodded, and I made a noise intended to sound encouraging. So she did know something.

Winnie picked up her glass, drained it, and said, "The first vote came up a couple of weeks ago. Coleman was there, of course, taking names. The next morning, I was out watering when he came by." She wrinkled her nose distastefully. "Edgar was about as subtle as a horny longhorn. He said he had some privileged information that might change my mind about the ranch project." She snorted. " 'Privileged information.' That man always talked big, trying to make folks think he knew more than he did. So I asked him what in the world he thought was privileged enough to change my mind, and he said he knew something about Johnnie that might be kind of hard for him to explain to his boss."

"Who's Johnnie?" Ruby asked.

"My younger brother," Winnie replied, in a matter-of-fact tone. An orange cat sprang onto the table and she took it into her lap. "He's an undertaker at Pauley's Funeral Home."

"And what did you say to Coleman?" I asked.

She laughed sharply. "I said that Johnnie wasn't my favorite brother and if he'd done something he shouldn't have, by golly, old Mr. Pauley ought to hear about it. And if Coleman thought he could make me change my vote on that ranch development by threatening to get Johnnie in trouble, he had another think coming." She stroked the cat, her eyes on my face. "I know I should have told Pauline, because it was an out and out bribery attempt, and that's illegal. But then I'd have to involve Johnnie, and I didn't exactly want to do that, for obvious reasons. So I just let it rest." The cat jumped off her lap, landing with a soft thud in a puddle of sunshine on the rug. "When I read in the paper that Coleman was dead, I was sorry I hadn't spoken up."

"Do you know whether Coleman approached any of the other Council members?" Ruby asked.

Winnie frowned. "Do I *know?* Well, not exactly. But I happened to be driving past Ken Bowman's Lincoln-Mercury dealership the day before the vote and I saw Edgar and Ken standing outside in the lot, having a talk. That afternoon, Ken called and said he was voting for the annexation proposal, and I should too." She paused. "Now, maybe Coleman was putting pressure on Ken, or maybe Ken was giving him a good deal on a new car. But Ken's phone call bothered me. If the vote had gone Coleman's way, I would've blown the whistle. I sure as the dickens wouldn't have let that sonofagun get away with rigging the vote." She gave us a calculating glance.

"You know, you two might be on the right track. If I'd wanted to cover up for Johnnie, I wouldn't have trusted Coleman to keep his mouth shut. Even if you gave him what he asked for, there's no guarantee that he wouldn't have wanted more. He was dangerous." She spoke without inflection, but there was something in her eyes that made me think she felt more passion than she showed.

"Ken Bowman is the only one Coleman might have tried to buy?" Ruby asked.

Winnie frowned. "Well," she said, "I got the idea from Darla McDaniels that she and Edgar might've had a private conversation recently, but I have no idea what they talked about." She picked up the pitcher. "She leased her bookstore space from him, you know. He was her landlord. Do you want some more tea?"

We lingered for another few minutes, sipping tea and admiring the garden. My nose was feeling better, and I thanked Winnie for the poultice. Ruby told her we'd give her a call and arrange a convenient time to collect the flowers, and we said good-bye. On the way out, I collected a couple more sprigs of lavender.

Ruby managed to contain her excitement until we got to the car, but just barely. "We're on to something big, China!" she exulted. "Pauline, Phyllis, Winnie, Ken Bowman — Coleman tried to blackmail all *four* of them — and maybe Darla and Wanda and Billie Jean, as well! Now all we have to do is find out which one of them had a secret they couldn't trust him not to tell, and we've found our murderer."

I got into the car and shut the door. "Ruby," I said quietly, "I want you to think about what you just said."

She stared at me. "Think about it? Why? What's wrong with it? Don't you agree?"

"Those people you just named — some of them are our friends, all of them are our acquaintances. They're people with children, people with families, people who have done a lot for Pecan Springs over a lot of years. There's a very good chance that Edgar Coleman was murdered by somebody we know and *like*." I paused. "Winnie, for instance."

"Winnie?" Ruby was horrified. "How can you think such a thing, China? Why, she —"

"She fed us jam cake and tea and said that she told Coleman to go fly a kite. Then she incriminated Ken Bowman and implicated Darla McDaniels."

"Incriminated? Implicated?" Ruby stared at me. "But she was only giving us the information we asked for. Don't you believe her?"

"It's not a matter of belief, Ruby. This killer isn't going to hold up a hand and say, 'Hey, it's me. I did it.' He, or she, is going to lie. Are you sure you can tell the difference between a lie and the truth — when the liar is somebody you know and like?"

Ruby frowned. "Maybe you're right. But I still don't believe that Winnie —"

"Maybe not. But we can't be taken in by her hospitality and her willingness to tell us what we want to hear. This is an ugly business. Now that we've started digging, we may unearth something that should have stayed buried." Having delivered this ominous remark, I slumped down into the seat. "Damn it. This is my wedding. Why can't the week be normal?"

Ruby turned the key. "Whoever heard of anybody having a normal week just before her wedding? Why, things haven't even *started* to get difficult. We haven't heard Sunday's weather forecast yet."

More headaches. I held the lavender to my nose and sniffed.

Chapter Six

Lavender in full bloom is a beautiful plant, and the Tuscan fields where it grows are famous for their beauty. But the workers who harvest the crop arm themselves with stout sticks because they know that poisonous snakes hide in the lavender's dry, fragrant shade. Perhaps for that reason lavender became a symbol of dishonesty, deception, and secret malice. In the Victorian language of flowers, a sprig of lovely lavender tucked into a bouquet might convey the warning "Beware of deceit."

"The Meaning of Lavender,"
by China Bayles
The Pecan Springs *Enterprise*
Home and Garden Section

The asp that bit Cleopatra is said to have been found lurking beneath a lavender bush.

Folk saying

140

The afternoon was almost over, and I had more to do than play Watson to Ruby's Holmes. Ruby took me back to the shop, where I checked on the afternoon's traffic (encouragingly brisk), counted the newly arrived punch bowls (six more), and unpacked the shipment of the herb books that Bertha and Betsy had agreed to autograph. By that time, it was nearly five, so I helped Laurel close, cleared the register, and headed home. McQuaid had a case to solve. I might be a successful small-business owner with an important event scheduled for the weekend, but I still had groceries to buy and dinner to make.

Howard Cosell was sitting, like a grumpier old man, in front of the kitchen door. I said hello to him, got a grunt in reply, then unloaded the groceries and poured myself a glass of sherry. Then I went out on the back porch, cut a leaf from an aloe vera plant, slit it, and rubbed the cool gel on my nose and under my eyes, not looking in the mirror. Sherry first, reality later.

But some realities have to be dealt with immediately. The answering machine was blinking furiously, and I pushed the button. The first message was from Brian, announcing that Melissa was coming to supper and hoping this was okay, because like he'd already told her it was, if I knew what he meant. Since a foot-long home-made submarine sandwich — my ingenious plan for tonight's supper — can be stretched almost to infinity, I wasn't worried about not having enough to go around, especially when the second message turned out to be from McQuaid, who said he'd be home late and not to wait supper, and hoped my nose was better.

"Hey," he added sternly, "I *love* you, remember? Whatever shape your nose is in."

The pleasant feeling generated by McQuaid's remark was abruptly extinguished by the third caller, the absent Harold Tucker, who owns our house. "We wanted to let you know that we're in the States," he said, in his clipped, dry, English professor's voice. He gave a mailing address in Indiana and added, "We came back a few months early to take care of some urgent business. We've had an unexpected and rather surprising change in plans. We'll be in touch with you to see what we can work out."

I hit the erase button with a vengeance. It sounded as if the Tuckers were hoping to move back home early. Well, if that was their idea, they could jolly well think again.

The lease stated clearly and unequivocably that McQuaid and I were entitled to live in their house through the first of January. A change in plans, phooey! I knew a first-rate lawyer — me — who would tell them exactly what they could do with . . .

These litigious thoughts were interrupted by a rap at the door. When I snatched it open, I saw Fannie Couch standing on the front porch. Fannie has always dressed like a sweet little lady in lace-trimmed grandmotherly dresses and flowered hats the size of Edwardian parasols. But a few months ago she celebrated her seventy-fifth birthday and announced that now that she was an old woman, she intended to wear purple, shock the Ladies League, and scare the horses. This evening, she was decked out in what looked like race-walking gear: brash purple shorts with a slick finish, a baggy yellow T-shirt, purple-and-white striped knee socks, and running shoes with treads that would have looked right at home on an eighteen-wheeler. But she hadn't jogged all the way out here. A car — not Fannie's old red Ford but a classy silver Lincoln — was parked in the drive. Somebody was sitting in the driver's seat, waiting for her.

Fannie frowned. "What in tarnation did

you do to your nose?"

I explained about the door.

"Oh," she said. "Well, I sure hope that purple under your eyes fades away before Sunday. If you've got an aloe vera plant, you might try cutting a leaf and —" She stopped. "Hell, you're the expert. Why am I giving you advice?" She pursed her mouth. "I'm not interrupting your supper, am I?"

"Not yet," I said. "Listen, Fannie, I don't mean to be ungrateful, but would you please tell your fans to turn off the punch bowls? We've got enough to serve punch at the next Texas-OU game."

"That's gratitude for you," Fannie said. She gestured toward the Lincoln. "Letty Coleman's out there. She wants to talk to you."

"Letty Coleman?" I was taken aback. "Why?"

Fannie fixed me with her bright blue eyes. "Letty's friend Charlotte is on the nursing home board of directors. Charlotte told her how you straightened out that bad business with Opal Hogge a few months ago, and Letty was hoping that maybe you could help straighten out some of *her* bad business."

I shook my head. "Sorry, Fannie. Letty's

husband is dead and she's a suspect, last I heard. She needs to talk to the police."

"Now, China." Fannie was patient. "You surely don't believe that Letty Coleman has enough gumption to shoot somebody. Anyway, she was with her sister on Sunday night. And she's already given a statement to the police. She's not a suspect anymore."

That was nonsense, and Fannie ought to have known better. Alibi or no alibi, the wife is always a suspect when the husband is blown away by an unknown assailant. A great many timid little women have been known to hire big bad trigger men to put an end to their husbands' philandering. But if Letty had already talked to McQuaid, there couldn't be any harm in —

"Straighten out what bad business?" I asked.

"I'll let her tell you," Fannie said, and skipped down the steps and out to the Lincoln. A moment later, Letty Coleman was sitting next to Fannie on my living room sofa. She had thanked me for my condolences and both had accepted my offer of a glass of sherry, which I brought in a decanter and set on the old pine carpenter's chest that serves as our coffee table. I like primitives because there's nothing you can do to them that hasn't already been done and left the scars to prove it. There's nothing fancy about them, either — and I'm not a very fancy person.

Letty was in her mid-fifties. She had been pretty once, and there was still something striking about her almond-shaped dark eyes and high cheekbones. Her coarse, graying hair was pulled tightly back and fastened in a low bun at the nape of her neck. She was predictably dressed in a black dress, black stockings, and black low-heeled shoes, and she wasn't wearing any jewelry. She looked even thinner than she did the last time she had come into the shop. Her hands twisted nervously, and there was a little tic at the corner of her right eye. She spoke with difficulty, in a tense, weary voice.

"Since Edgar died . . . that is, since he was . . . killed, I've been thinking . . ." She dug a tissue out of her black bag and wiped her eyes. "I mean, I've been terribly worried about . . . well, some of the things he was . . ." She swallowed and used the tissue again. "But I don't think anyone can help, really." Her thin voice broke, and she put one trembling hand to her mouth. "Everything is in such a terrible mess. I re-

146

ally shouldn't be bothering anybody with my troubles." That last bit sounded, I thought, a little forced — but she had been through a great deal in the last few days. She was entitled.

"Drink your sherry," Fannie advised. "China will help if she can." She smiled at me. "Won't you, China?"

I took my cue and made a reassuring noise that Letty seemed to take for assent. She sipped her sherry, straightened her shoulders, and made a fresh start. "Edgar was involved in a great many things I didn't understand," she said. "He was always getting phone calls in the middle of the night and he rented mailboxes in three or four cities. I know of at least three bank accounts, and —" She broke off.

"It sounds as if he may have had some unorthodox business dealings," I said cautiously. "But I'm not sure how that affects you, Letty. The police will check the mailboxes and the bank accounts to be sure there's nothing criminal and —"

"— and there was another w-w-woman, too," Letty said, in a choked voice, not hearing me. There was a silence.

After a moment, Fannie leaned forward. "I heard something about Edgar and his secretary," she prompted. Her voice was sympathetic. "Iris Powell — isn't that her name?"

"Iris?" Letty gave her a distant look. "Edgar was only playing around with her. He did that quite a bit, but it didn't mean anything."

"You knew about Iris?" Fannie asked in surprise.

Letty nodded bleakly. "Pauline Perkins, too." She straightened and returned Fannie's look with something close to defiance. "Maybe you think I was a fool. But that was the price I paid for falling in love with a younger, good-looking man who was, well, oversexed." She gave an apologetic little cough. "Unfortunately, I've never been . . . that way. In fact, for me it's just the opposite. I was afraid I would lose him if I didn't let him —" Her face was burning and she dropped her eyes. "If he couldn't find an outlet for all that . . . sexual energy. So I told him he could have his affairs as long as he was discreet. As long as it was just a . . . well, just a physical thing. I couldn't have tolerated it if he'd had any *real* feeling for anybody else. That's what I would consider infidelity." She sighed. "But in the past month or so, I began to think that maybe he . . ." Her voice trailed off.

"That he had fallen in love with some-one?" I asked gently.

"Yes." She raised her dark, anxious eyes to mine. "That's why I've come to you."

I returned the look, wondering what special strengths — or what particular weaknesses — were required of a woman to acknowledge and accept her husband's adulterous games, one after another. But Letty wasn't the first and she wouldn't be the last to tolerate such behavior within the confines of her marriage, even after it became public knowledge. That must be the worst of it, actually — knowing that other people know, thinking about what they're saying, feeling the humiliation of their curiosity or their censure or their pity.

I cleared my throat. "What made you think there was somebody else?"

"Edgar was . . . different. Moody, preoccupied. Most of the time, he was so easygoing and jovial, always making jokes. But lately, he had something on his mind, and it was bothering him."

"Maybe it was the annexation proposal. The Council turned it down — that couldn't have made him happy."

"It wasn't that." Letty sighed. "Anyway, there were other things. A note, a couple of phone calls. He was very secretive about it."

"Do you know who she is?"

"I think so," she said. Her voice was taut, her fingers twisted into a knot. "But I'm really only guessing about their relationship. I want you to find out if I'm right."

Fannie leaned forward. "Hold your horses, Letty. This is a matter for the police. If Edgar was seriously involved with somebody else, they need to know."

Letty whirled to face her. "But what if I'm wrong?" she cried in an anguished voice. "Just look what's happened to poor Pauline Perkins! I learned today that her husband is filing for divorce, and all because of what Edgar did to her." I wanted to point out that Pauline herself wasn't totally blameless, but Letty was going on, becoming more passionate. "You know what people are like in this town. Once you've crossed the line, they never forgive you. Pauline's political career is finished. This other woman . . . she's married, and active in church and volunteer work. Her husband is a professional, and they have a child. They're decent people, and I don't want to see their marriage wrecked." Her mouth tightened and her voice became hard, knife-edged. "Unless it's true. Then I'll tell the police myself, with pleasure. I swear I will." She held out her hands to me, imploring. "Please — will you help?"

"You need a private detective," I said.

She shook her head. "I need somebody I can trust. Somebody who lives here and knows people and can find things out without stirring up suspicions. Somebody who understands about investigations and the way the law operates. You used to be a criminal attorney, and Fannie and Charlotte say I can trust you. You're the perfect choice."

"Aren't you forgetting that the man I live with happens to be the temporary chief of police?" I asked. "How do you know I won't go straight to him with anything I find out?"

"I trust you not to tell him what he doesn't need to know," Letty said.

I sat back. I wanted to tell Letty that I had a wedding to attend to, which was far more important than discovering which of her dead husband's sexual infidelities had been fired by love rather than lust. But if I took her plea at face value, there was both wisdom and compassion in it. For the sake of all concerned, it would be far more sensible to conduct a speedy private inquiry. If I found out that there had been another affair, I would turn the names, dates, and serial numbers over to Letty, who would then go to McQuaid with the information. Or I could tell him myself, at any time it seemed appropriate.

But there was something else. For some reason — I wasn't sure why — I couldn't quite take Letty's proposal at face value. I couldn't get over the feeling that there was another motive behind it, something she wouldn't or couldn't reveal. Maybe it was guilt; surely she had to acknowledge to herself that if she had refused to accept her husband's behavior, he might still be alive. Or maybe it was a flaming anger, deep down inside, where she couldn't reach it. Fortunately or unfortunately, even the merest whiff of deception or self-deception intrigues me. I'm tantalized by the thought that somebody is hiding something from me or from themselves, and I want to know what it is. And more: I had come away from this afternoon's conversation with Winnie with the distinct idea that several people knew more about Coleman's recent activities than they were likely to tell the police. Plenty of murder cases are never solved, especially when the suspect list numbers in the double digits and every suspect has something important to hide. This case was beginning to smell like one of them.

I looked at Letty. "I think you may have the right idea," I said slowly, "but I need to think about it. I'm getting married this Sunday, and I'm pretty busy."

Fannie gave a short laugh. "That's the understatement of the year," she said to Letty. "China already has more on her plate than she can say grace over." She frowned, and I knew she was sorry that she'd allowed Letty to inflict herself on me. "Letty, if I'd known what you intended to ask, I wouldn't have —"

"It really won't take much time," Letty said, almost desperately. "Maybe all you have to do is ask her and she'll tell you. Her name is —"

I shook my head. "I don't want to know who she is unless I'm going to do something about it." The way things turned out, it was a dumb response, and if Ruby had been there, she would have given me a sharp kick in the shins. But Fannie was right. I already had too much to do without getting involved in Letty's problem, and I wanted to make that point.

Letty put her hand on my arm. Her fingers were like claws, and there was an enormous power and passion behind her *Please*.

"Let me think about it overnight," I said.

So that was how we left it. I got her phone number and promised to call her in the morning. Fannie gave me a hug, hiked up her running shorts, and the two of them drove off. With a sigh of relief, I headed for the kitchen. Constructing designer sandwiches for a pair of ravenous kids is hardly the world's most demanding job, but after that session with Letty, I was ready to throw myself into it, heart and soul.

Throughout my life, I have lived in a number of apartments, condos, and houses and cooked in kitchens that ranged in size from microscopic to midget. This kitchen, however, has enough sink and counter space to build a twelve-course dinner, with room left over for a large fridge, a scarred pine table that seats eight comfortably, my beloved Home Comfort gas range (which is old enough to qualify for Social Security), and an oak rocking chair beside a floor-to-ceiling window, where Howard Cosell can lie and grind his teeth over the mockingbirds diving for bugs in the grass. I sighed as I got out sandwich fixings and a head of cabbage, thinking with regret that there would soon be another kitchen in my life. But no sooner than January, the lawyer in me vowed, no matter what the Tuckers had up their devious sleeves. In the mean-time, I would enjoy every minute of this one.

So I happily shredded cabbage for cole slaw, arranged cold cuts, and sliced Swiss cheese and huge Big Boy tomatoes and a sweet yellow onion the size of a grapefruit, humming "Whistle While You Work" and refusing to think about rascally husbands, ruined marriages, and murder. Until Brian and Melissa walked in and put the gun on the table in front of me.

"We didn't touch it, honest," Brian said earnestly. "Except with the stick, that is."

"That's how we carried it," Melissa elaborated. "With the stick in that trigger thing. We didn't want to mess up the fingerprints. If there are any."

"The trigger guard," Brian said importantly, reaching down to pet Howard Cosell, who had come away from the window to see what was going on. "Hi, Howard Cosell, you good old dog." He headed for the phone, leaving a trail of muddy footprints on the floor.

"I was afraid it would go off," Melissa told me, her face sober. "Brian said it wasn't loaded, so it wouldn't. But we were careful anyway."

"Wasn't cocked," Brian corrected her,

dialing. "I could tell by looking at the hammer."

"Right," Melissa said respectfully. "Cocked. Brian knows all about guns." She shrugged out of her backpack, and I saw that she was muddy to the knees. Howard Cosell abandoned Brian and came over to sniff Melissa's jeans. "We kinda thought," she said, "that it could be the same gun that killed that guy in the garage. That's why we didn't want to mess up the fingerprints. We didn't want anybody to see us, either, just in case."

I stared at the gun — a .32 Beretta caked with mud — where it lay beside half a head of cabbage, an onion, and a plate of sliced tomatoes. I could see tiny dried blood spatters on the top of the barrel. "Where did you find it?" I asked.

"On the bank of the creek," Melissa replied. She frowned. "There was somebody who saw us, though. A woman in a car. She was watching."

"Hey, listen, Dad," I heard Brian say.

Dad? I whirled around. "Brian, I think you'd better let me talk to —"

"Hey, man," Brian said into the phone. "Melissa and me, we like found this pistol and kinda thought maybe it's the one you're looking for. You know, the one that killed that guy you and China didn't want to talk about last night."

I could hear McQuaid's explosive *What?* from where I stood.

"Yeah," Brian said. "Cool, huh? Anyway, we brought it home. It's here on the table. What time are you coming for supper?"

Melissa tilted her head, regarding me with a worried look. "What happened to your nose?"

"A door," I said to her. To Brian, I said, "He's not coming for supper. He's working late."

Melissa stopped looking at my nose, reached into her pack, and pulled out a lidded quart jar. It was filled with dirty water and a dozen greenish creatures with big eyes and long tails. "Tadpoles for the snakes," she explained, setting the jar on the table. "They look like sperm, don't they? With eyes." She dove back into her pack and came up with a small wasp's nest. "Don't worry," she told me reassuringly. "There aren't any grown ones in there. Just a bunch of grubs."

"Okay," Brian said into the phone. "I'll tell her. See ya." He hung up.

"And this," Melissa said with pleasure, "is a present for *you*." She pulled out a bread wrapper filled with muddy leaves and handed it to me. "It's mint. We found it growing wild, where we found the gun. A great big patch of it. We thought you could make some tea with it." She eyed me thoughtfully. "Or maybe you could put it on your nose. You know, like they did in the old days. It might be good."

"Thank you," I said. "Sounds like a fine idea." I looked at Brian. "What did your father say?"

"He said he'll see us when he gets here." Brian squatted down so that his eyes were level with the glass jar. "Some tadpoles," he said admiringly. "Man, they're really big. Like wow."

"Yeah," I said. "*Tadpolis giganticus*. Where did you find the gun?"

"Same place we found the tadpoles. Hey," he said to Melissa, "they look like that sperm stuff we saw on TV, don't they?"

"Yeah," Melissa said, very seriously. "Except they've got eyes. Sperm don't have eyes, do they?" She appealed to me. "Do they, China?"

"I don't know," I replied. "I never looked." When I was their age, the thought of sperm had never crossed my mind.

"Probably not," Melissa said thoughtfully. "The egg is so big, all they have to do is bump into it. They don't need to look where they're going."

Lord deliver us. I turned to Brian. "Where exactly did you find the gun? Like where on the map?"

"Jordan's Crossing." Brian unscrewed the lid and poked the tadpoles with his finger. They began to wiggle madly. "You know, where the creek goes through those big concrete pipes. It was just laying there, like maybe somebody threw it out of a car window or something."

"Lying," I amended.

"Not," Brian said indignantly. "It's the truth, ain't it, Melissa?"

I sighed. "Go on."

"That's all. It was just laying there, and we saw it." He held the jar up. "I wonder how many we got. A couple of dozen, at least." He began to count. "One, two, three —"

"Fifteen," Melissa said. "I counted them when I put them in." She frowned. "Be careful, Brian. That jar is really slip—"

The good news is that the tadpole jar did not fall on the gun and destroy whatever evidence it might have offered. The bad news is that it fell on the table, bounced and splashed, then rolled off the table and onto the floor. Shortly after we had put out the dog, rounded up fourteen frantic tadpoles and restored them to a new quart jar, and cleaned up the mess, McQuaid hobbled in. Marvin Wallace was with him.

"Where's the gun?" Marvin demanded. "I want to see it."

"Good evening," I said pleasantly. "So *nice* of you two to take time out of your busy schedule to drop in. Would you like to stay for supper, or shall I pack you a brown bag?"

Marvin had the grace to look embarrassed. McQuaid gave me a tentative grin, testing my mood. "Mind if Marvin joins us?"

"Of course not," I said. The gracious hostess. "I'll put on another plate."

"Here's the gun, Dad," Brian said. He and Melissa proudly displayed their find. There was a brief consultation, then McQuaid sacked and labeled the gun.

"Good job, kids," Marvin said, clapping his hand on Brian's shoulder and smiling at Melissa. "You did the right thing — although you might have left the gun there and gone to a phone to call us."

"But we were afraid somebody might take it," Brian objected. He turned to his dad. "Is it the gun you're looking for?"

"Could be," McQuaid said noncommittally. "We won't know until the ballistics tests are run." He didn't mention the blood, which the children might not have seen.

Melissa was staring at Marvin, who was still wearing his white Stetson. "I've never met a Ranger before."

Marvin took his hat off and bowed. "At your service, little lady," he said, sounding like a character in a grade-B Western.

Melissa gave him a dark look. "I'm not very little," she said. "And I'm not a lady." I smiled. Out of the mouth of babes.

McQuaid straightened up, leaning on his canes. "Okay, you guys did good. Now we'll go to the creek and you can show me where —"

"No," I said firmly. "*Now* we eat supper, *then* you go to the creek."

Marvin looked at his watch. "I don't mean to be rude, but do you suppose we could hurry it up a little?"

"Sure," I said. "If you and McQuaid will set the table, we can get dinner out of the way in a jiffy."

Marvin gave me a startled look, but followed instructions. I put the food on the table, and we all sat down. I very much wanted to tell McQuaid about my conversations with Winnie and Letty and find out what was going on at his end of the investigation. I also wanted to know what he had learned when he interviewed Phyllis's husband, and whether it was true that Darryl had filed for divorce. But I wasn't about to ask questions in front of the kids, so the guys got to keep their cop-secrets to themselves. With Brian and Melissa monopolizing the dinner table conversation, we heard more about the sexual habits of reptiles than we wanted to know. To change the subject from the striking similarity between tadpoles and sperm, I asked Melissa how she liked living in Pecan Springs.

"It's better than Syracuse but not as fun as Boise," she said. "Mountains are nice." She tilted her head. "Dad says that Atlanta wasn't so nice, but I was too little to care."

"You've moved around a lot, then," I said. I was surprised. Most doctors and dentists I knew tended to settle in one place.

"We're moving," Brian announced.

"Where?" Melissa asked. "When?"

"Somewhere," Brian said vaguely. "Soon."

This was a perfect opening for me to remark that Harold Tucker had called and made noises about getting his house back early. But I didn't want to let Marvin in on our private family business, so I kept quiet. Anyway, Brian was going on.

"Wanna come to a wedding?" he asked Melissa. "It's on Sunday. It's outdoors, and we're gonna have lots of cake and stuff. But you gotta wear a dress." He made a face. "That's because I gotta wear a tie."

"Well, maybe," Melissa said, "if I don't have anything better to do. Who's getting married?"

"Dad and China," Brian said, past a mouthful of sandwich.

Melissa looked at me, confused. "I thought China was your mom already."

"She is," Brian said. "She's the mom who lives *here*. My real mom lives somewhere else. She sends me presents sometimes, mostly clothes and stuff." He brightened. "She sent me a model of the *Enterprise*, though. That was cool."

Marvin tapped Melissa on the arm. "I'll take some more of that coleslaw, little lady," he said.

Melissa gave him a look. "What's the magic word?"

Marvin colored. "Please," he said. I smiled.

"I'll ask Jennie if I can come to the wedding," Melissa said. "She isn't my real mom either," she went on, with a now-

163

that-you-mention-it confidentiality. "My real mom died when I was born. She had blond hair and blue eyes and she was always laughing. She was prettier than Princess Di. Dad says people thought she ought to be in the movies, she was so pretty. She never would've done that, though," she added. "He says she just wanted to be my mom. I dream about her a lot. I wish she hadn't died."

"Yeah," Brian said thoughtfully. "My real mom is pretty too. She's got long red hair." He gave me a matter-of-fact, comparing look. "Actually, she's a lot prettier than —"

"Have your parents been married long, Melissa?" McQuaid asked hastily.

"They got married when we lived in Seattle," Melissa said. "Jennie's nice, except when she's trying to get me to be a lady." She wrinkled her freckled nose. "I don't want to be a lady." She gave Marvin a long look. "I believe I'll be a Ranger. Like you."

"I thought you were going to be a botanist," I objected, feeling hurt. Kids can be so fickle.

Marvin looked stern. "If you're planning to go into law enforcement, you need to study hard and do a lot of sports. You have to believe in yourself all the way, because it's harder for girls."

"Not for me," Melissa said. "My grades are already better than Brian's, and when I get into a fight, I hit *hard*." She paused. "What's the matter? Are you sick?"

Marvin was staring at his coleslaw. "Something seems to be . . . wiggling."

Brian got up to see. "It's the tadpole," he said.

"Cool," Melissa said, and giggled.

"We'd better be going," Marvin said, pushing his plate away.

I stood up. "We're celebrating Melissa's birthday tonight." I brought out a cupcake for Melissa with twelve candles, and cupcakes each with a single candle for the rest of us. We all blew out our candles and made our wishes.

I wished for clues. Sunday was getting closer.

Chapter Seven

Because of its uses in various kinds of dyes, the herb bugloss became a symbol of false-hood and deceit. The roots of dyer's bugloss (Anchusa tinctoria) were used to color wool and women's faces. The deep red color was long lasting, and washing actually brightened it. Bugloss grew to have an unwholesome reputation among those who felt that a woman who tinted her cheeks could hardly be trusted to tell the truth.

China Bayles
China's Garden

Arranging a wedding is a lot like throwing a big party, except that people tend to have an emotional investment in weddings and want to see their favorite fantasy rituals played out. While McQuaid and I were determined to keep things simple, I also had to think about the other people who were involved — McQuaid's parents, Leatha, Ruby. Each of them had an idea of what our wedding ought to be, and I wanted to satisfy them, within reason, of course. I drew the line at Leatha's plan for me to wear her wedding dress, which had a train long enough to reach to San Antonio. And at McQuaid's mother's suggestion that her friend Erma could sing "I Love You Truly," and at Ruby's idea that the guests should release a hundred white balloons with our names on them in pink letters. I had no intention of littering the jet stream with personalized rubbish. Otherwise, I was trying to be accommodating.

So after McQuaid and Marvin went off with the kids, I sat down at the table and began scanning my latest list. Clothes, food, flowers, license and rings, music, Bertha and Betsy — Good grief, I'd almost forgotten about Bertha and Betsy, who were due in tomorrow afternoon. They'd be sleeping here, sharing the guest bedroom next to the one my mother always occupies. My mother, Leatha, would be arriving, too, although I wasn't sure when, along with her husband, Sam.

I rushed upstairs, found the clean sheets I'd tucked away with lavender sachets, and hurriedly changed all three beds. While I was at it, I flicked the dust off the bed tables and put out fresh towels, the rose-geranium soap I'd made in one of my soap-making classes, and citrus and spice potpourri. I was on the way to the kitchen, thinking that it would be nice if we had dinner at home tomorrow night, when the phone rang. It was Ruby.

"Darla said she could talk to us tonight," she said without preamble. "Are you free?"

"Darla who?" I asked, still thinking about tomorrow night's dinner. Something easy and quick, yet elegant. Roast chicken with lemon and rosemary, maybe, and fresh vegetables. There would be breakfasts, too, Continental style. Betsy and Bertha were doing something very nice for me, and I wanted them to enjoy themselves while they were here. Meals meant another list. And maybe I'd better call Leatha and find out what time she planned to show up, and whether Sam was coming early, with her, or later, for the wedding.

"Darla McDaniels," Ruby said patiently. "City Council member, former Pecan Springs High cheerleader. Possible target of Coleman bribery attempt, according to Winnie. You *do* remember our investigation, don't you?"

"Oh," I said. "Sure." I glanced at the clock. It was after eight. "It's not too late?"

"She's still working. I'll pick you up."

I'd been so engrossed, first with Letty's story and then with the discovery of the gun, that I'd more or less forgotten about Ruby's determination to interview the Council members. On the way to Darla's, I filled Ruby in on the new developments. She was intrigued with the gun and the blood droplets I had spotted on the barrel.

"Will they be able to find out who owns it?" she asked.

"The records will probably show who bought it originally — although that person may not own it any longer. It could have been sold, stolen, or lost. Anyway, it might not even be the murder weapon. Who knows? It may have been lying there for weeks. It may be totally unrelated to —"

"Spoken like a defense attorney." Ruby swung down the alley and into the parking area behind Darla's store, which is on the west side of the square. She parked next to a blue Mercury that bore BOOK 1 vanity plates — Darla's, most likely. "Poor Letty," Ruby said, turning off the ignition. "I must say, Edgar Coleman was one hardworking Lothario. Pauline Perkins, Iris Powell — and now a third woman? Whew!" She dropped the keys in her purse. "Letty didn't tell you her name?"

"I didn't want to know," I said. "At that point, I wasn't sure I wanted to get involved."

She shook her head disgustedly. I knew she was thinking that Kinsey Milhone wouldn't have missed a chance like that. "But you've changed your mind."

"Yes," I said. Seeing a blood-spattered gun lying on my kitchen table between an innocent cabbage and an irreproachable tomato might have piqued my curiosity. Or maybe it was the recollection of Letty's ambiguous glance. I was positive she was concealing something. "Yes, I'm sure."

"Good," Ruby said. "Let's go talk to Darla."

We got out of the car and headed toward the back of the store, where a light was burning in what I assumed was the office. Darla McDaniels owns Bluebonnet Books, the only independent, full-service bookstore between Austin and San Antonio. When Darla leased the century-old building a few years ago, she had to sweep out the bat droppings, refinish the original wooden floor, repair the pressed-tin ceiling and limestone walls, and install new lighting and windows, as well as bookcases and shelves. She had obviously made a major investment in renovations, not to mention what she'd tied up in her sizable inventory of books and gift items. That's a big hunk of change, plus her emotional investment, which is incalculable. Darla probably spends more hours in her store than she does with her husband — the former jock she had once shared with Ruby.

Ruby rapped four times on the alley door, and after a moment Darla opened it. There is no trace left of the trim, athletic cheerleader she was once. Now, she is a very large woman with broad shoulders and hips. But rather than play down her size, Darla plays it up, with a sizzle. She wore a gauzy royal-purple tunic and matching piazza pants with a cranberry-and-orange chiffon scarf looped around her neck. She had outlined her eyes in purple liner and used purple shadow and black mascara liberally. The effect was, well, striking.

After a casual hello to me and a cheek-to-cheek with Ruby that paid tribute to their longtime friendship, Darla led us past a closet-sized office in which a gray-haired woman was hunched over a checkbook and a calculator, to her own slightly larger office, littered with computer printouts, boxes of old invoices and records, and stacks of books. A gold plaque on her desk read DARLA J. MCDANIELS, PRESIDENT. I wondered briefly what she was president of.

Darla lowered her hefty bulk into an office chair and gestured at the two straight chairs against the wall. "Haven't seen you around lately, Ruby," she said. "Keeping yourself busy?" She pushed aside the remains of a take-out hamburger. The odor of french fries filled the stuffy room, overlaying the musky scent of Darla's perfume. High on the wall, a portable air conditioner labored noisily, but it didn't do a thing to dispel the odors.

"The tearoom is opening in a couple of weeks," Ruby said, sitting down. I sat down beside her. "It's been a lot of work. And China and Mike McQuaid are getting married on Sunday."

"Getting married!" Darla said, with an inflection that suggested surprise. She added, with a chuckle, "I don't know that I'd want to be a cop's wife, but if you do, well, congratulations."

"He's only interim," I said, remembering that Darla, too, was one of McQuaid's bosses.

She shrugged. "Some of the Council would love to have him stay on." Under the pitiless fluorescent light, her purple costume was garish, her rouge streaked, her lashes clumped with mascara. The sizzle looked tawdry.

"You must be pretty busy too, Darla," Ruby said. "I don't know how you juggle everything — the store, the Council, your family." She smiled reminiscently. "But you were always good at the balancing act. Remember that pyramid formation we used to do, with Piggy and me on the bottom and you on top?" She giggled. "Those were the days, huh? Drove the crowd crazy, didn't we?"

Darla's laugh was a little sour. "I'm still on top, thank you very much. Only nowadays, it takes brains. And will power. A little capital doesn't hurt, either." She glanced at Ruby. "So. What's so urgent that it couldn't wait until tomorrow?"

"We talked to one of your colleagues on the Council this afternoon," Ruby said. "She thought you might be able to help us."

"Hmm," Darla said. She focused on the cold french fries, reached for one, then restrained herself. "Help you what?"

"Help us out of a dilemma," Ruby said. "China and I have uncovered something — in an unofficial way, of course — that might speed up the police investigation of Edgar Coleman's murder."

Darla's gaze fastened on Ruby, her hand still poised over the french fries. "Edgar Coleman?"

"The person we talked to mentioned that Coleman had dealings with several members of the City Council." Ruby leaned forward. "She said, for instance, that he had been talking to you. We wondered if you could —"

Darla's eyes narrowed. "To me? What would Edgar Coleman want to talk to me about? Why, we hardly knew one another." She pushed the french fries away. "And just who the hell is this Council member who goes around spreading stories about —"

"I understood," I said quietly, "that Edgar Coleman was your landlord."

She stared at me, her teeth catching her lower lip and working it for a moment. Then she realized what she was doing and rearranged her mouth. "Yeah, sure," she said, straightening her shoulders and becoming very businesslike. "But I had no idea you were talking about *that*. That's totally separate. It's got nothing to do with Council business. I would never —"

"Darla?" The three of us looked up to see the gray-haired woman standing in the door. She held a pencil in one hand and a piece of paper in the other, and a pair of plastic-rimmed reading glasses dangled around her neck on a gold-colored chain. "I'm sorry to interrupt your conversation, but it's late and you know how men are. Charlie throws a fit if I'm not home to cook his supper. I won't be writing checks again until the fifteenth of next month, and I wanted to mention something important that you might want to attend to before —"

"What is it, Marge?" Darla asked, cutting off the flow of words. I didn't blame Darla for her impatience. Marge was obviously a talker.

Marge held out the paper. "Well, I was writing the rent check for October when I saw a reminder on the invoice saying that November's rent has been doubled. I know you and Mr. Coleman worked out a compromise before he . . . passed on. So I thought maybe you'd better call Iris and let her know what the two of you arranged, so she can correct the billing, which was obviously mailed before you two came to your agreement." She pursed her mouth, tapping her lips with the pencil. "Such a total shock, his going that way. Why, I've never in my entire life known anybody who was *murdered*. And to think that only the day before it happened, he was here, in this very office! Sure brings it home, doesn't it? Mortality, I mean. Death and all that." She rolled her eyes and made a sad, clucking sound with her tongue, *tch tch tch*. "Poor Letty. I feel for her. It must be so *hard*."

Darla was suddenly struck by a fit of coughing. I was next to Marge, so I took the statement out of her hand and handed it to Darla. It was an invoice from Coleman Enterprises.

"Totally separate, huh?" I remarked idly.

Darla picked up a paper napkin and blew her nose. "Thank you, Marge," she said. "I'll see you on the fifteenth."

"Sure," Marge said. "But don't forget to call Iris and get it straightened out. You *did* sign the new lease, didn't you? Both you and Mr. Coleman? If so, you need to make sure she has a copy of —"

"Thank you, Marge," Darla said sharply, biting off the words. She opened a drawer and shoved the invoice into it. "Go home before Charlie starves to death."

When the bookkeeper had left, I said, "Maybe you could tell us about that compromise, Darla."

Darla's firm jaw was set and her eyes were narrow. "Why should I? Just because some nosy Council member decides it's a crime for a tenant to talk to her landlord? I don't think so."

"Just because," Ruby said, very thoughtfully, "we might be able to help you keep

176

this information from becoming a matter of public record. If people found out about it, they might think you had something to do with his death. Which might make trouble for you in the next election. Might not be good for business, either."

"Something to do with his death?" Darla was spirited. "That's bullshit, Ruby. You can't possibly imagine that I —"

"Oh, of *course* not," Ruby said, with an excess of reassurance. "Anyway, I'm sure you have a what-do-you-call-it . . . an alibi? He was killed on Sunday night."

In the silence that followed Ruby's question, the lines on Darla's face noticeably deepened and she grew paler under her makeup. "I didn't kill him," she snapped, "and I have no idea who did. And what's more, I resent your implication. You've got a lot of nerve, Ruby, considering all we've been through over the years." No alibi, I thought, with interest — and the lack of it was worrying her.

"What did Edgar Coleman offer in return for your vote on the annexation project?" I asked.

"My vote?" There was an edge of panic in Darla's voice, but she clung to her defenses. "I'd like to know what gives you the right to —"

"We've learned that Coleman attempted to bribe other Council members," I said. "But I can understand why you don't want to talk about it — to us, anyway. I'm sure you're saving the information for the police. Bribery of a public official is a felony." I nudged Ruby. "Come on, Ruby. We can tell McQuaid to —"

"Other Council members?" Darla asked nervously.

"Right," Ruby said. "The cat's out of the bag."

"Shit," Darla said. She closed her eyes for the space of a couple of heartbeats, then opened them with a sigh. "What the hell," she said, resigned. "Marge will spread it all over town, anyway. She's a good bookkeeper, but she doesn't know the meaning of the word 'confidential.'" Her hand went to the french fries, took two, and stuffed them in her mouth. "He gave me another five years with no increase."

"And if you held out?"

Her nostrils flared. "He was going to double it."

"That's robbery!" Ruby exclaimed heatedly. "What a jerk!"

Ruby's sympathetic response seemed to collapse Darla's last defense. She took four more french fries and dredged them in a little paper cup filled with catsup, blinking back tears. "With Barnes and Noble moving into the mall last month, it would have killed me. I'd have lost everything I've invested — money, time, all my hopes and dreams." Four more fries. "I wasn't going to take that lying down."

"So you made a deal," I said. "You traded your vote for a break on the rent."

The food seemed to give her courage. "You're damn right I made a deal," she said fiercely. "You would've done the same thing, in my place." She opened another drawer, pulled out a sheaf of papers, and slapped them on the desk. "See for yourself."

It was a five-year lease agreement, with terms that I supposed she'd found acceptable, since her signature was on the last page. The document was dated the day before Coleman died.

"But Coleman didn't sign it," Ruby said, pointing to the line left for the lessor's signature.

"Of course he didn't sign it," Darla said bitterly. "Do you think that scumbag would put his name on paper before he got what he wanted? He was holding off until after the next Council vote. *Then* he'd sign." She sighed wearily. "I almost cheered out loud when I heard somebody had shot the bastard, but I wish to hell the killer had waited until the lease was signed." She paused, reflecting. "Well, it probably doesn't matter. I figure Iris will let me renew at the old rate for another year, and by that time, the building will be up for sale. Who knows? I might even be able to buy it."

"Well, then," Ruby said brightly, "it sounds like things are going to work out just fine after all."

There was silence in the room. "Do you know," I asked after a moment, "how far Coleman got with the other Council members?"

Darla took a whole handful of french fries. "You said it didn't have to become public record." She looked at me. "Does that mean it'll be kept quiet?"

I knew very well what she was angling for. She wanted me to use my influence with McQuaid to see that her name would be kept out of the newspaper. "Nobody can say what direction the police investigation will take," I said cautiously, "but they might be able to treat this information as background."

The statement was vague and meaningless, but it seemed to satisfy Darla. After a moment, she said, half-defiantly, "Well, why shouldn't I tell you? The question didn't come to a vote, which means that nobody is guilty of anything, right?"

Without waiting for an answer, she pushed on. "I don't know what kind of leverage he used with the others, but he certainly approached most of us. Ken, Winnie, Wanda, Pauline, Phyllis." She stopped. "Hang on. I don't know for sure about Phyllis. She's such a Girl Scout, I doubt Coleman thought he'd get anywhere with her. Winnie was definitely a holdout — she kept talking about how much damage he was doing to the environment — and Billie Jean had already voted yes." She looked down at the lease. "It's weird the way things work out, isn't it? Coleman had the votes he wanted, but he didn't live to count them."

Ruby looked at her intently. "Who do you think killed him, Darla? It had to be somebody who hated him, or was afraid of him, or . . ." She frowned. "Maybe it was somebody who had something to hide and knew he couldn't be trusted."

Darla gave a hard, bitter laugh. "Who killed him? Who the hell cares?" With a violent gesture, she swept the lease off the desk and into the drawer. "Good riddance to damned bad rubbish."

Chapter Eight

Lavender's green, diddle diddle,
Lavender's blue
You must love me, diddle diddle,
Cause I love you.
I heard one say, diddle diddle
Since I came hither
That you and I, diddle diddle
Must lie together.

Variation of "Lavender's Blue"

Ruby took me home, promising that she would talk to Ken Bowman first thing in the morning and reminding me that I had an eight-thirty appointment with Billie Jean at the House of Beauty. "Looks like McQuaid's home," she remarked, as we pulled into our drive. She was right. McQuaid's van — the specially equipped one we've leased for the duration — was parked in front.

"Want to come in?" I asked. "There are some cupcakes left over from dinner."

"I don't think so," Ruby said. "I'd better go on home." She cleared her throat. "But speaking of cake," she added, with a great show of carelessness, "do we need to check back with Adele?" I had ordered the wedding cake — a three-layer confection with the traditional bride and groom on top — from Adele Toomes, at Sweets for the Sweet. The shop began as a bakery, but Adele has expanded it to full-scale catering.

"Is there a particular reason," I asked warily, "for checking back with Adele?"

Ruby wasn't looking at me. "My friend Lulu called tonight and said that Annie quit and took the bus to Tucson this morning. Which leaves Adele with nobody but Maureen. And Maureen doesn't do cakes."

"Ruby," I said with a sigh, "I don't need to hear this."

"Oh, I'm sure everything's just fine," Ruby said hurriedly. "Just the same, I think I'll stop in and have a chat with Adele tomorrow morning." She put the car in gear. "Don't fret, dear, and don't forget about your beauty appointment."

Brian's light was still on upstairs, so I made a quick detour to give him a goodnight kiss, stumbling over Howard Cosell on the way out. Back downstairs, I found McQuaid at the kitchen table, with a can of Coors, a bag of tortilla chips, and a bowl of his favorite incendiary salsa, made from some of Blackie Blackwell's home-grown Rica Reds. They're only a little cooler than the temperature on the surface of the sun.

"Glad you're home," McQuaid said, sounding as if he meant it. "What have you been up to?" He grabbed my hand and pulled me down for a quick kiss. His lips were like fire. Literally.

"Oh, just girl stuff," I said. "You know how it is the week before a wedding." Surreptiously rubbing my tingling mouth with the back of my hand, I opened the re-frigerator to look for a beer and found a plate containing three small sunfish, each about the size of a silver dollar. "The kids went fishing while you checked out the creek," I guessed.

"Right," McQuaid said. There was mud on his jeans and a smear of mud on his shirt. "They were lucky." He scratched his leg above his boot. "All I got is chiggers."

I brought my beer to the table. "So what do you figure?"

"The gun was probably tossed out of a car as it went over the low-water crossing," McQuaid said. "No clues in the area. The computer's down tonight, so we don't have a make on the registration yet. Marvin took the gun to Austin for ballistics, blood work, and prints." He gave me a glance. "Sorry about that scene at supper. He means well, but he can be a real ass sometimes."

"A real ass most of the time," I said. I sipped my beer. "If that's Coleman's blood on the gun, he must have been shot at point-blank range."

"Yeah," McQuaid said shortly. "Left side of his face, above the upper lip. Tattooing around the entrance wound. The back of his head wasn't pretty, either."

"So it was somebody who knew him well enough to get up close," I said. "Somebody he wasn't afraid of." I frowned, thinking back to our lunchtime conversation. "What's the situation with Darryl Perkins? Is he still one of your suspects?"

"Darryl's got an alibi, of sorts," McQuaid said, dunking a chip in salsa. "He was in Waco, at a Lions Club conference that went on through Monday evening. Or rather, that's where he was *supposed* to be. He claims he got food poisoning from a bad bologna sandwich and spent Sunday evening in his hotel room, throwing up."

"Waco's only a couple of hours' drive," I said. "He could have driven back here, shot Coleman, then hot-footed it to Waco again."

"He *could* have," McQuaid said, "but I've got my doubts." He drained his beer. "Darryl's all hat and no cowboy. I can see him jealous and spoutin' off to his buddies about what he's going to do when he gets his hands on a gun. What I can't see is him shoving it in Coleman's face and pulling the trigger." He frowned. "Hate to say it, but I'd sooner put my money on Pauline. It isn't true," he added, "that Darryl filed for divorce. Apparently he never quite got up the nerve — and now they've patched it up. Makes you wonder, doesn't it?"

I nodded. Pecan Springers think of Darryl as a big man because he owns the car dealership and a piece of the radio station. But behind the scenes, Pauline has always been the bigger man. Darryl might have a fit of jealousy every now and then, but if Pauline's passions were stirred, she'd be far more likely to do something about it.

"So what about Pauline?" I asked. "Where was *she* on Sunday night?"

"Home alone," McQuaid replied. "No phone calls, no visitors, no way to verify."

"Does Darryl own up to knowing that Coleman was blackmailing his wife?"

186

McQuaid shook his head. "There's no way to say for sure who knew what, or exactly when they knew it. Darryl denies knowing it. Pauline denies telling him."

"Pauline may just be trying to save his bacon," I said.

"Yeah." McQuaid sighed heavily. "God, I hate small-town murders. Especially when the victim is the town bully and most of the suspects are Mr. and Mrs. Clean." He made a wry face. "Give me a drive-by drug killing any day of the week."

I frowned. "What about Jorge Garza? Did you talk to him?"

"Both Marvin and I interviewed him." McQuaid was somber. "The man is a powder keg. Nervous, angry, volatile. Looks like he could blow at any moment. Apparently, after he got suspended at work —"

"Suspended?" Phyllis hadn't told me that.

"Yeah," McQuaid said grimly. "I haven't confirmed the details with his supervisor yet, but he apparently got involved with a family of migrant workers and tried to help them by supplying a set of phony documents. He's under investigation for forging immigration papers — which means that Coleman's threat hit him at the worst time. It's not hard to see Garza pushing a gun into the man's face — not to protect Phyllis, but to keep Coleman from causing him more grief."

"Maybe Phyllis can vouch for his whereabouts on Sunday night," I said.

"Nope. Her mother was in the hospital with a suspected heart attack, and Phyllis was with her. Garza has no alibi." He reached for my hand. "Thanks for getting that letter to us, China. If it hadn't been for you, this stuff on Garza wouldn't have turned up."

Yeah, thanks, China. Nice of you to implicate your friend and her tough-luck husband. I hoped Jorge wasn't taking out his angst on Phyllis and made a mental note to give her a call and see how she was holding up. Maybe McQuaid was right. Maybe big-city drive-bys were preferable to small-town murders, where everybody knows everybody else and the facts are tangled up in old friendships, ancient rivalries, and secret debts.

I leaned forward. "I hate to complicate your investigation, but you need to hear what Ruby and I have dug up."

McQuaid groaned. "Don't you two ever lay off? We've already got enough suspects to hold a square dance."

"I thought you were on the side of law

188

and order," I said. "Do you want to hear or don't you?"

He nodded, bemused. "Shoot."

I shot, giving him a summary of the conversation with Winnie, Letty's late-afternoon visit, and Darla's interview, with as much verbatim as I could recall. When I finished, McQuaid sat for a few moments, thinking.

"Letty didn't say a word about another love interest when I talked to her," he said at last. He gave me a long look. "What I want to know is how you got all that information out of those people without a badge or a warrant."

"A badge would've gotten in the way." I paraphrased Ruby. "Did you ever, in all of the years you were in Homicide, hear of a single living soul who actually volunteered to be a suspect in a murder investigation?"

"Well —" McQuaid said.

"I want to talk to Letty," I said. "I agree with her that there's no point in getting the other woman involved unless there's something to it. And it isn't the sort of investigation the cops do best." I grinned. "Can you picture Letty saying *anything* to Marvin but 'yes sir' and 'no sir'?"

"I suppose you're right," McQuaid said slowly. He made up his mind. "Okay, talk to her, and report back." McQuaid pushed himself out of his chair and reached for his canes. I stood too, and slid my arms around him. He lifted my chin and kissed me, hard. I could still taste the chile pepper on his mouth, but now its heat mingled with the other warmth rising up inside me. He slid his right hand down the front of my shirt to the first button, his fingers cool against my throat. "We've got a wedding night coming up pretty quick," he whispered into my ear. "Want to get in a little practice?"

"I haven't bought my honeymoon nightgown yet," I objected. "How can I rehearse without a costume?"

"Easy," McQuaid said. "We both get naked."

"Best offer I've had all day," I murmured.

On school mornings, Brian dashes to the kitchen to toss down a bowl of cereal with fruit before he grabs his books and sprints for the bus. In nice weather, McQuaid and I usually take our breakfasts onto the back deck, sharing the *Enterprise* and the sweet, early coolness, the air heavy with the scent of lavender and brightened by the yellow rose that climbs over the trellis. This morning, though, McQuaid didn't linger. He ate his cereal leaning against the counter, frowning as he listened to my report of the message Harold Tucker had left on our answering machine the afternoon before.

"Guess we'd better have a look at that lease," he said. "Wonder where I put it."

I looked around the kitchen with a sigh. "I hate to think about moving. We'll never find another place like this one." I straightened my shoulders. "But we're staying put until January. The Tuckers will just have to rent a house." I changed the subject. "Don't forget about the marriage license. Today's Wednesday — we really have to get it."

"Yeah, sure." McQuaid chugged the rest of his orange juice. "Why did Coleman have to get himself knocked off the week before our wedding? The department has gone for a couple of months with nothing nastier than petty theft and a few drunk and disorderlies, and now this."

I flipped a slice of bread into the toaster. "Is the Council making progress on their search for a chief?" I asked the question very casually.

He took an apple out of the bowl on the table. "Haven't heard anything about it lately." He wasn't looking at me. "I guess they'll tell me when they've found somebody."

I folded my arms and faced him. "McQuaid," I said quietly, "you know my feelings on this subject. You have a perfectly good teaching job. It pays more money than wearing a badge and does not require you to risk life and limb."

He reached for his canes. "Apprehending a D-and-D isn't very risky." He bent toward me, gave me a quick kiss, and limped toward the door.

I raised my voice. "Did you hear what I said?"

"Sure," he replied lightly. "Eleven-thirty at the courthouse. I'll be the one with the eager look. Love you."

That wasn't quite the reassurance I wanted, but it was all I was going to get. I went upstairs and checked out my nose in the mirror. The abrasions were still evident, but the blue under my eyes was fading. With luck, I wouldn't have to listen to any more favorite remedies. I reached for the phone to dial Letty's number and told her that I agreed with what she'd proposed the night before. It was a good idea to find out whether Edgar had been involved with anyone else, and I'd like to talk to her about what she knew.

"Oh, *thank* you!" she exclaimed. "And I learned something else, just this morning. It's confirmed what I guessed." Once again, there was that odd tension in her voice. Anger? Fear? Considering all of Coleman's extracurricular activities — women, real estate deals, bribery, maybe even drugs and organized crime — nobody could fault her for being afraid.

"Maybe you ought to go straight to the police," I said. "If you know something important, you might be in danger."

She backpedaled. "Well, I'm not *that* sure. And I don't think there's any danger."

"I've got an appointment to get my hair cut," I said. "I'll come over around ten."

"Fine. As soon as you can." She paused. "And maybe I'll arrange —" Another pause, then: "Well, we'll see. Ten o'clock. I'll be waiting."

I was in our bedroom, wrapping myself into a denim skirt and thinking ruefully that maybe I should be out running a few of the extra pounds off, when the phone rang. It turned out to be Smart Cookie. She was glum.

"I've told Blackie I won't take the police chief position," she said. "I'm withdrawing."

"Oh, no, Sheila!" I exclaimed. "You'd be terrific for the job! Surely you and Blackie can work it out. Anyway, it's not fair for you to give up something you want so badly, just because it doesn't fit Blackie's idea of what his wife ought to be doing. That's no way to run a marriage."

Sheila cleared her throat. "What Justine said about the political angle . . . well, she made me think, China. I could cause a lot of trouble for Blackie just by doing my job. I might even keep him from getting re-elected. And you know how much he loves what he does. I would never want to get between him and his work."

"Yeah," I said. "Being sheriff is almost a mystical experience for him." I didn't want to say so, but I was afraid that the same thing was true for McQuaid. If Sheila got the nod, he'd bow out gracefully. If she didn't, he might be persuaded to take the job.

Sheila laughed, but without humor. "Actually, I didn't call about that," she said. "Do you happen to know Iris Powell?"

"Edgar Coleman's secretary? I don't know her, but I know who she is." I paused. "Why are you asking?"

"She's more than his secretary," Sheila said.

"So I understand," I said dryly.

"I didn't mean *that,* either. She was his office manager. She knows his business, inside out."

I wondered briefly whether Iris knew about the deal that Darla had made with Coleman. "How are you connected with Iris Powell?"

"Paula, my administrative assistant, is Iris's sister."

I remembered Paula. She had joined Sheila and me for lunch once or twice. "It's a small world," I said.

"It's a small town. Paula's very worried about Iris."

"Worried?"

"According to Paula, Iris has a pretty good idea who killed Coleman and why. She says Iris is afraid that she might be the killer's next target. She wants us — you and me — to talk to her."

"You I understand, since you're Paula's boss and a cop — sort of. But why me?"

"Paula says Iris needs to talk to a lawyer. You keep up your bar membership, don't you?"

"Yes, but that's neither here nor there," I said firmly. "Iris needs to talk to Mc-Quaid."

"She has, already. But Paula says that

Iris was afraid of telling him too much. She didn't want him to guess how deeply she was involved with Coleman's business. I got the impression that she has information about illegal activities, and she's not sure what to do with it."

"Paula strikes me as the exaggerating sort," I said. Actually, this was an understatement, for the time or two I had seen Paula, she had related a couple of sensational stories involving dramatic psychological crises that might have been drawn from *All My Children*. Her tale about Iris might have more to do with an overactive imagination than with the facts of the matter.

"Paula's inclined to blow things out of proportion," Sheila admitted, "but I've got the feeling there's something to this." She paused. "I know you're busy, China, but I think we ought to go see Iris. Paula could let her know we're coming."

"Okay," I said. "Can you pick me up at the shop at eleven-thirty?" I stopped. "No, that won't work. McQuaid and I are getting our license today, and I've got three or four other urgent things to do, starting with a hair cut." The day was already so full, I wasn't going to have time to breathe. "How about late afternoon? Want to pick me up, say, at four-thirty?" Laurel was closing today, so I could leave a little early.

"I'll ask Paula to set it up and leave a message at the shop to confirm." Sheila paused, shifting gears. "Speaking of weddings, we really have to make some decisions about the music. What do you think of using 'Greensleeves' before the ceremony, and the old Dinah Shore song about lavender — 'Lavender's Blue.' Then the *Bridal Chorus* for your entrance and the *Wedding March* afterward."

"I like 'Greensleeves,'" I said, "and 'Lavender's Blue' is perfect. But I wish we could think of something besides the traditional marches."

"Everybody expects them," Sheila said. "That's why they're traditional."

"That's why I'd rather have something else." I thought for a moment. "For the recessional, how about 'Home With the Armadillos'?"

Sheila groaned. "This is serious, China. The wedding is only three days away."

It was my turn to groan. "Okay, okay. Scratch 'Armadillo.' How about Beethoven's *Ode to Joy* for the recessional?"

"I guess that would work," Sheila said, sounding doubtful but relieved. "That just leaves the bride's entrance."

" 'At the Hop'?" I suggested. I glanced at my watch and stuck my feet into my leather sandals. "Oops, gotta go. I'm late for my hair appointment."

"Have fun," Sheila said, sounding resentful. "I wish I didn't have anything to do but loaf around getting beautiful."

"You're already beautiful," I said with a sigh. "I've got to work at it."

Chapter Nine

O! And I was a damsel so fair,
But fairer I wished to appear.
So I washed me in milk,
and dressed me in silk,
And put sweet thyme in my hair.

Old Devonshire song

The fair maid who, the first of May
Goes to the fields at break of day
And washes in dew from the hawthorn tree
Will ever after handsome be.

Folk Saying

Pecan Springs may not be much bigger than a peanut, but where essential services are concerned, we've got our bases covered. We have two banks, three Baptist churches, four barbecue joints, five auto dealerships, and more beauty shops than you can count. There's the unisex shop in the mall, which is frequented by adolescents with green hair and rings in their noses, and a couple of dozen small shops in garages and rec rooms, where neighborhood women flock to trade gossip and get their hair shampooed and set while their preschoolers scribble in coloring books on the floor. And there is Bobby Rae's House of Beauty.

To appreciate Bobby Rae's, you have to have lived in a small town at one time or another in your life — and you have to be a woman. Although Bobby Rae does the occasional man, her House of Beauty appeals mostly to the female of the species. From the pink plastic flamingo outside the door to the powder-pink decor inside, from the dotted swiss pink-ribbon-trimmed curtains to the bouquet of pink silk flowers on the magazine table, from the hair fashion photos on the wall to Nora's Nail Fashions table in the corner, Bobby Rae caters to the small-town Aphrodite. A fly-specked sign on the wall promises that a trained beautician or spa specialist will cut, style, set, and blow dry your hair; bleach it, color it, correct it, curl it, or straighten it; color your eyelashes and your eyebrows; peel your face and wax your legs and painlessly relocate your "bikini line"; and cover your real nails with gel, acrylic, fiberglass, silk wrap, or just plain plastic. Or, if you prefer, you may purchase a Bountiful Beauty

Package to pamper yourself or a friend: a Lady Executive Escape, a New Mom Morning, or a Bride and Groom Getaway. I was contemplating this information in some amazement when I was accosted by a sizable woman in pink jeans and a silky pink smock, a basket of sausage-sized foam curlers in one hand.

"Mornin', dear," Bobby Rae said cheerily. "How can we do you today?"

I looked up at the sign. "Bride and Groom Getaway? What's that?"

"It's everything yer heart desires times two. Sauna, spa, a do for two — plus a catered lunch from Terri's Takeout. Fancy sandwiches, salad, the works. When you get back from the Getaway, you're ready for the weddin'."

"I'm afraid the groom would be too busy," I said.

"Yeah. Men." With a look of infinite scorn, Bobby Rae squeezed behind the counter of the reception desk and put down her basket of foam sausages. "That's whut they all say. Too busy. No time." She snorted. "Skeered, that's whut *I* say. 'Fraid their friends'll say they're sissies. But that's okay, honey. You kin pay half and get the Bride's Getaway."

Bobby Rae Ritter is of a generous girth,

with Dolly Parton–sized breasts and arms like Troy Aikman. On her head she wears a pile of pink hair like a prodigious pouf of cotton candy, back-combed and teased and tousled and moussed, with pink tendrils curling festively around her cheerful, moon-shaped face. If there were a Texas Hall of Fame for Big Hair, Bobby Rae's photograph would be in it, front and center with former Governor Ann and the Dallas Cowboy cheerleaders. Styles may come and go in Hollywood and New York, but Big Hair remains the grand Texas passion.

"I'm afraid I don't have time," I said.

Bobby Rae smiled warmly at me. "It don't take much time to get beautiful, hon. Listen, we'll fix you up so gorgeous, he'll think it's Farrah he's marryin'. Hair, nails, facial, a wax job —" She opened the appointment book. "When's the big day?"

"Sunday," I said. "But I've already got an eight-thirty with Billie Jean to get my hair cut."

"Why, that don't make no nevermind," Bobby Rae said comfortingly. "You can take your Getaway in little bites, 'stead of all at once. Billie Jean can cut you today, I'll color you tomorrow, and Nora'll do your facial and your nails on Friday mornin'." She took my right hand and examined my nails, a momentary look of consternation crossing her face. But she recovered herself quickly. "Maybe we better schedule them nails for Friday afternoon," she said with genuine sympathy. "Might take a little longer than usual." She glanced up at my face and her eyes fastened on my nose. "And maybe we oughta tack on an expert makeup session, just in case that face don't fade fast enough. When's the weddin'?"

"Thanks, but I don't want a Getaway," I replied firmly. "I'll just have to live with my face."

Bobby Rae gave me a long, pitying look. "Hate to see you anything but beautiful for your weddin' day, sweetie," she said, reluctantly abandoning me to my ugly fate. "But whutever you say." She gestured. "Billie Jean was a little late this morning, but I think she's here now. Through that pink door. She'll do you in a hurry, if that's whut you got your heart set on."

You may be wondering why a City Council member is cutting hair in the back room of Bobby Rae's House of Beauty, so I'd better explain. Last year, an unusual event took place in Pecan Springs. For the first time in recorded history, voters rebelled against the conservative Old Guard who have dominated local politics since the railroad came to town. In one massive heave-ho, the citizens tossed out four conservative incumbents who were up for re-election and elected Phyllis Garza, Darla McDaniels, Winnie Hatcher, and Billie Jean Jones, each of whom reports, more or less, to a particular segment of the Pecan Springs voting population. Phyllis was elected by the Hispanic community, Darla by the small business lobby, Winnie by the local Greens, and Billie Jean by her customers. When Billie Jean decided to run for election, she simply added a thirty-second political commercial to the usual shampoo-and-snip. She cuts a lot of hair, and her margin of victory was bigger than anybody else's. The power of beauty is not to be taken lightly.

Unlike Bobby Rae, Billie Jean is not a walking advertisement for her art. She is twiggy and sallow-faced and her hair is an ordinary light brown, about the color of mine. This morning, she was wearing a wrinkled white T-shirt, sneakers without socks, and baggy green pants that tied around the waist, like men's pajama bottoms. She is nervous by nature, and being late this morning seemed to make her more so than usual. She gave me a small smile. "What're we doin' for you today, China?"

"Shampoo and cut," I said. "I'm getting married on Sunday."

"I heard. You're braver'n me. I wouldn't marry a cop, no matter how many times he got down on his knees to beg." She lifted a handful of my hair. "Pretty dry. And maybe you oughta do something about that gray streak. Let me fix that up for you, it'll take off prob'ly five years."

"He's only a temporary cop," I said. "When you guys get around to hiring a chief, he can quit." I hesitated, tempted. "Do you really think it would take off five years?" I asked.

"Easy," Billie Jean said. "Maybe ten. We could do it temporary. By the time it washes out, you'll know whether you want to do it permanent." Now that she was into the swing of things, she sounded less tense. "I could lighten you up, oh, three-four shades. Look real nice."

My usual hair-care regimen is home-made and simple. I concoct my own herbal castile shampoo with aloe, camomile, and lemon juice, and occasionally I beat up an egg yolk and rub it in after a shampoo. When my hair is really dry, almond oil is good, which usually takes care of dandruff as well. If not, I massage in mint vinegar three or four times a week until it clears up. But I hadn't had time this summer to do more than grab a bottle of shampoo at the grocery store, and my hair was looking dark and dry.

So the Aphrodite in me agreed to a lightening and conditioning, while my cynical self went along, bemused, to see what would happen. The whole affair took less than an hour and when it was over, the gray was gone and what was left was a head of very light brown hair with fetching gold highlights. It wasn't five years and it wasn't Big Hair, but I wouldn't throw a stick at it.

And in the process, I heard an interesting story. At first, Billie Jean held her lips pressed tight and it wasn't as easy as I'd expected to get her to talk. Once we got on the subject of Edgar Coleman, though, she seemed almost eager, as if she had a story to tell and had just been waiting for the right person to tell it to. Billie Jean had been cutting Coleman for three or four years — one of the few males she did — but she hadn't realized just how much he thought of her until a couple of weeks ago, when he asked her how come she didn't

206

have her own shop.

"What did you tell him?" I asked. By this time, she was blow-drying me, and I was watching her face in the pink-framed mirror. Her lips weren't pressed tight anymore, but there was a scowl on her face.

"I said I sure as shit aimed to, the minute I scraped together enough to pay for equipment. He said that was extremely coincidental, because just the day before he'd had to take over one of the clip joints in a strip mall he owned."

"Oh, yeah?" I said. "That *is* a coincidence."

She ruffled my top hair with her fingers and waved the dryer across it fast. "You damn betcha. He said he'd let me have the place, which still has all the equipment and the sign and everything. In fact, he'd make it real easy for me, like he'd just forget about the first six lease payments, which would let me get my feet on the ground before I had to make rent."

"Mmm," I said. "You must have been tempted."

"Extremely." She flipped a brush through my hair, fluffing it out on the sides. Most of the time it just lies flat. I had to admit that fluffy was an improvement. "I'm damned sick of Bobby Rae and her Pepto-Bismol pink. Oh, it might be all right if a person only had to put up with it for a couple of hours every month or so. But it's pretty friggin' miserable to look at eight hours a day five days a week. I've got so that pink turns my stomach. You damned betcha it was tempting."

I looked up and caught her eye in the mirror. "So when's the grand opening?"

"Ha," she said bitterly.

"Ha?"

She made a face at me in the mirror, cupping her hands around the sides of my head to shape it. "Yeah, ha. Turns out Coleman wasn't setting me up in a shop because he liked the way I cut hair, oh no. There were strings tied all over that nifty little present he was holding out. To get those six free months, all I had to do was vote yes on the Blessing Ranch annexation when it came up for a final vote. Hair spray?" Without waiting for my No! she picked up a can and began to spray my hair in short bursts. "Coleman was there when we voted the first time, you see, and he heard me say yes." She considered my head critically, patted it here and there, and sprayed again. "He was buying insurance. He figured if I got that shop space, I'd vote yes again." Disgustedly, she thumped the can down and whipped off my pink plastic cape. "Trouble was, Coleman didn't know me. I am an ethical person. I told him he could take that shop and shove it, and I was gonna vote no."

"I guess I don't understand," I said. "You voted for the annexation once, so you must have thought it was a good idea."

"Well, sure." She shook out the cape with a snap. "I got a couple customers live out there that need water. They told me their problem and asked could I help, and I said yes, because I felt like they had a valid point. I do what I can for the folks who voted for me." She curled her lip scornfully. "Some sucker tries to *buy* my vote, though, he's got trouble. Big time." She inspected my neck. "Sit back down there and let me run the clippers."

"So you told off Edgar Coleman, and then what?" I asked, while she was buzzing up and down my neck.

"Then nothing. He said he was gonna try to change my mind and I said good luck, sarcastic, you know. So he walked outta here mad, and a coupla days later, somebody blew him away." She took up a brush and whisked my neck. "So. Do you like it?"

I stared at the blond stranger in the

mirror. "Wow," I said.

"Color turned out just right," she said, pleased. "Five years. I was right, huh?"

"Oh, absolutely," I lied. I stood up and reached for my purse, then paused. "Any idea who might have killed Coleman?"

She scrunched up her mouth and pulled down her brows. "You know, I've been thinking about that," she said slowly. "If I'd been the type to get pissed off, I sure as hell would've been mad at that sonofabitch for trying to bribe me. But 'spose he made a offer to a person who *was* the type. Or 'spose he had something he could hold over that person, and wanted to trade. He'd be quiet, if the person would vote his way. But you couldn't trust Coleman any farther than you could see him, so the person killed him. Something like that happened on *Murder She Wrote* not too long ago." She reached for a broom and began to energetically sweep up drifts of my hair. "Good thing I'm not the type. Matter of fact, I was down in San Antonio when it happened, takin' care of my granddaughter while my girl had herself another baby." She looked up with a grin. "She got a boy this time. I'm takin' the next couple of days off to help her out."

"Congratulations," I said. "Let me know

210

when you open your new shop. What are you going to call it?"

She had obviously given the matter some thought. "The Best Little Hair House in Texas," she said with satisfaction, putting the broom away. "That oughta get some attention."

Edgar and Letty Coleman lived in Mesquite Meadows, Pecan Springs's newest upscale neighborhood. The houses are all custom-built on open, three-acre lots that are short on trees but long on limestone rock and wildflowers. In the spring, the curving streets are bordered with bluebonnets and paintbrush; in summer, the blues and reds give way to glowing sweeps of goldenrod and coreopsis and brown-eyed Susans. By autumn, the flame-leaf sumac are heavy with the fruit that the raccoons find so tasty and the yaupon holly is already studded with its bright red berries, tart enough that the robins and cedar waxwings leave them until last, after they've eaten all the juniper berries. Some years, they don't get around to them at all, and you find November's berries still clinging to the branches in July.

The Colemans' house — a stylish white Southwestern adobe with a red-tile roof —

was set back from the street behind a circular drive xeriscaped with drought-resistant natives — yucca and sotol, rabbitbrush and agarito and desert willow. Letty's elegant silver Lincoln Continental sat in front of the garage, which still sported a strip of yellow crime-scene tape. I looked around. No wonder the neighbors hadn't heard the shot that killed Edgar Coleman. The nearest house was a half-block away, on the other side of a deep ravine.

I parked, went up the walk, and opened the gate into a walled courtyard that stretched across the front of the house. The courtyard was hot and bright and paved with smooth river rock, with a few large boulders scattered artistically here and there. In the center, a large artificial waterfall plunged into a rocky pool surrounded by showy clumps of grass, a fifteen-foot green cactus with many branches and symmetrical ribs, and a tornillo mesquite with twisted limbs, hung with odd-shaped corkscrew beans. It was an interesting landscape, and its designer had achieved a striking effect — the plants and rocks and even the water all carefully composed, with not a weed to be seen. But that's all it was, somehow: an effect, like a still life, finished, complete, season-less. To appreciate it, all the viewer had to do was stand and gaze. Not my sort of garden. I prefer plants that invite me to get involved with them, love them or hate them, dig them up and move them around, deadhead and divide them, mulch them, and root out weeds. I wondered whether Letty liked this garden. Perhaps it had been her husband's idea.

But I wasn't here to ponder the relationship between the style of a garden and the personality of its owner. I needed to find out what Letty knew about the "other woman" who might or might not have been one of Edgar Coleman's lovers — and to discover what Letty was hiding. I had thought about my conversation with her off and on all morning, while Billie Jean was turning me into a blond hussy, and I was sure she was concealing *something*. Some sort of knowledge, or an emotion she didn't want to reveal: a deep-seated, far-reaching anger, perhaps, or fear. Still thinking about this, I walked toward the front door. If I hadn't been thinking, hadn't had my eyes on the ground, I doubt that I would have noticed the discreet little plaque: GARDEN DESIGN BY WANDA RATHBOTTOM, WANDA'S WONDERFUL ACRES.

Wanda Rathbottom, another City Council member. I paused, wondering whether Edgar might have offered Wanda a landscaping contract in return for her vote on the annexation proposal. It wouldn't surprise me.

I went to the front door — a heavily carved, oaken affair — and rang the doorbell. After a minute, I rang it again. After the third ring, I pushed the door open, put in my head, and called Letty's name. She was expecting me — in fact, when we talked that morning, she'd made it very clear that she was anxious to see me.

Well, I was here, but Letty obviously wasn't waiting. Calling her name again, I went down the hall and into a large open room with a cathedral ceiling, a stone fireplace at one end and a glass wall that looked out onto a patio. The room was furnished with leather Mission-style sofa, chairs, and occasional tables, and decorated with handsome handwoven rugs and wall hangings. Over the mantel, a massive stuffed longhorn stared out at the room with glass eyes — a man's room, full of man-sized furniture. Off to the right was a doorway into a dining room filled with a heavy pine Mission-style table, chairs, and sideboard, more rugs on the wall and a chunky pottery sculpture on the sideboard. Surely this wasn't Letty's style. There wasn't a trace of her in anything I had seen so far. Didn't she claim any space of her own in this house?

"Letty?" I called again. No answer. In front of me, a sliding door opened onto the patio and I pushed it open and went outside. The patio was paved with bleached white flagstones and decorated with heavy terra-cotta pots filled with a variety of cacti — more of the Southwestern motif, uncomfortably stark, it seemed to me. On a table shaded by a yellow umbrella sat a pitcher of iced tea, three glasses and plates, a small tray of cookies, and a pair of sunglasses — but no Letty. The late-morning sun was bright, and the stunning glare from the white adobe and the stone paving patio made me slit my eyes as I looked around.

The house was built on the edge of a rocky ravine. The patio was edged by a knee-high rock wall, but there was an opening where stone steps descended, perhaps to a garden area below. I went to the top of the stairs to call again, and that's when I saw her, spread-eagled and face-up at the foot of the stairs twenty feet below, arms outflung, eyes wide open, staring blindly at the blazing sun.

Chapter Ten

Lavender has a long tradition of magical use as a herb of purification, of love and of protection. . . . In Tuscany lavender was used to protect children from the evil eye, while in North Africa the Karbyll women used lavender to protect themselves from mistreatment by their husbands.

Lavender, Sweet Lavender
Judyth A. McLeod

"Of course she's dead," I said grimly. I was clutching the cell phone so hard that my fingers hurt. I changed hands.

"You've already called EMS?" McQuaid asked.

"Yeah, for all the good it will do. Looks like a broken neck." My throat hurt. I shut my eyes, but I couldn't shut out the sight of Letty, with her blank face and blind eyes, sprawled at the foot of the stairs.

"Signs of foul play?"

"Death is foul."

McQuaid sighed. "Yes, I know. But —"

Tough. I should be tough. Dead bodies don't bother Kinsey Milhone. "If she was pushed," I said, "the pusher didn't leave any obvious clues. But then I didn't take time to do a detailed forensic analysis. I flew down the stairs to see if she was as dead as she looked, then flew back up to the car to use the phone. I didn't want to use the one in the house."

"Good girl," McQuaid said approvingly.

I repressed the urge to tell him that I wasn't a girl and said, "I did notice something, though. There's a pitcher and three glasses on the patio table. It looks like I wasn't the only guest she was expecting. And now that I think about it, she did start to tell me that she might arrange something. She didn't say what it was, though."

"Ah," McQuaid said. It was the pleased "ah" of a cop who is on to something. He paused, and his voice softened. "Are you okay, China?"

I thought about this. "I don't find a dead body every day of the week, if that's what you're asking, and I *was* expecting to have a conversation with Letty." I tried out a chuckle. It sounded normal. "I guess I'm as okay as a person can be after discovering that her hostess has cashed it in."

"Hang around until I get there," he said.

"I'm on my way."

It took him about twenty minutes. Meanwhile, EMS showed up, followed by the nearest neighbor, Mrs. Burnett, who came over when she heard the siren. She was a round-faced woman in a tastefully tailored gray suit, a little snug across the hips, carrying a gray fake-leather briefcase stamped with the name Rena Burnett, Adams County Realty.

"Her *too?*" Mrs. Burnett asked. Her moony face was flushed with distress. "Poor Letty. Poor, poor Letty. How did it happen? She didn't . . . well, slit her wrists or anything like that, did she?"

That idea had not yet occurred to me, and the question gave me something to think about. "I found her at the foot of the patio stairs."

"Those stairs," Mrs. Burnett said, in the same tone she might have used for *that snake.* Her nostrils flared. "I told Edgar he ought to put up a railing." She set her briefcase on the ground beside her tasteful gray pumps. "He told me to butt out."

"Did Letty give you any reason to believe she might be thinking of suicide?"

"Well," she said. She stopped, eyeing my denim skirt and plaid blouse. "You're not from the police?"

"No," I said, then added, "I'm a lawyer. But this wasn't a business call. Letty wanted to talk to me about something that was bothering her."

"Oh, well, that's all right, then," Mrs. Burnett said. "I just don't want to volunteer — Well, you know." She gave a nervous laugh, remembered what we were talking about, and pulled down her mouth. "I don't make a practice of sticking my nose into people's private business, no matter what Edgar thought."

"She must have been under a lot of strain," I said sympathetically.

"Poor, poor Letty," Mrs. Burnett said again. "It was terrible, just absolutely *awful,* her finding him the way she did. She was hysterical, you know." She gave me a sideways glance. "Out of her head."

"I'm sure you're right," I said. "I know *I* would be, if I found my husband dead."

"Oh, yes. It was early in the morning and I was just going to the office — I'm a real estate agent, you know, with Adams County Realty." She opened her bag and handed me a business card. "She was down at the foot of the drive, waiting for the EMS, crying and screaming like a madwoman. Some man was with her — he turned out to be the editor of the *Enter-*

prise, the one who wrote all that awful stuff about blood on the wall." She shuddered. "Poor Letty. She just kept going on about —" Mrs. Burnett stopped.

"About —" I prompted.

She narrowed her eyes and drew in her mouth. Her face was flushed. "Well, about Edgar's women friends," she said, with a show of great reluctance that wouldn't have fooled anybody. "Names and stuff. It's a good thing that man didn't put what she said in the paper."

Names and stuff. "Pauline and Iris, you mean?"

"And Jean. I know it sounds crazy, but she had it in her head that they were the ones who shot him. She said they plotted to kill him because he was cheating on all three of them. Four, counting her." She screwed up her face. "Sex gets people in all kinds of trouble, doesn't it."

"You're absolutely right," I said, in a tone of great earnestness. "But I guess she didn't say that to the police."

"I don't think so." She pursed her lips. "By the time they arrived, she'd gotten hold of herself, more or less. I mean, it was obviously the sort of accusation only a crazy woman would make. Nobody would really think that three grown women would put their heads together and decide to *shoot* somebody." She paused, considering. "Although I don't suppose you could blame them if they did. Edgar was just asking for it, the way he carried on. I swear to God, that man was *such* a womanizer. You never knew where he would strike next." She made a huffing noise, fished in her shoulder bag for a tissue, and blew her nose. "How anybody could be so sweet and handsome on the outside and such a shark on the inside, I'll never understand."

"He had a terrible reputation," I agreed, wondering if Rena Burnett had first-hand knowledge of Edgar Coleman's sharky seductiveness.

"Lower than a snake's belly." Mrs. Burnett finished with her tissue and disposed of it in her bag. "Letty and I go — went — to the same church, you know, which gave me all the more reason to try and help her. I have never believed in divorce, because I think two people ought to work out their problems. But her marriage was a hell on earth, and I told her, straight out, she ought to get rid of him. If ever a husband mistreated a wife, it was Edgar Coleman."

Get rid of him. It was a resonant phrase. "Do you think," I asked, "that he abused her physically?"

Mrs. Burnett's face had grown redder and she was perspiring. "I don't know about that. But in my book, you don't have to actually hit a person to abuse them. Letty couldn't see it, naturally, but it's been my opinion all along that he only married her for the money her first husband left her, which Edgar forced her to invest in the Blessing Ranch. Of course, she'd deny it, but I know for a fact that she gave him the money because she was afraid to tell him no, for fear he'd leave." Mrs. Burnett blew out an explosive breath. "Anything he wanted, he got, and I do mean *anything*. And lots of times he wasn't even nice about it."

"Such a pity," I said, wondering whether Letty had grown so tired of always giving and never getting that she had picked up that shiny little mouse gun and blown her abusive husband away. And then, suffused with guilt and shame for what she had done, had thrown herself down the stairs. But while that theory was attractive, it didn't fit Letty's demeanor when we'd talked yesterday and this morning, or the fact of that pitcher and three glasses.

Mrs. Burnett reached down and picked up her briefcase and I cast an eye toward the street. McQuaid's arrival would probably put a stop to our girl talk. I'd better move her on to specifics.

"It's a good thing Letty had you to talk to," I remarked. "It must have made her feel better to get it off her chest." I frowned. "Of course, she spoke about Iris and Pauline to me, but I don't think I heard her mention anybody named Jean."

Mrs. Burnett sniffed. "That was a new one on me, too. I asked Letty, because Jean is such a common name. She said she got it off the answering machine and maybe didn't get it right. Then she said she actually didn't know for sure about their relationship, and maybe she was wrong."

A stab at a name, a guess at a relationship. Still, Letty hadn't sounded doubtful when she'd talked to me this morning. I made a mental note to tell McQuaid to check the machine and look around the phone for any scribblings she might have left, then went back to our earlier subject. "Did Letty actually talk to you about suicide?"

Mrs. Burnett glanced at her watch. She was obviously worried about being late to something, but she also wanted to talk. A woman in conflict. "Not in so many words," she replied. "If she'd said anything really specific, I would've called our minister and asked him to come and counsel with her. She said she didn't want to go on living without Edgar, she wished she was dead, that sort of thing." She looked grim. "Although if you ask me, she was well rid of him. Without him, she had a chance at a new life. It's too bad she didn't get to take it."

"Did you notice a car in the drive this morning?" I asked, fearing I was about to lose her before I ran through all my questions. "Or see anyone around the house?"

"No," she said slowly. "The only car I saw all morning was the one that turned around in my drive. A blue car. I saw it from my kitchen window."

"What time?"

Mrs. Burnett gave me a puckered frown. "About nine-thirty, I guess. I was rinsing the breakfast dishes. We were a little late this morning. My husband was going off on a business trip. You know how men are about traveling. He couldn't find anything he needed, including his skivvies."

"A dark blue car? Light blue?"

She blinked. "Sort of dark. Medium, I guess." She shook her head, frowning. "You don't think — You can't mean —" On the third time, she got the whole sentence out. "Oh, good Lord. You're not saying that somebody *pushed* poor Letty down those stairs?"

"I don't know," I said honestly. "But if I were going to kill myself, I don't think I'd trust a flight of stairs to do the job — even those stairs. Would you?"

She chewed on that for a moment, then shook her head, *tch-tch*ing. "But who would do such a thing? And why? The only bad thing Letty ever did in her life was to marry Edgar. I can't imagine why anybody would want to kill her." More headshaking, more *tch-tch*ing.

If she couldn't, I could.

Because Letty had learned who Jean was. And then she had arranged for a three-way discussion of the pertinent questions between herself, Jean, and me.

"Thank you, Mrs. Burnett," I said. "You've been very helpful."

"Well, I don't know," Mrs. Burnett said doubtfully. She paused. "This is a little premature, but maybe you could tell me about Letty's will, being a lawyer and all?"

"Her will? No, I'm sorry, I don't know anything about it. Was there a specific question?"

Mrs. Burnett clasped her briefcase in both hands. "Well, I was just wondering about the house. Places around here are in great demand, and we don't get vacancies too often."

"You'd like to list it?"

She looked relieved, as if she were glad that the words had come out of my mouth, not hers. "It really is rushing things and I hate to mention it, but, well, yes. I have a buyer who just adores Southwestern style. I'm sure she'd be crazy about this place. We don't see a lot of adobe around here, and that courtyard makes the property unique. Edgar had it done by a garden designer. He was proud as a peacock about it."

"I'll see what I can find out," I said. McQuaid's siren split the air, ending the conversation between us.

"Your nose looks pretty good, considering." Laurel eyed me narrowly. "Your hair looks great. What a difference a day makes." She glanced at the clock, which read eleven-thirty. "But I thought you and Mike were supposed to be at the court-house, getting your marriage license."

"Yeah." I rang the register to see how we had done for the morning. It could have been better. Much better. "But there's been a complication."

"Another one?" Laurel asked. She was

226

wearing her brown hair loose today, and it hung forward over her green Thyme and Seasons T-shirt. We had them made to wear and sell in the shop last spring.

"I'm afraid so," I said. I told her what I had found at Letty Coleman's house; she expressed dismay, and we mused for a moment together on the impermanence of life. Then I frowned. "What do you mean, *another* complication?"

Laurel gave me a rueful glance. "For starters, Bertha and Betsy called. They've gone to Houston to visit Lucia's Garden." Lucia's Garden is a wonderful herb shop run by my friends Lucia and Michael Bettler. Their Basil Festival, which is held in August, is not to be missed. "They'll be here Friday morning."

"Will that be enough time?" I asked anxiously. Khat, who can be remarkably empathic when he's in the right mood, jumped up on the counter, arched his back, and announced that he would allow me to stroke him, if it would make me feel better. I knew that Ruby and Sheila and I could handle the basic stuff — the flowers, the music, the food. After all, Ruby and I have collaborated on enough classes and celebrations to qualify us as certified professional event planners. But Bertha and

Betsy have a magic touch with weddings. I was counting on them for the finishing touches that would make everything perfect.

"Bertha said to tell you not to panic — things will turn out just fine." Laurel tossed her hair back over her shoulders. "And Betsy said that two days are plenty, since it's not a huge wedding. And since the Merryweathers are helping with the flowers."

"It feels huge to me," I said. "A whale of a wedding. But they've had a lot of experience. They're probably right." Khat, having allowed me a full five strokes, decided I'd been sufficiently soothed and dropped to the floor. "Do I want to hear about the other complications?"

"Probably not." With a swift gesture, Laurel took a plastic clip out of her pocket, swept her hair into a pony tail, and fastened the clip around it. "Remember that stack of punch bowls we left in the corner of the tearoom? It fell over during the night. We don't have to worry about returning them. But we *do* have to figure out how to let people know that their punch bowls got broken. I'm going to call Fannie and see if she can help."

"Rats," I said feelingly.

Laurel's dimple flashed. "Mice, actually. That's the other complication. They got into that big box of cookies Ruby dropped off for the reception and made a mess." She gave me a regretful look. "I was supposed to put the cookies in the freezer last night, but Ben's mom called to say that she has to go in for more blood tests tomorrow, and I was so flustered I forgot. I had to throw them out."

I scowled at Khat, who was delicately washing one black paw. "What are we keeping you for?" I asked him, irritated. "Why didn't you eat that mouse?" Khat looked up at me, blinked twice, and gave an incredulous *mrrrow* — Who, me? Eat a mouse? How plebeian! — and began washing the other paw. He prefers chicken livers cooked with garlic.

To Laurel, I said, "I'm sorry about your mother-in-law. Do you need to take some time off? If you do, I'm sure I can manage."

"I don't think so. At least, not just now." Laurel sighed. "There's a lot to think about, though. I'm having trouble keeping track of it all."

"I guess everybody's in the same boat," I said. All but Letty. She didn't have anything to think about or anything to do, ever again. That disquieting thought made a pile of broken punch bowls and a box of mice-munched cookies seem trivial. "Have you seen Ruby?"

"Oh, yeah." Laurel made an impatient noise. "What's happening to my mind? I forgot to tell you that she wants you to come over at the end of her meditation class. She has some news for you — about the case, whatever that means."

I glanced at the clock. "Is her class over?"

"I think it's just ending." Laurel began rummaging through the items on the counter. "Also, a woman left a card and a note for you — if I can locate it in this mess." She sighed hopelessly. "After the wedding, I've *got* to get better organized. All this chaos is driving me crazy."

"After the wedding," I reminded her, "the tearoom will be open, and we will be even more disorganized."

"Go talk to Ruby," Laurel said, with a wave of her hand. "I don't want to think about it."

If you've never been inside the Crystal Cave, you've missed an intriguing experience. The shop is stocked with crystals and rune stones, tarot cards and dragons, New

Age music and goddess greeting cards and fantastic jewelry and magazines and books on spirituality and astrology and the mind-body connection and healing herbs. This morning, the shop's air was delicately scented with the magical aroma of Ruby's favorite incense and brightened by the celestial sound of a Celtic harp. A group of women were just leaving, moving quietly, with peaceful smiles and gentle good-byes — Ruby's meditation students, who meet once a week in the carpeted area at the back of the shop, sitting silently on their zafus and meditation benches, focusing their attention on the breath. No mantras, no humming, just silent focus, allowing the stress to seep away. I join the class every so often, but it's hard for me to sit still for more than about five minutes and harder yet to concentrate my attention. My mind is always zip-zip-zipping from one thought to another: my monkey mind, Ruby calls it, swinging crazily here and there, chattering away even when I'd prefer it to be quiet. I keep telling myself that when I have more time, I'll get serious about it and learn how it's done. God knows, I could do with a little less stress.

Ruby saw the last of the students out the door and turned to me, smiling slightly.

She was wearing loose white cotton pants, a white cotton loose-sleeved jacket, white sandals, white hoop earrings. Her hair was a frizzy red halo. She wore a look of ethereal purity.

"Have a good session?" I asked.

"Mmm, wonderful," Ruby said serenely. She focused her eyes and seemed to come back from somewhere far away. "Oh, hey, I *like* your hair!" she exclaimed. "It makes you look five years younger — no, ten, don't you think? Has McQuaid seen it? What did he say?"

"Let's not go overboard," I said cautiously. "Five, maybe, but not ten. McQuaid saw it but he didn't say anything. He was paying more attention to Letty than to me."

Ruby looked amused. "To Letty? You mean, you have competition?"

"Letty's dead," I said.

Ruby stared at me. Her lower jaw dropped.

"I found her at the bottom of a twenty-foot stone staircase at the rear of her house. Her neck was broken."

Ruby gulped, started to say something, swallowed, and tried again. "Murder?" she squeaked.

I leaned against the counter. "McQuaid

is trying to figure it out. A neighbor suggested suicide, but it could've been accidental. Those steps are treacherous." I thought of Letty on her back, blind eyes staring at the sky, and I shivered. She had endured what must have been bitter years of marriage to a man who exploited her cruelly. And now, on the threshold of freedom and a new life, she was dead.

Ruby shook her head. "Uh-uh. An accident is just too convenient."

"Convenient for whom?" I said. "Not for Letty. It was pretty inconvenient for her."

"You know what I mean," Ruby said. She went to her CD player and turned it off, silencing the harp.

"I suppose I do," I said, and told Ruby about my conversation with Rena Burnett, including the information about Jean, Suspected Lover Number Three, and the blue car that had turned around in her drive while she was rinsing the breakfast dishes. "Of course," I added, "the car isn't necessarily related."

"Three!" Ruby exclaimed hotly. She folded her arms across her chest. "What a louse! If he'd been my husband, I'd have kicked the jerk out on his philandering butt." Ruby's been there, done that. When she caught Wade Wilcox, her ex, taking out-of-town weekends with his secretary, she called a lawyer, filed for divorce, and never looked back.

"It doesn't say much for the institution of marriage," I agreed quietly, thinking of Letty and Edgar and Pauline and Darryl and Ruby and Wade and wondering how many other families have been fractured beyond repair by sexual avarice. Fidelity may be an old-fashioned virtue, but it speaks to something deep and true in the heart. I sighed. "I wish I'd been a little more willing to listen to Letty yesterday. She was ready to tell me the woman's name, and I told her to keep it to herself."

"We have one Jean on our suspect list already," Ruby said. "Billie Jean Jones. You talked to her this morning. Were she and Edgar getting it on?"

Billie Jean! Why hadn't I thought of her? "I was with her from eight-thirty until ten," I said slowly. "When I left, she was still sweeping my hair off the floor. So unless she pushed Letty down the stairs before she came to work —"

I stopped. Bobby Rae had said that Billie Jean came in late this morning. Billie Jean herself had seemed unusually preoccupied while she was doing my hair, and it had been hard to get her to talk. I had accepted her story at face value because I know her, and because I hadn't had any reason to question it. But maybe she hadn't told me the whole truth about her relationship to Edgar Coleman or the deal he'd offered her. Her alibi certainly wasn't as airtight as she made it sound. She could easily have put her granddaughter in her car and driven back to Pecan Springs from San Antonio. Was Billie Jean Jones the "Jean" Letty had mentioned to Rena Burnett? Had it been her gun that killed Edgar? Had she gone to see Letty before she came to work and pushed her down the stairs?

Ruby was watching me narrowly. "What are you thinking, China?"

"I'm wondering what time Letty died," I said. But we wouldn't know that until after the autopsy, and maybe not even then. She had been lying in the sun on the warm ground — the medical examiner probably wouldn't be able to come any closer than a three-hour range. "I guess we can't rule out Billie Jean," I added. I summarized for Ruby what she had told me about Coleman's offer of six rent-free months.

"*No* rent?" Ruby asked wryly. "That's a better deal than the one he offered Darla." She paused, her brow furrowing. "Do you remember the plaque on Darla's desk?"

"Yeah. I wondered what she was president of."

"That's not what I mean. Her middle initial was J. Do you suppose it's Darla Jean?"

"Good grief," I said. "Not another one. Don't people have any imagination when it comes to naming their kids?" I regarded her. "Hey, your middle initial is J, isn't it?"

"J for Janine," Ruby said. "And if you're thinking that *I* might have been Edgar Coleman's sweetie, you can stuff it." She unbuttoned her white jacket, shrugged out of it, and hung it up. Beneath it, she was wearing a tight-fitting sleeveless silk tank top, the same fiery red as her hair. She slipped out of her sandals, reached under the counter, and pulled out a pair of bright red wedge heels. "I think it's worth a trip to Bluebonnet Books to find out what the J stands for," she added, stepping into the wedgies, which added another three inches to her six-feet-plus. Instant character change, from guru to foxy lady. Ruby is astoundingly versatile.

"I'd go with you," I said, "but I need to go over to the courthouse and see if I can get the marriage license and *take* it to McQuaid. That might be the only way I'm going to get him to sign it." I sighed. "I also have to see Wanda Rathbottom some-time today. And Sheila and I are supposed to have a talk with Iris Powell this after-noon."

"Iris Powell?" Ruby looked bemused. "How'd you manage that?"

"Sheila suggested it." This involved an-other explanation, at the end of which I re-membered that Ruby was supposed to have done some investigating of her own that morning. "Did you get a chance to talk to Ken Bowman?"

"Oops, I forgot," Ruby said, snapping her fingers. "When you told me about Letty, it flew right out of my mind. Yeah, Ken came over to help me light the pilot light on my hot water heater."

"I thought he was going to jump-start your car."

Ruby took a red felt hat off a peg and put it on her head, tilting it rakishly over one ear. "The pilot light went out by itself, so I didn't have to monkey with the car. I couldn't get past first base, though. Ken admitted that Edgar bought a new Lincoln from him, and that's *all* he would say."

I remembered the classy silver Lincoln Letty had been driving. "I wonder if the new car was Edgar's end of a trade for Bowman's vote."

"My thought exactly," Ruby said. "But when I probed, Ken got all huffy and said that the sale had nothing to do with anything."

"At least his name isn't Jean," I said dryly. "I'm not in the least surprised that you didn't learn anything. Nothing is going right. Did Laurel tell you that the punch bowls fell over and broke, and the mice got into your cookies before the cookies could get into the freezer — and that Bertha and Betsy won't be here until tomorrow?"

Ruby looked dismayed. "You know, I didn't check the stars when you set your wedding date. I'd better do that right away. Just to make sure what's going on. I suspect that Mercury's gone retrograde, at the least. Or maybe Pluto is acting up."

"I'm glad there's a logical explanation," I replied.

"Don't be tacky," Ruby said, going to the front door to lock it and put up the Out to Lunch sign. "Some things are going reasonably well. All the work in the tearoom is done, and I went through the herb garden today — it looks very nice. Even if we don't do any extra decorating, it will still be lovely. Unless it rains, of course."

I shuddered. "God forbid." Pecan Springs is normally dry — we get less than thirty inches of rainfall a year — and I'm always hoping for a nice all-day rain. Not this weekend, though. This weekend, I was praying for sunshine and decently cool temperatures.

"Amen," Ruby said vehemently. "But I'm afraid we've got a major problem with the wedding cake. It turns out that Annie wasn't the only one who took the bus to Tucson. She and Maureen have been having an affair and Maureen went with her. Which leaves Adele all alone to cater the Mayor's Prayer Breakfast on Friday and bake four wedding cakes for the weekend. To top it all off, somebody crunched her delivery van in the First Baptist parking lot. She says this just wasn't her week. She's doing the prayer breakfast, but canceling the cakes."

Ah, the drama of small-town life. "Maybe we could get the Mayor's Prayer Breakfast to pray for Annie and Maureen to come back and bake cakes," I said, "and ask the Baptists to take up a collection to fix the van." I grinned. "Although the Mayor's Prayer Breakfast might be busy praying for Pauline's forgiveness. After all, she is now a fallen woman. She needs all the prayers she can get."

Ruby scowled. "Be serious, China. This

is your wedding we're talking about, for pity's sake."

"Right. It's only a wedding, not the event of the century."

"Oh, yeah?" Ruby laughed cheerily. "Think again, sister. It's the event of *your* century. After Sunday, you'll be a married woman. You're beginning a whole new phase of your life. Take it from me. Things will never be the same."

I shuddered. I like myself as I am, plus or minus a few minor personality flaws. I like McQuaid, too, and the way we are together, friendly, comfortable, argumentative. If I thought marriage would change me, or change him, or change us, I'd cancel, even at this late date. Instead of a wedding, we'd have a party, and our honeymoon would simply be a great vacation. Which would be a whole lot easier, come to think of it. I could stop worrying about wedding cakes and marriage licenses and flowers and enjoy the party.

But I was gambling that McQuaid and I, married, could remain our independent, autonomous selves. I wasn't entering a marriage like Letty's, where one partner dominates the relationship so completely that the other is forced to give up what she wants in order to keep the thing going. I sighed. In the beginning, at least, Letty must have had great hopes for her marriage. When had she realized that it closed down her options, rather than enlarging them? At what point — if ever — did she understand that she had yielded up her will to his?

Thinking of Letty made me sad, but it also put this latest wedding-day glitch into perspective. "Relax, Ruby," I said. "Let's not sweat the small stuff. If we can't find anybody to bake a cake, we'll put out peanut butter and jelly."

It's a good thing the Mayor's Breakfast bunch couldn't hear Ruby's response. They would have added her to their prayer list.

Chapter Eleven

Lila Jennings' Greater Garlic Mashed Potatoes

16 cups peeled white potatoes, quartered
4 cups peeled garlic cloves (Lila says this
   is right, even if you don't think so.)
2 cups milk
$1/2$ pound butter
Chopped fresh parsley
Salt and pepper to taste

Simmer the potatoes in salted water until tender. Drain and mash with the butter. While the potatoes are cooking, simmer the garlic and milk in a saucepan until soft, or about 30 minutes. Puree in a blender. Beat the puree into the mashed potato, and season with salt and pepper. Garnish with chopped fresh parsley. [Lila says this recipe makes enough for 16 people, and she usually makes it twice, to handle her lunch crowd. To serve your family of four, divide by four.]

It was just noon, so Laurel and I closed up for lunch too. She went off to eat and I headed for the Adams County Court-house, which sits in the middle of the town square, surrounded by statues dedicated to the memory of dead soldiers, and benches where the survivors can sit and remind one another of past glories. The building itself is constructed of slabs of pink granite hauled to the site from Marble Falls, seventy miles to the west and north. It's a fine example of turn-of-the-century Texas political architecture, looking as if it will endure for centuries to come. The granite, which was quarried out of Granite Mountain, is likely to be around somewhat longer. It was born of Precambrian fury more than a billion years ago and buried beneath a half-mile thick layer of limestone rock that was deposited in the warm and shallow Mesozoic seas that extended west to New Mexico and north to Oklahoma. The granite was exposed after the land began to rise, the seas were drained, and Cenozoic erosion stripped off the overlying sediments. In various shades of gray-pink, it is found now in weathered heaps on the surface and in domes of unimaginable size beneath. By such picturesque names as Texas Sunset, Prairie Rose, Texas Star, and

Texas Red, it has made rather a reputation for itself in the world. You can see polished slabs of it on buildings in such far-away places as Osaka, Singapore, and Atlantic City, as well as the Texas State Capitol building in Austin. If you're looking for Texas Red in the raw, you can find a 500-foot-high, 640-square-acre hunk of it a few miles north of Fredericksburg, on Farm to Market Road 965. It's called Enchanted Rock. When you climb it, you'll see how layers of the stone have peeled off like layers of an onion in a process called exfoliation, which is caused by the heating and cooling of the rock's surface.

But there's no peeling stone on our local courthouse, which attracts tourists from far and wide. A chattering flock of them — blue-rinsed ladies and balding men with cameras around their necks — were gathered in front of it today, being instructed by Vera Hooper, the town docent. Twice a day during tourist season, Vera meets groups at the Chamber of Commerce office on Pecan Street and leads them on a walking tour of the historic buildings around the square, including the Sophie Briggs Historical Museum, which houses Miss Briggs's famous collection of ceramic frogs, the boots Burt Reynolds wore in *The*

Best Little Whorehouse in Texas, and a four by five–foot bronze casting of a fire ant nest, made near Dime Box, Texas. (If you don't believe me, come and see for yourself.)

I, however, was headed in the other direction, to the county clerk's office, which is on the second floor of the courthouse, up the creaky staircase and down the hall to the far end. I counted myself lucky to find Melva Joy Stryker behind the marble-topped counter upon which generations of Adams County couples have leaned their elbows while they got licensed to marry. If Roseann Tice had been there, I probably wouldn't have dared to make my request. Roseann, a transplant from Missouri, is narrow and nervous and never breaks a rule for fear that the bureaucratic gods will frown at her. But Melva Joy is a plump, pleasant third-generation Texan with tight brown curls and a generous personality, the sort who offers to take care of your cats and water your African violets while you are on vacation. We worked together last year on the Myra Merryweather Herb Guild bazaar committee, so we consider ourselves friends.

I started off by reminding her that I still had the large potted marjoram that I'd

245

promised her some weeks before, whenever she wanted to stop by the shop and pick it up. Then I gave her my request.

"You want to take the license *where?*" she asked, startled.

"I'd like to take it to the police station for my fiancé to sign," I said meekly. "He's the temporary chief of police, and he's on a case. I really wouldn't ask, but it's pretty hard for him to get away just now and the wedding is coming up on Sunday."

"Oh, it's Mike you're marrying," she exclaimed. "Well, why didn't you say so? He's cute." She paused. "I hope he won't have to use those canes forever."

"We hope not too," I said. "But we're glad he's improved as much as he has. There for a while it was touch and go." It wouldn't hurt to play on her sympathies, with which Melva Joy is abundantly supplied.

She pulled her brows down in a frown. "The case Mike's on. It's that Coleman business, isn't it?"

"Yes," I said. "And now that Letty Coleman is dead too, I'm afraid we may have to be married by proxy." I chuckled, to show her I was only joking.

Melva Joy stared at me. "Letty's *dead?*" Her eyes widened, her eyebrows went up, and her jaw dropped, registering dramatic surprise and shock. "Holy smoke! How'd it happen? Car wreck or something?"

I gave her a bare outline of the events of the morning.

"Well, my goodness," Melva Joy said sorrowfully. Her substantial bosom rose and fell under her floral-print dress. "A broken neck. Would you believe? That is just too sad for words." She tilted her head, giving me a sharp look. "She wasn't pushed, was she? I mean, with her husband gettin' shot and all, it makes you wonder."

"I don't know," I said. "The police are looking into it." I leaned on the counter. "You knew her?"

The brown curls bobbed. "Oh my, yes. Letty was a very sweet person. My heart went out to her, all that trouble she had with that tomcat husband of hers." Melva Joy paused and gave me a look that inquired whether I knew about Edgar's philandering. I gave her a look back that said I did, and she went on, a little more confidentially, "We sang together, y'know. In the Sweet Adelines. Soprano."

"No, I didn't know," I said. "I'm glad she had something to do — to keep her mind off . . . well, things."

"That Letty," Melva Joy said, "she had

perfect pitch. Which is awfully important when it comes to sopranos. You got one standing next to you who sings flat, it'll pull you both down."

"I can imagine." Somehow, I was touched by the thought of Letty having perfect pitch. I was glad that something had been right in her life.

Melva Joy reached beneath the counter and took out a form. "Roseann would say it's against the rules, but I'm doing it anyway. A man's got a murder case to solve, he don't need to be over here doing paperwork." She sat down at an IBM typewriter and expertly rolled in the form. "You get close to a person when you're both sopranos. Letty and me, we'd go for ice-cream cones afterwards, over to the Baskin and Robbins. She always had chocolate chip." She looked up. "Names?"

I gave her mine and McQuaid's, and added, "Did Letty talk much about her husband?"

"Only when she was feeling low," Melva Joy said. She attacked the keyboard with energy, recording our names in a staccato burst. "Iris Powell I could understand. But I never could feature Pauline Perkins, somehow. Date and place of birth? I wouldn't mention Pauline," she added, "if it wasn't common talk."

I told her our dates. I was born in Houston, McQuaid in San Antonio. "Just out of curiosity, did Letty ever mention anybody named Jean?"

"Well, yes." She frowned, backed up and hit the correction key. "But she didn't know who Jean was — just her name, is all." She looked down at the dates she had just typed and grinned. "Younger than you, is he? Roseann says that's the kiss of death in a marriage, but I like to see it. Shows we don't get older, we just get better." She sighed heavily. "It didn't work out just real well for Letty. He was younger than her, you know. But I expect you'll do better."

"I expect so too," I said firmly. We went through the remaining items and I handed over the blood test forms we'd gotten back from the doctor the week before. "How much?" I asked, reaching for a pen and thinking of the symbolism of my writing and signing the check for our marriage license. This was not an indicator of things to come, I hoped.

"Thirty-five." Melva Joy made an apologetic face. "It went up five dollars last month. Seems like everything is going up."

I gave her my check. She turned it over,

stamped it smartly, and put it in her desk drawer, then pushed the form across the counter. "When you come back with it all signed, be sure you give it straight to me," she said. "Don't let on to Roseann that I let you take it out of the office, or she'll have a hissy at both of us." She closed the drawer, shaking her head regretfully. "I really hate it about Letty getting killed. I mean *really*. It's hard to find anybody with perfect pitch anymore, let alone a soprano."

When I left the county clerk's office, it was just past twelve-thirty. If I was going to get any lunch, it had better be quick. I walked over to the police station to see if McQuaid was back. Dorrie the dispatcher said I'd just missed him, but he'd told her to tell me he'd be at the Nueces Street Diner, catching a quick bite. That's where I found him, sitting at the end of the red Formica counter with Hark Hibler.

The Nueces Street Diner is owned by Lila Jennings and her daughter, Docia, who recently came down from Dallas to take over the kitchen. The menu isn't likely to be reviewed in *Texas Monthly*. Today's comfort-food special, posted on a blackboard out front, was fried okra, meatloaf and garlic mashed potatoes, coleslaw, and apple pie. But the diner itself is a sight for sore eyes. Lila and her husband, Ralph (gone from this world after succumbing to a two-pack-a-day habit), bought an old Missouri and Pacific dining car and furnished it with post–World War Two collectibles: chrome-and-red chairs and red Formica-topped tables, a Wurlitzer jukebox, postwar light fixtures and ceiling fans, old soda pop signs, and framed newspaper clippings from a time when Tom Dewey was touted to beat Harry Truman and Texas hadn't discovered air-conditioning. Even Lila's gotten into the act. She got Bobby Rae to give her bleached blond hair a do that makes her look like one of the Andrews Sisters, and her green nylon uniform, ruffled apron, and little white hat are pure fifties.

I sat down on the empty stool next to McQuaid and pulled the license out of my purse. "The mountain comes to Mohammed," I remarked. I took out a pen and pointed to the designated space. "Sign here."

"What am I signing?" McQuaid asked, past a mouthful of apple pie.

"Your license to marry me," I said. "Lucky you."

"Well, well," McQuaid said. "Hand-delivered, no less, by the light of my life." He put down his fork, picked up my pen, and signed with a flourish. "How'd you get Roseann to let you take this official piece of paper out of the county clerk's office?"

"What Roseann doesn't know won't hurt her," I said primly, and put the license in my purse.

Hark leaned forward to peer around McQuaid. "Speaking of delivering, am I going to get next Thursday's Home and Garden page before you fly off on your honeymoon?" Hark, who lost something like forty pounds last year, looks the way a small-town newspaper editor ought to look: wrinkled white shirt with collar unbuttoned and sleeves rolled up, rumpled slacks, a half-day's growth of dark beard, dark hair in need of a trim. There's something real and comfortable about him, though. What you see is what you get, no frills, no psychodrama, just plain Hark.

"The page is done," I replied, "all but the piece on lavender. I'll get it to you this afternoon. Tomorrow morning at the latest. Do you want it on disk, or hard copy?"

Hark grunted. "What do you think we are, some backwater weekly that still turns out copy on typewriters? I'll take it on disk." He frowned at me. "What did you do to yourself? Face lift?"

Lila approached and set a glass of ice water on the counter in front of me. "Hark don't have room to put good stuff in the paper anymore," she said sourly. "He's too busy coverin' crime and murders. He's hopin' to get a Putzer prize to hang on his wall."

"A Pulitzer," Hark said, and slid his iced tea glass suggestively in her direction. He was still looking at me. "You lose some weight?"

"That's whut I *said,*" Lila replied with a dark look. "Don't we git enough murders on tee vee without readin' about 'em in the paper? Arnold Seidensticker must be turnin' in his grave like a whistlin' dervish, seein' whut's happened to his newspaper."

"Nothing's happened to his newspaper, Lila," Hark said, "except that the circulation's gone up."

Lila laughed scornfully. "Oh, yeah? When it was a weekly, there was plenty of good news to fill it, family reunions and parades and beauty contests and stuff. Now it comes out every day, there's nothin' but crime. Can't you find anything *good* to write about?"

Hark shrugged. "We cover the news, Lila, we don't cover it *up*. Pecan Springs isn't the sleepy little town it was when Arnold ran the paper. The college is big, Walmart's moved in, there's a lot more traffic up and down the Interstate. We print the news we've got, and what we've got is crime. Which includes vandalism, drugs, and a couple murders every now and again." He gave his glass another nudge. "Now, how about some more iced tea?" He glanced back at me, light dawning. "I know. You got your hair cut. It's shorter. Looks real nice."

"Thank you," I said modestly. I turned to McQuaid. "How do you like it?"

McQuaid didn't hear me. "*One* murder, Hark. There's no evidence that Letty Coleman was pushed down those stairs, and don't you go saying anything else. We've got enough problems without the newspaper complicating the situation."

"So you didn't find anything," I said, feeling regretful and ambivalent. I didn't want to hear that Letty had been murdered, but I agreed with Ruby that an accident seemed like a too-easy explanation. What's more, I couldn't help feeling that Letty's death ought to *mean* something — at the least, that it should give us a clue as to who killed her husband. But an accident was a dead end. As far as Edgar Coleman's murder was concerned, it took us no-where.

"Miz Coleman?" Lila asked in alarm. "Pushed down what stairs? Whut's happened to her?"

"She *fell* down the steps behind her house," McQuaid said briefly. "Broke her neck."

"Omigawd," Lila whispered, shocked. "Why, she was just in here this morning!"

"This morning?" McQuaid asked. "What time?"

Lila shook her head. "Sittin' right there where you are, on that very stool, talkin' to Doc Jackson. She had a cheese and mush-room omelet and biscuits and —"

"What *time*, Lila?" McQuaid pressed. "This is important."

"This is your chief talkin', Lila," Hark said in a theatrical growl. "Tell him what time."

"Whut time?" Lila twiddled a strand of blond hair that was falling down in front of her ear. "Well, let's see. It had to have been after the first pan of biscuits, 'cause the oven wasn't set right and Docia burned 'em on the bottom and Miz Coleman had to wait for the second pan to get hers.

Which she did without complainin', unlike some folks I know who pitch a fit when they don't get whut they want right when they want it." She threw a baleful look at Hark. "Make it, oh, seven. Pretty early for her to be out." She swiveled her attention to me. "You decide what you're gonna have?"

Seven. So Letty had been here even before we talked on the phone this morning, which meant that Billie Jean was still in the running as far as opportunity was concerned. I sighed. Quite apart from any personal feelings I might have for Letty, I agreed with Melva Joy when she said it was a pity to lose a soprano with perfect pitch. I would hate to lose somebody who knew how to cut my hair. I looked up. Lila was still waiting, her mouth pursed, her head held to one side.

"The special looks pretty good," I said.

"You come in at the tail end of the lunch hour, you got to take potluck," Lila replied. "We got plenty okra and meatloaf and mashed potatoes, but the last piece of pie is gone. On desserts, we're down to tapioca pudding and green Jell-O." She sighed. "Lord, I just plain don't believe it about Miz Coleman. I don't."

Green Jell-O. I suppressed a shudder.

256

"I'll take the meatloaf and okra and pass on dessert. And a double helping of mashed potatoes." Lila mashes potatoes with garlic. Very tasty. Good for you, too.

"Still got to charge you," Lila said. "You don't like Jell-O, have some tapioca." She eyed McQuaid. "Fell down the steps, did she? Just like that?"

"Far as we can tell," McQuaid said blandly. "Nobody saw or heard anything that would suggest otherwise."

"Make it tapioca," I said, choosing the lesser of two evils. I turned to McQuaid, thinking of those three waiting glasses on the patio table. "Did you check around the phone?"

He gave me a rebuking look. "Of course we checked around the phone. All the phones, in fact. We found a pad with numbers for the guy who mows the lawn, the dentist, and Pauley's Funeral Home. They're handling Edgar's cremation. Guess now they'll make it a double funeral."

"A double funeral," Hark said. "Now, that's a human interest story." He tapped his empty glass with a fork. "Lila, ain't you *ever* goin' to get me some tea?"

"There he goes, pitchin' that fit," Lila said darkly, and stalked off, muttering under her breath. She was back in a minute with a pitcher of tea and my plate. The fried okra, which I have never in my life managed to do just right, looked wonderful. The meatloaf could have used a little more tomato sauce and some thyme and basil would have worked wonders, but you can't have everything. She put the plate down in front of me. "You lettin' your hair grow for the weddin'?" she asked. "I gotta say, long hair looks good on you."

"Thank you," I said. When she had gone, I lowered my voice and spoke to McQuaid. "Did you turn up anything on the gun?"

"Yeah," McQuaid said. "I got the report right after I got back from the Colemans'. The ballistics checked out. It was the gun that killed Edgar Coleman, all right."

"Prints?" I asked.

"One. They're still looking for a match in the FBI file. Marvin is hauling our suspects back in to get their prints."

"That's the gun that the kids found at the creek?" Hark asked.

"That's it," McQuaid said. "Piece of luck, their stumbling on it. That area is wild and weedy. It might never have been found." He frowned. "How'd you hear about that?"

Hark looked shocked. "You don't expect me to reveal my sources, do you?" He paused. "If you've got a fingerprint, you oughta have your man pretty quick."

"Maybe, maybe not," McQuaid said. He finished his pie and pushed his plate away.

"What about the registration?" I asked. I picked up the crust McQuaid had left on his plate and nibbled it. He never eats the crust, which for me is the best part.

"According to the manufacturer's records, the gun was originally purchased about ten years ago by some guy in Miami, Florida. No current address, so that's a dead end, at least for now." McQuaid leaned over and gave me a peck on the cheek, signaling that he was ready to go back to work. "Okay if I leave you with this sex maniac?"

"Hey," Hark said, offended, "who you callin' a sex maniac?"

"Listen, McQuaid," I said, "I've got a couple of things I need to tell you. Sheila and I are going to see Iris Powell this afternoon. Her sister seems to think she might have some information. Is that okay?"

McQuaid was studying his bill. "Yeah, sure," he said absently. "I've already seen Powell. Her alibi checks out." He frowned.

"Since when has Lila started charging for coffee refills?"

"Since yesterday," Hark said. "I already complained. It's your turn."

"Another thing," I said, "I talked to Billie Jean Jones this morning, and she told me —"

He put down a tip and reached for his canes. "Sorry, China, if it's not critical, I don't have time." He gave me a glance. "Looks like your nose is a lot better. Everything's under control, I hope. The wedding stuff, I mean."

"Everything's under control but the groom," I said nastily. "I'm counting on his being there on Sunday afternoon, in spirit as well as in body. *And* getting on that airplane on Monday morning."

He slid off the stool and propped himself up. "The wedding's no problem. I can take a half-day break from the case. But the honeymoon —"

"McQuaid," I said grimly, "the honeymoon is no problem either. If the investigation isn't completed, you can leave it in Marvin's capable hands. I'm sure he'd be pleased to wrap it up for you."

Hark drained his glass and set it down. " 'Life of Crime Forces New Husband to Abandon Honeymoon,' " he said with gusto. "Another great human interest story, right up there with kids finding murder weapons and double funerals."

"Try 'New Wife Forces Husband to Abandon Life of Crime,' " I said, and pitched into Lila's fried okra. "And while you're out playing cops and robbers, McQuaid, just remember the job's only temporary. *I'm* a permanent fixture." I lifted my chin. "What do you think of my hair?"

"Your hair always looks fine to me, whatever you do to it," McQuaid said, with the air of a man who has delivered the ultimate compliment. He grinned at Hark. "You can hang around and keep China company, Hark. I've got a killer to catch."

Hark gave a heavy sigh. "McQuaid, you dadgum sonofagun, you don't deserve this pretty woman. If she'd tell me she's a permanent fixture in *my* life, I'd step right up and say 'Yes, ma'am, here I am. You just tell me what you want me to do and I'll do it.' "

"Wonderful," I said enthusiastically. "How do you feel about the Hawaiian Islands?"

I finished my lunch (except for the tapioca pudding), paid my bill, and walked with Hark as far as the *Enterprise*. We said good-bye and I went on to the county courthouse to deposit the signed marriage license with Melva Joy. As I was going up the stairs, I met Sheriff Blackie Blackwell on his way down.

In his white hat, cowboy boots, and brown leather vest with a silver star, Blackie is a familiar figure around the Adams County Courthouse. His father, Corky Blackwell, was elected sheriff in every election for twenty-five years, and his mother, Reba, was the unofficial deputy, cooking for prisoners in the county jail and handling the phone and the paperwork. Blackie grew up riding shotgun with his father and carrying tin plates for his mother, and he never gave a minute's thought to a career other than law enforcement. He's stocky, with solid shoulders and sandy hair cut very short, a square jaw, a square chin, and a four-square sense of honesty and fairness that comes from believing in the law and enforcing it with impartiality and singleness of purpose. But beneath his unemotional and mostly uncommunicative exterior, he has a compassionate heart. Even people who don't like cops like Blackie.

He took off his hat and grinned. "All

ready for the big day, China?"

"We're getting there," I said, displaying the license. "Now, if only McQuaid could wind up the Coleman case —"

Blackie sobered. "That's a tough one. Sorry it had to happen when it did. Makes it rough for you, with the wedding and all."

"You've heard what happened to Letty Coleman?"

"Yeah. I was in the county clerk's office a minute ago, and Melva Joy told me. Hard to believe it's an accident."

"That seems to be a generally held view," I said dryly. "It certainly complicates the investigation."

"I'm on my way over there now to talk to McQuaid," Blackie said. "If I can help, I'd be glad to. Maybe another man or two would make a difference."

"It might — if you can get him to accept." I gave him a searching look. "What's this I hear about Sheila withdrawing her candidacy for chief of police?"

Blackie shrugged. "That's what she told me last night. I've got to say I was disappointed."

"Disappointed!"

He sighed. "Yeah. But I'm afraid some of it's my fault. When she first told me she wanted to have a shot at the job, I said I didn't think there was room for two law enforcement careers in the same family. Since then, though, I've got to thinking about the way my mom and dad worked together. Mom didn't have an official title and she never acted like she wanted a career. But she was right there, all the way, doing what had to be done to keep Dad's office going. He couldn't've hired somebody to do what she did."

He paused, gathering his thoughts. For Blackie, this was an extraordinarily long speech, and it looked like more was coming. I waited.

"Way I see it," he said finally, "Sheila's got a lot of experience, she's sharp, and she's talented. It's not fair for me to ask her to hold back on anything she wants just because she's my wife. In fact, it wouldn't be good for our marriage if either one of us got the upper hand. We've got to be free and equal or it won't work."

Such a generous wisdom, I thought admiringly. "Have you told her this?"

His steady gray eyes met mine. "I told her," he said, "but I don't think she believes me. She thinks I just want to make her happy. She's got this idea that there might be political problems, her being chief, me being sheriff." He chuckled.

"Like the county might not be big enough for both of us, politically speaking."

"You don't agree?"

He looked at me incredulously. "Are you kidding? I've never played politics and I never will. I run on my record as a law enforcement officer. If folks don't like it, they can vote me out and vote somebody else in." He shook his head, bemused. "I wish I knew where Sheila got that stupid idea. I'd tell 'em to go stuff it."

I sighed. I knew where Smart Cookie had gotten the idea. She got it from somebody named Justine Wyzinski, on my front porch. "Want me to tell her about our conversation?"

"Yeah, that might help," Blackie said. "Sure, you talk to her. Tell her I want her to go for it. If you don't mind, that is."

"Are you kidding?" I said, feeling that for once, things were working out just the way I wanted. "I'd do anything to keep McQuaid from staying on as police chief a minute longer than necessary. He's got a nice, quiet, *safe* job waiting for him at the university. I'll be glad when he goes back to it."

Blackie regarded me thoughtfully. "Maybe. But what if he's tired of that nice, quiet, safe lecturing job and wants to go back to law enforcement?"

I stared at him.

He put his hat back on his head. "It's not right for me to tell Sheila what to do or hold her back from what she's got her heart set on. Don't you try holding McQuaid back, either, China. You'll be sorry if you do."

Chapter Twelve

Cactus. Grow in the garden and inside the house as a safeguard against burglary and unwanted intrusions. Grow in the bedroom to guard your chastity. Fill a jar with cactus spines, rusty nails and old tacks, pins and needles. Add rue and rosemary leaves to fill the jar, seal tightly, and then bury under your doorstep as a powerful protective device.

Scott Cunningham
Magical Herbalism

Ruby was right when she said that the shop garden looked very pretty. Now that the days were cooler and the nights longer, the salvia had come into its fall bloom and the calendula and Mexican marigold splashed orange along the fence. The Shasta daisies were blooming too, big patches of white among the greens and grays of the herbs. Unless Betsy or Bertha had other ideas, there wouldn't be much for the wedding helpers to do but decorate the arbor where Mc-

Quaid and I would take our vows — if everything went the way it was supposed to.

I walked down the path, noticing that there was more than enough rosemary — of all wedding herbs, the traditional favorite — to decorate the tearoom for the reception, as well as use it in the bouquets and boutonnieres. Sometimes our Pecan Springs summers seem so unendingly hot that I wonder why I live here, but one sniff of rosemary, a Mediterranean herb that flourishes in hot, dry summers and mild winters, reminds me. I was fingering a fragrant sprig and remembering what Blackie had said, when Ruby came down the path, wearing a distressed look.

"Darla Jean," she said.

"What?" I asked, startled out of my reverie. "Who?"

"Darla Jean McDaniels. Jean is Darla's middle name. Which means that we have to consider her a suspect. Especially since she doesn't have an alibi for Sunday night." Frowning intently, she sat down on the wooden bench beside the apothecary garden and stretched out her legs. "What's more, she didn't get to the store until after eleven this morning, and she wouldn't say where she'd been. And she *looked* as if she might have pushed Letty down those stairs, China. Her face was flushed and she was nervous as a cat on a hot stove. When I asked what she'd been up to — just casually, you know, nothing that ought to have caused suspicion — she practically chased me out of the store."

"Maybe she had second thoughts about telling us so much last night," I said, recalling Darla's last words. *Who killed him? Who the hell cares?* "Or maybe she just wants to forget the whole thing. After all, her problem is solved now that Edgar Coleman is dead. He can't raise her rent from the grave."

"That's true," Ruby said. She pulled off her hat and began to fan herself with it. "But look at it this way, China. Suppose Darla Jean was having an affair with Edgar. It was perfect ammunition for him. If she doesn't vote his way, he'll raise her rent and tell what they'd been up to into the bargain. But even if she gives him what he wants, she knows she can't trust him, so she goes to his house and shoots him. Darla Jean's big problem is solved, once and for all — until Letty finds out about the affair and begins to suspect whose finger pulled the trigger. In which case Darla Jean has another big problem. Right?"

"It's all circumstantial," I said. "There has to be something, some piece of evidence . . ." I stopped.

There was one thing, of course. The fingerprint on the gun. It was time to tell McQuaid what we had found out, whether he wanted to hear it or not. He could question and print both Darla and Bonnie Jean. Darla might refuse to talk to Ruby about where she'd been that morning, but she'd have a harder time evading McQuaid's questions. And then I thought of something else. Darla's car.

"Ruby," I said thoughtfully, "what color car does Darla drive?"

"What color?" Ruby screwed up her mouth. "Blue, maybe. I noticed it in the lot last night, but it was dark and I didn't pay much attention."

"If that was her car I saw, it was blue," I said. "A blue Mercury. Rena Burnett reported that a blue car turned around in her drive at nine-thirty this morning. And McQuaid told me at lunch that they've found a print on the gun. It's time to call in the big guys."

"The big guys?"

"The law. McQuaid and Marvin. It's obvious that Darla isn't going to phone us and confess, and I don't think you and I should try breaking her fingers all by ourselves. I'm speaking metaphorically, of course," I added, at Ruby's raised eyebrows. "I don't know about Marvin, but McQuaid doesn't break fingers."

If Ruby was disappointed, she managed to contain herself. "All I want is for this to be over," she said, "so we can concentrate on getting you married and off on your honeymoon. *With* your husband."

I agreed with that, too. We went back to the shop, to the crowded closet that serves as my office, and I called McQuaid. He and Marvin were out, Dorrie informed me importantly, on a missing-person call. When I asked who was missing, she grew coy.

"I don't think I ought to tell you," she said. "It's classified. Breaking news."

"Come on, Dorrie," I said. "This is China. The boss's wife. It's all in the family."

She was stern. "Not until Sunday."

"Pretend this is Monday. Anyway, he'll tell me when I see him, so what's the harm?"

I could hear her chewing her gum. "Okay," she said at last. "But keep it under your hat, will you? I mean, I don't want the chief to think he's got leaks."

"No leaks," I promised. "Who's missing?"

She lowered her voice. "Mr. Garza. Ranger Wallace called to get him to come in and be fingerprinted, and his wife said he was gone."

"Gone!" I echoed blankly. "Gone where?"

"Mexico maybe. He left some sort of a note, but I haven't heard the details yet. Miz Garza was pretty upset." She paused. "Whut do you want me to tell the chief?"

"Tell him," I said slowly, "that I need to talk to him about Darla McDaniels and Billie Jean Jones. He questioned them both earlier, but I think he ought to talk to them again. Have him call me when he gets the chance, and I'll fill him in."

Dorrie agreed, and I put down the phone with a profound regret. Whatever had prompted Jorge Garza to leave town, it would have the effect of bumping him up to the top of McQuaid's suspect list. And if he'd gone to Mexico, the chances of finding him were very slim. That was his home territory, and he had family there. He'd know where and how to hide out, and the Mexican police aren't known for their diligence in ferreting out missing persons, especially those with Spanish surnames. I thought once again, sadly, of Phyllis.

"What was all that about?" Ruby asked

curiously. "Somebody's missing?" When I told her, her face changed. "He's run away to Mexico? Why, that almost amounts to an admission of guilt!"

"It might," I said. "But he's been in trouble at work — in fact, he was recently suspended for getting phony papers for some of his clients. Maybe it all began to pile up, and he just decided he didn't want to stick it out."

"Maybe we should call Phyllis and see if there's anything we can do," Ruby said. "After all that's happened, she must be devastated."

"We'll have to wait. McQuaid and Marvin are over there now. They're probably lifting his fingerprints off various items in the house, for comparison with the print on the gun." If they found a match, they'd know they had their man, of course — but *not* finding it wasn't equally conclusive.

Ruby looked at her watch. "Laurel agreed to watch the shop for me while I put in some time on the advertising for the tearoom. Are you driving out to Wonderful Acres to talk to Wanda?"

Wanda Rathbottom. I'd forgotten all about her. "Do you think that's necessary? McQuaid has enough suspects to keep three cops busy. And I need to do something about the wedding cake."

Ruby looked superior. "I thought we were having peanut butter and jelly."

"A figure of speech. I'll call Fannie. She probably knows somebody who can pinch-hit for Adele."

"And don't forget that you and Sheila are going to see Iris Powell," Ruby continued. "I think you should talk to Wanda, too — for the sake of completeness, if nothing else."

"Oh, all right," I said. Interviewing Wanda was probably a waste of time, but she was the last of the City Council members that Coleman appeared to have compromised. I might as well wrap it up. Anyway, it was a slow afternoon. Laurel could handle things by herself for an hour or so.

But I didn't get out of the shop right away. I needed to talk to Fannie, and then my mother came in, announcing that she had driven up from Kerrville with the intention of helping with the last-minute wedding details. "So here I am," she chirped brightly, "ready to go to work."

Leatha and I have not had an easy time of it over the years. When I was young, I used to envy the girls whose mothers did motherly things, like making cookies for the Girl Scout bake sale or attending parent-teacher conferences. Leatha didn't have the time or the energy to do those things because she was far too occupied with her problems, which she marinated in Scotch until both she and the problems were ripe. As you might imagine, I developed a great anger toward her, and focused all my love and attention on my absent father. The fact that he was never around didn't keep me from adoring him, and the greatest joy of my preteen years was to sit in the back row of the courtroom and watch him at work, feeling an enormous pride. As I grew up, I did all I could to please him and to be like him, an effort that earned me a great many successes: a law degree, a legal career, a lot of money, and a totally lopsided life. It took a long time to outgrow this adolescent hero worship and recognize that my father was just as addicted to his profession as my mother was to her alcohol and that his compulsion had annihilated our family just as surely as hers. It took even more years for me to accept Leatha and to try to build something approaching a normal mother-daughter relationship (whatever that is). We've been closer since McQuaid was shot, and his slow recovery has also marked a time of healing for us.

Still, things are dicey. When Leatha shows up, I get a clutchy feeling in my stomach and I want to be somewhere else. This was especially true this afternoon, because Leatha opened the door to my tiny office just as I was asking Fannie whether she could come up with an alternative to Adele. Fannie said she couldn't rattle any names off the tip of her tongue, but she'd take the matter under advisement.

"Let *me* bake your cake, China, dear," Leatha said, in her slow, honey-sweet drawl. She was raised on a Mississippi plantation, and her years in Texas haven't parched the Deep South out of her speech.

I put the phone down and gave her the first excuse I could think of. "That's very nice of you, Leatha, but it's really too much to ask. Don't worry, we'll find somebody." In other words, thanks but no thanks.

To understand my response, you probably should know that of all the many motherly things Leatha didn't do when I was a child, baking a cake was at the very top of the list. My absentee father, by virtue of his diligent attention to a high-paying profession, made enough money for us to hire Aunt Hettie, who ran our kitchen as if she were cooking at the Governor's Mansion, and baked every birthday cake I ever got. My dream mother (who more closely resembled June Cleaver in *Leave It to Beaver* than I now like to think) would not only have baked those cakes, but would have brought cookies to the Troop bake sale, fed me hot soup when I was sick, and made fried chicken and potato salad for picnics. Leatha might manage Sunday night sandwiches and maybe an instant pudding now and again, but I never once saw her put a complete dinner on the table, let alone bake a cake. Much less a *wedding* cake.

"But I've been taking a cake course," Leatha said eagerly, "and it just so happens — a marvelous coincidence, really, just as if it were predestined! — that our class project was a wedding cake. A lovely three-layer cake, decorated with frosting flowers and with the groom's cake on top. So I know just how to do it." She pushed up the sleeves of her chic green floral-print dress. "I'll call my instructor and get the recipe. It doesn't have any herbs in it, but we can make a rosemary-and-lavender wreath for the plate — which is what we did for our class project. Rosemary and lavender are wedding herbs."

"I know," I said, wondering if the people who thought up these things also knew that snakes were supposed to hide in both plants.

"The cake will be my contribution to your wedding day, China. Heaven knows, you haven't let me do anything else."

"You're getting Brian's clothes."

"Oh, that." She waved her hand dismissively. "To tell the truth, I've felt positively *helpless*. But now I've got something worthwhile and fun to do."

Now, I grant you that Leatha has accomplished a great many admirable changes in the past few years, metamorphosing from a wealthy River Oaks matron to the practical wife of a Kerrville rancher, from daily drunk to recovering alcoholic. She's let her hair go from bleached blond to natural silver, and she grandmothered Brian at the ranch this summer while I was trussed up in traction. But from kitchen klutz to wedding-cake baker? The mind boggled.

"I really think it's too big a job —" I began, but Leatha cut me off.

"Of course you do," she said matter of factly. "You're just like your father. He always thought I couldn't do the least little thing. But he was wrong then and *you* are wrong now, and I'll show you. I'll bake you a three-layer wedding cake you'll never forget."

That was exactly what I was afraid of. But if I didn't let Leatha bake the wedding cake, her feelings would be hurt and I would feel guilty, which was the very last thing I needed. Laurel opened the door at that moment, and Leatha announced that she had just been appointed official wedding-cake baker.

"Can she really handle a wedding cake?" Laurel asked, after Leatha had left, her signature scent of White Shoulders lingering after her. My mother may have moved to a ranch, but I'll bet she wears White Shoulders while she's out branding dogies, or whatever.

"If she can't, we can always fall back on peanut butter and jelly."

Laurel's eyebrows edged upward.

"Well, then," I said, "how about Sara Lee? I'll go to the supermarket and get a dozen or so frozen cakes. We can stack them up like a row of bricks and pour a bucket of frosting over them. It won't be round, but we can tell everybody that rectangular cakes are in fashion."

Laurel shook her head. "I don't understand you, China. If this were my wedding, I'd be going absolutely bananas. The groom is too busy to show up for the license, your mother has volunteered to bake your cake, there's rain in the forecast —"

"*Rain?*"

"You haven't been watching the Weather Channel?" Laurel's tone softened. "Gosh, China, I hate to be the bearer of bad news, but there's a storm brewing out in the Gulf. Her name is Josephine. She's still a tropical storm, but they're saying she may intensify to hurricane strength today. The best guess for landfall is somewhere along the Texas Gulf coast late Saturday or early Sunday. Of course, she could shift to the northeast and head toward Louisiana, in which case we'd be out of the woods. But still —" She shrugged. "Who knows?"

"That's all we need," I groaned. "A hurricane!" Pecan Springs is far enough inland that we don't usually get hurricane winds, but a big tropical storm can dump eight or ten inches of rain on us in just a few hours. What a mess! Then I thought of Letty, whose blank, staring eyes would never see another sky, another sun, another storm. What was a little rain, compared to a long death?

I straightened my shoulders. "Time to come up with Plan B," I said. "If Josephine shows up, we move the ceremony into the tearoom. It'll be a bit crowded, but we're all friends."

"A *bit* crowded?" Laurel asked doubtfully. "How about a *lot* crowded?"

"We'll open the shops," I said with determination. "We'll all stand close together. We'll make it work."

"Right," Laurel said. "We'll make it work." She didn't sound convinced, but she didn't argue. Anyway, what choice did we have? I checked in with Ruby to tell her — without going into the details — that she could take the wedding cake off her list of things to do. I didn't mention Josephine.

There might be a tropical storm out in the Gulf but there wasn't a cloud in the sky over the Hill Country and the temperature was in the nineties. I got in the car and turned on the air conditioning, letting it wheeze for a few minutes before I drove off.

Wanda's Wonderful Acres is located on Redbud Road, on the east side of I-35 and the Balcones Fault. The fault divides the Edwards Plateau to the west from the Blackland prairie to the east, a rolling, grassy plain that was easily transformed by the plow into Texas's principal cotton-producing region. But then the pink boll worm chewed the heart out of the Cotton Kingdom and the droughts of the fifties finished it off. Now, the land produces animal feed. The fields are kept green by mobile irrigation systems that pump millions of gallons of water up from the aquifer and sprinkle it on the hay and sorghum that fatten the beef cattle that provide the cholesterol that clogs American arteries. I've heard that it takes twenty-five hundred gallons of water to produce a pound of beef, and when I drive past a huge field when the sprinklers are spouting like a hundred Old Faithfuls, I believe it. I resent it, too, especially at the height of a summer's drought, when the aquifer levels have dropped like a rock, the springs have dried up, and we've gone to a flush-only-when-necessary status. Today, though, I wasn't thinking about irrigation systems or clogged arteries or even the dwindling aquifer. I was thinking ahead — not very happily — to my conversation with Wanda Rathbottom.

Mostly through the efforts of Quentin Craven, the long-time manager, Wanda's Wonderful Acres has become Pecan Springs' premier nursery. Sales have no doubt been hurt by the big home-and-garden warehouse that opened on the Interstate last year, but the competition has been good for the nursery at least in one sense, forcing it to expand into new markets. Until last year, Wonderful Acres stocked only easy-dollar sure sellers — summer and fall annuals, predictable perennials, basic shrubs. Now Wanda has branched out, so to speak, into Texas natives and drought-resistant plants, which the home and garden store doesn't carry. She also brings in potted herbs every spring and fall, and in that sense we're rivals. Our competition doesn't bother me particularly. Even rivals can enjoy amicable relations. But Wanda has always been a sharply competitive and very prickly person.

Quent was nowhere in sight when I drove up and parked in the lot out front. There were only one or two other cars, suggesting that Wanda — if she was there — would not be occupied with customers. The heat had been bad all summer, which is not good for nursery traffic. Browsers won't hang around hot, humid plant tables when they might be lounging in the air conditioning with a cold lemonade, and experienced gardeners don't like to see their new plants keel over with heat stroke.

In our part of the country, fall is the big perennial season. If you plant in early or mid-October, you can count on a couple of good rains to settle the plants in before the first hard freeze halts new growth.

It was definitely too hot for browsing in a nursery. After a search, I found Wanda, red-faced and irritated, in the cactus house. She was giving orders to a couple of youngsters — horticulture interns from CTSU, I guessed — who were handling the watering. Apparently they had not been doing the job to her liking, and she was reading them the riot act in no uncertain terms. Wanda is a large, strong woman with spiky brown hair, narrow eyes, and almost no eyebrows, and when she gets emotional about something, which she does quite often, her nose twitches. She wore a red denim apron over green twill pants and an extra-size T-shirt that hung to her knees. Her nose was definitely twitching.

"Hi, Wanda," I said with robust cheer. "Got a minute?"

Wanda glanced at the large man's watch she always wears. "Only just," she said pointedly. "I've got to make some phone calls." She motioned with her head. "We'll go into the office. It's *hot* out here."

It was almost too hot for comfort, in

spite of the large exhaust fan at the far end of the greenhouse, which kept the air moving. But I trailed behind as Wanda bustled down the rows of plant tables. I don't much like cacti because they have so many defense mechanisms, but their forms intrigue me. I lingered, bending over a tray of something that looked like a bunch of green mushrooms covered with dense white prickles.

"What's this, Wanda?"

Wanda paused in her hurrying exit. "*Escobaria leei.* Dwarf Snowball. It has salmon pink flowers in the spring." She took a couple of backward steps and pointed to another cactus, which was covered with a symmetrical net of stout white spines, like touching stars. "This is *Coryphantha echinus.* West Texas Spiny Star. I collected the seed myself in Howard County, which is about as far north as it grows." She touched the cactus affectionately. "In the spring, it has the most incredible yellow and orange flowers. Isn't it gorgeous? And look at this one." Her voice was slowing down and getting softer. "*Echinocereus dasycanthus.* He's a real sweetie."

A sweetie? This was Wanda Rathbottom talking? I looked at her sideways. "He's cute," I agreed. "What do his friends call him?"

She actually giggled. "Rainbow Hedgehog. When he gets older, his stem will be banded with different pastel colors. His big yellow flowers display red stripes when they close up, like peppermint candy. *Soooo* spiffy," she added, verbally chucking the cactus under the chin.

This was a side of Wanda I'd never seen before, and it intrigued me more than the cacti. I turned, catching sight of a long row of large pots filled with the very same ribbed green cactus I'd seen in the Colemans' walled garden. "Now, that's a handsome plant. What is it?"

"*Cereus hildmannianus*," Wanda said. "Hildmann's Cereus. It's native to Brazil." She looked ruefully at the row of pots, about twenty of them. "I have quite a lot of it, as you can see. If you know of anybody who wants some . . ." Her voice died away. The pleasure was gone. Her nose was twitching sadly.

I waxed enthusiastic. "Isn't this the same cactus you used in the Colemans' garden? I *love* the strong vertical element it provides there. So architectural. And the skin — wonderfully leathery and interesting. Really, Wanda, you outdid yourself with that garden. The design, the plants — the whole effect is nothing short of stunning."

If Wanda was surprised by my hyperbole, she didn't let on. "Thank you, China. Yes, that little garden came off quite beautifully, if I do say so myself. *Cereus* is an absolutely fabulous plant." She stroked the cactus as if she were fondling a familiar friend. "She's a night-blooming plant, you know. Huge white flowers as big as a saucer and so delicate, like porcelain. Letty Coleman hated her, though," she added, with a small, sour smile. "She said she didn't like the smell, and she doesn't like cactus. She didn't tell Edgar that, of course. The garden was his idea, and he always got his way. He said he wanted to see how it looked before he finalized the contract for —" She stopped. A shadow crossed her face.

Contract? I waited, but nothing else was immediately forthcoming. "What happened was so terrible," I said after a moment. "Just tragic. And so unexpected, too."

Wanda's smile faded as if it had been turned off by a dimmer switch. Her eyes became watchful. Her nose grew still. "Yes," she said, very quietly. "It's hard to believe he's actually dead."

"Actually, I wasn't thinking of Edgar. I was thinking of Letty."

She wiped her forehead with the back of her hand, smearing dirt across the place where her left eyebrow would have been, if she'd had one. "Letty?"

"You haven't heard?"

"Heard what?" she asked irritably. "Don't talk in riddles, China. You've got something to say, say it."

"Letty Coleman is dead," I said.

The effect of this information was really quite interesting. Wanda's lower jaw dropped, her eyes widened, and she made an audible gulping sound, like a fish out of water.

"Would you like to sit down?" I asked solicitously, taking her elbow.

Her jaw snapped shut, her eyes narrowed, and she yanked her arm out of my grasp. "Of course not. How did it happen?"

"Broken neck," I said. "The back stairs."

"Oh, those stairs. Very dangerous. I nearly fell on them myself once." Her nose twitched. "When did it happen?"

"This morning." I paused. "I'm sure the police will be checking with you."

Wanda was startled. "With me?"

"Well," I said judiciously, "they haven't

wrapped up the investigation into Edgar's murder, you know. And now that Letty's dead —" I gave her a sympathetic look and, on a hunch, added, "People who had contractual dealings with Edgar will be on their suspect list. The police always go for the business associates. And since you're also on the Council —"

My remark about the police was an unfounded and unconvincing assertion, and under other circumstances, Wanda would have given me a smart, sarcastic "Says who?" But her emotions had taken over for her brain. Her shoulders slumped and her eyes began, unexpectedly, to fill with tears. "Oh, God, what a mess! And just when I thought it was all over and done with."

"A landscaping contract?" I asked, still guessing.

"The most important one of my life," Wanda said bleakly. "It would have saved the nursery. But as things stand . . ." Her nose twitched faster.

I could finish the sentence in my head. As things stood, she was going to lose Wonderful Acres. "Why don't we sit down?" I said. There was a wooden bench in front of the cereus.

Wanda sank down on the bench with a weary sigh. I upended a five-gallon bucket and sat down on it where I could see her face. Our long silence was broken only by the metallic whir of the big exhaust fan and the manic chirping of a bird that had managed to find its way into the greenhouse and couldn't get out. The twenty cereus were a line of silent witnesses.

"About the contract," I prompted, and waited for her to tell me to shut up and get the hell out of there — as she would have, under other circumstances. But she didn't. This had been tormenting her and she was ready to get it off her chest.

"A friend of Edgar's," she said, "a man named Shepherd, manages a five-acre office complex in San Antonio. He planned to remove the shrubs and install a xeriscaped landscape. What he wanted was low-maintenance, drought-tolerant native plants he wouldn't have to hire a landscape service to water and weed, along with some large succulents — prickly pear and agave and some showy cacti. He wanted a desert look." She glanced sadly at the waiting cereus, obviously destined for the project. "Edgar set it up so I was low bidder on the project."

"So you got the job?"

"That's what he said," she replied dully. She wiped her twitching nose with the back of her hand. "In fact, he showed me the contract. It was all filled out — all it lacked was Shepherd's signature."

"And you purchased the plants for the project on the basis of that unsigned contract."

She looked at me as though I were a mind reader. "How did you know?"

"It's an old scam," I said. I paused. I already knew the answer to the next question, but I had to ask it anyway. "What did Coleman want from you to persuade Shepherd to execute the contract?"

Her mouth opened, but she couldn't seem to say anything. She put her hand to her nose as if to hold it still.

"He wanted you to change your vote on the annexation project?"

She closed her mouth, dropped her hand, and thought about it. "Yes," she said finally.

"What did you tell him?"

"What *could* I tell him?" she wailed. Her eyes were screwed almost shut. "To get the best price, I bought the plants on a nonreturnable basis. I've got a lot of money tied up in them, and no way to get it out. The contract would have kept the nursery alive for another six months, maybe more."

"So you agreed to vote his way?"

She pulled at her already spiky hair with both hands. "What other choice did I have?" she asked shrilly. "Don't go taking the moral high road with me, China Bayles. If some sleazy snake cornered you and ordered you to do something for him if he'd save your business, you'd do it."

"I'd do almost anything," I said, reserving some wiggle room.

"Bullshit. I'd do anything I had to do to hold it together. So would you. What does a stupid vote matter, one way or the other? What does the Council matter? It's all a political game."

I'd do anything I had to do. Her words sliced the still air. What had she done? To pry the truth out of her, I needed some leverage.

"I might be able to help you, Wanda," I said slowly. "One of my friends practices law in San Antonio. She specializes in fraud. A letter from her would probably convince Mr. Shepherd that it's in his best interest to sign that contract. If a letter doesn't work, a phone call will. She can be very persuasive."

Wanda stared at me, taking this in. Her face showed her inner struggle: She was hopeful, then afraid to hope, by turns. Finally, hope won out. "It might work. It's *got* to work!" She leaned forward eagerly. "Oh, thank you, China. You can't know how much this means to —"

I held up my hand. "Hang on," I said. "Before I put my friend to work, I want to know where you were on Sunday night."

She gave me a blank look. "Sunday night? Why, I was home. With my husband."

"From when to when?"

"All day, actually. Our son and his wife were supposed to come for dinner, but I was feeling pretty down about this whole thing, so I called them and canceled." She frowned, realized why I was asking, and sucked in her breath. "You want to know if I killed him, huh? Well, let me tell you, if I'd had a gun, I certainly would have considered it."

"Where were you this morning?"

Her mouth tightened. "This morning?" she asked suspiciously. "Why do you want to know?"

I gave her a big smile. "I'd like to feel I'm getting a little something in return for my phone call to my friend in San Antonio."

"No, I mean, what's it to *you?* Why are you so interested in the Colemans?"

I remembered an old line that Perry

Mason used when he moonlighted as a detective. "Let's just say that I'm acting as a friend of the court."

She thought about that and decided that it sounded right. "Well, anyway," she said sullenly, "I don't have anything to hide. I was in the office this morning. I had a lot of stuff to deal with."

"Can anybody verify that?"

Her jaw was working back and forth as if she were gritting her teeth. Her nose was twitching. "Quent was with me most of the time. We were going over the books."

By now, it was pretty plain that Wanda hadn't had anything to do with Letty's death. But it wouldn't hurt to push her a little. "Where is Quent?" I asked. "Just in case he's needed to confirm your statement."

Wanda put her hand to her nose. "He's not here. He won't be back." She swallowed hard. "He got another job, in Houston."

"In Houston!" I said, shocked. "But why?"

"Because I don't have the money to pay his salary." Wanda began to cry. "I had to let him go."

Chapter Thirteen

There are many folk traditions for the protection of small children. For instance, a cross made from lavender, or a bundle of lavender, rosemary, and dill, might be hung in the cradle to keep the infant from being carried off by witches. Peony root was carved into beads and hung around the neck to protect against evil, or a child might be given a bracelet of cloves strung on a red thread to repulse the devil. An amulet containing mistletoe, holly, and hazelnuts protected against lightning and sudden storms.

"The Meaning of Lavender,"
by China Bayles
The Pecan Springs *Enterprise*
Home and Garden Section

From time to time, I have enjoyed poking fun at Wanda Rathbottom, whose efforts to corner the nursery trade in Pecan Springs have often seemed intemperate. But now that I've heard her story, it won't be so easy to be sarcastic. As I drove back along Redbud Road, I kept thinking of how tough it was going to be for her without Quent, who had single-handedly transformed Wonderful Acres into a fine nursery. Chalk one more disaster up to Edgar Coleman. I used my cell phone to put in a call to the Whiz and left a message on her answering machine. If anybody could force Shepherd to honor his contract with Wanda, it was Justine Wyzinski. The money wouldn't bring Quent back, but it might keep Wonderful Acres afloat a little longer.

Back at Thyme and Seasons, everything seemed pretty normal. Business had picked up while I was gone, and we'd had a respectable afternoon. Laurel reported that a quartet of wandering tourists had come in, browsed for a half-hour, and gone away with a stack of books, some gift items, and a selection of essential oils, leaving a nice bit of cash behind. I was momentarily sorry that the tearoom wasn't open yet — they might have left even more cash. Not to be greedy, of course, but I *am* in business to make a profit.

"Remember the woman who was here this morning?" Laurel asked, when she had finished telling me the news. "The one who left you the note I couldn't find?" She took the clip out of her hair and shook her head, brown hair rippling down her back.

I picked up the mail. "Uh-huh," I said, leafing through it. There wasn't much — several mail orders, a couple of invoices, a newsletter from the International Herb Association, and an envelope with an Indiana return address. "Did you find the note she left?" I asked absently, studying the envelope.

"No," Laurel replied, pulling her hair back and clipping it into another ponytail. "I didn't have time to look. But she's out in the garden. She wants to talk to you."

"What about?" I opened the envelope. There was a typed letter inside. It was from Harold Tucker, our absentee landlord.

"She says it's personal." Laurel paused, frowning a little. "Actually, today isn't the first time I've seen her. She's been here a time or two, although I think mostly she just walked around the garden."

Still holding the letter, I looked up at the clock. The visit with Wanda had taken longer than I'd thought, and it was nearly four-fifteen. "I won't have long to talk to her," I said. "Sheila will be here in a few minutes. We're going to see Iris Powell."

"That reminds me," Laurel said. "Sheila

phoned to confirm. Your mother called too. She got the recipe for the cake, and she was on her way to the grocery to pick up supplies. She sounded excited."

"I'm excited too," I said. I folded the letter without reading it, stuffed it back in the envelope, and stuck it at the back of the stack. Harold Tucker could go fly a kite. He was not getting his house back before the first of January. And that, by damn, was that.

"Ruby is *very* excited," Laurel said significantly. "She got her outfit for the wedding this afternoon."

I handed the mail to Laurel. "A couple of these look like orders. If you get time, you could process them." I paused. "I didn't know Ruby went shopping today."

"She didn't. The outfit came in the mail. From one of those weird catalogs she buys from. Sexy Secrets, I think it was called."

"Oh, God," I said. Ruby buys her clothes from two places, the vintage shop in the Emporium next door and catalogs, some of which offer very odd items. Some of Ruby's most exotic clothing comes from catalogs.

"Right." Laurel's expression was grim. "I wouldn't be the one to tell her so, but the outfit looks like a nightgown. All she'd need is a retinue of slave girls and some palm fans and she could go as the Queen of Sheba. One good thing, though," she added with a little laugh, "you won't have to worry about people finding fault with your wedding dress. They'll be too busy criticizing Ruby." She stopped. "And then there's Josephine."

Josephine? I frowned. "Who's Josephine?" Then I remembered. "Oh, yes. The tropical storm."

"Not any longer," Laurel said. "They've promoted her to a hurricane. She's still way out in the Gulf and doesn't show any sign of going anywhere special. But there's a high pressure ridge to the north, and the steering winds are likely to send her in our direction. She's getting stronger, too. They say she might be Force Three when she hits the coast."

"It figures," I said. "This is shaping up to be the wildest wedding Pecan Springs has ever seen. The groom may or may not show up, the bride's mother is baking the cake, and the matron of honor plans to come as the Queen of Sheba. What the hell. Get out the umbrellas. We'll have a hurricane party instead."

The woman was waiting for me on the stone bench beside the fountain, in the shade of a chaste tree. A breeze swayed the fragrant blue blossoms, but the afternoon was still much too hot for the navy blue suit she had on, and she was perspiring. She wore her sandy-red hair in a tidy pageboy cut. When she turned her head sharply at my footsteps, her hair swung away and I saw that the right side of her face had been extensively reconstructed, with only partial success. I had automatically taken the hand she held out before I realized, with a start, that it was a prosthetic. But she stood and smiled with the poised assurance of a professional woman who is used to meeting and dealing with people on her own terms, and handed me a business card that said she was Rachel Lang, a psychologist who specialized in counseling women and girls, from Orlando, Florida.

I pocketed the card, on which she had written a local phone number. "What can I do for you, Ms. Lang?"

By any stretch of the imagination, the woman was definitely not pretty. The reconstruction had left her face scarred and misshapen, her nose was oddly chunky, and her right shoulder drooped. But her clear gray eyes met mine steadily and her voice was low-pitched and deliberate.

"You can help me reconnect with my daughter, Elena," she said.

Of all the things the woman might have asked me, this was the least expected. "Your . . . daughter?"

"Yes," she said. "She was abducted eleven years ago. I'd like to tell you my story, if you have the time."

I looked at my watch. "I have a few minutes."

"Thank you," she said. "I'll be brief. At the time Elena was taken, I was serving a prison term for tax fraud. The court had granted temporary custody of Elena to my mother. The child's father, Jim Carlson, took her out one afternoon and never brought her back. My mother called the police, but they couldn't or wouldn't do anything. The shock of it nearly killed her then, and she died of a heart attack six months later."

"I'm sorry," I said. I was also surprised, because while there was a resonant tone of deep feeling in Rachel Lang's voice, she spoke straightforwardly and factually, with a firm control. This was a woman who knew herself.

She nodded, accepting my sympathy without comment. "When I was released from prison and began to look for my daughter, the trail was cold. It was as if she had vanished in thin air. Unfortunately, a couple of months after my release, I was involved in a nearly fatal automobile accident. My car was hit head-on by a drunk driver, and I spent most of the next year recovering." She touched her face with the fingers of her left hand. "As you can see, it involved quite a bit of reconstructive surgery, as well as physical rehabilitation. I wasn't able to resume the search for another year. Finally, I contacted the National Center for Missing and Exploited Children. We did manage to turn up a lead, but by the time I arrived on the scene, Elena and her abductor were gone."

Her story was tragic — tragedy heaped on tragedy. But I couldn't see where I fit into it. "I don't mean to be insensitive," I said, "but what in the world makes you think I can help you find your daughter?"

She smiled crookedly. "You know Elena very well, better than I do, in fact. Last weekend, she worked for you here in your garden. She spends a great deal of time with your son, Brian."

"Melissa?" I gasped. "You're talking about *Melissa?*"

"That's the name her abductor gave her. Her real name is Elena Lorraine Lang."

302

Beneath the businesslike words, the woman's voice had grown sad, as if she were still grieving for something precious, something lost. "She was born twelve years ago yesterday, in the Women's Unit of the Florida State Prison." She smiled a little. "I've been absent from my daughter's life, but I recall every moment of her birth. It was an incredible, glorious event. I loved her instantly, with every cell of my body."

Twelve years ago yesterday. And last night we had celebrated Melissa's twelfth birthday. I shook my head helplessly. "I . . . I don't know what to say."

"I know it's a surprise," the woman said, "and I understand that it may be hard to believe. I can provide confirmation of my claims. And of course you are free to contact the Center and check my assertions with the case worker who has been monitoring this search. I can give you her name and the Center's telephone number. The hot line answers calls twenty-four hours a day." She opened her purse, holding it with her prosthetic and reaching into it with her left hand. "I can show you Elena's birth certificate and the custody papers, as well as an age-progressed photo that the Center produced. It's not exactly like her, but pretty close."

"An age-progressed photograph?"

She pulled a large manila envelope out of her purse. "They used a photograph of Elena at eighteen months, just before she was abducted, and a photo of me. They put them together with a software program that creates an image of what she might look like today." She opened the envelope and took out a photo and some papers. "And here is a 'To Whom it May Concern' letter from the Center and my Florida driver's license."

I scanned the papers and the license quickly and lingered over the photograph. It wasn't perfect, a little off in the chin and eyes, but it was Melissa, with her chunky nose — unmistakably, eerily, her mother's nose. Looking at the photo, I felt an immediate and sweeping sympathy for the young girl I would love to call my daughter, who had long ago accepted the idea that her own mother was dead. Over the years, she had created a fantasy around that mother, transforming her into a beautiful illusion, a gorgeous princess. How would she cope with the reality of a real mother who was a convicted felon, facially disfigured and partially disabled, who had given birth to her in prison? Melissa might have been better off if this woman had never found her.

I handed everything back to Lang except the card with the Center's phone number and the case worker's name. "Granted that what you've told me is true," I said distantly, "I still don't know what you want from me. Have you contacted the local police and asked for their help?" I didn't think she had — surely McQuaid would have called me immediately.

"Not yet." Lang put the papers back in her purse. "My first concern is Elena. She is deeply attached to her abductor, and perhaps also to his wife. Emotionally, this could be catastrophic for her, just as she's entering adolescence. She will need a great deal of support when she learns the truth." She paused. "I'm not in a great hurry to confront Dr. Jackson — that's what he's calling himself. I think the risk of flight is considerably less now than it was when he left Seattle."

"Seattle?"

"Yes. I said that we turned up a lead some time ago. Someone recognized Elena's picture and phoned the Center. I flew immediately to Seattle, but by the time I got there, they had gone. They didn't leave any traces."

"Melissa said that she lived in Seattle," I said slowly, remembering last night's conversation. "She said that was where her dad remarried." I found myself wondering, somewhat irrelevantly, what was going to happen to Dr. Jackson. He was a very good dentist. It was a damned shame to lose him. And Rachel Lang was right: Melissa loved her father very much. When she found out the truth, she would be devastated. If Jackson was convicted of kidnapping, how would she cope? I doubted if the discovery of her real mother would compensate for the loss of the father she loved.

I was jolted out of these thoughts. "—not her father," Rachel Lang was saying.

"What?"

"Dr. Jackson is not Elena's father," the woman said. She shook her head, smiling a little. "I'm sorry. This is all very complicated. You see —"

She stopped. We could hear the sound of footsteps on gravel, and we both turned. It was Smart Cookie, cool and self-confident in a lemon-yellow blazer, black blouse, and trim black slacks.

"Laurel told me you were out here," she said. She nodded a greeting to Rachel Lang. "I'm sorry to interrupt your conversation, but I think we'd better be going, China. I told Iris Powell we'd be there at a quarter to five, and it's a fifteen-minute drive."

"I'm afraid I have to go, Ms. Lang." I glanced at the card. "Is this the phone number where you're staying?"

"Right. It's the Pack Saddle Inn." Her voice became urgent. "I know you're terribly busy with your wedding plans, but can we possibly get together tonight? I would like to tell you the whole story, from beginning to end, so you can better understand what I hope to achieve." She pressed her lips together and a shadow of sadness crossed her face. "Elena admires you so, Ms. Bayles. I think you may be the *only* one who can help her. This is going to be so hard for her to understand and accept."

"I'll give you a call later in the evening," I said. "I can't promise to see you, though. Things are a little hectic just now." That was the understatement of the month. Of the year, probably.

"That's what your counter-person told me," the woman said. She held out her hand again, and I took it. "I'll be at the inn after seven o'clock. Please call. I'll be glad to drive to your house to see you, if that would be better."

Sheila and I said good-bye and left her standing there beside the fountain as we walked down the path. "What was that all about?" Sheila asked, as we neared her car.

"Her daughter was kidnapped," I said. "It's a heartbreaker."

"Oh, God," Sheila said compassionately. "That's the very worst thing I can think of." She took out her keys. "Why did she come to you?"

"Because I know the girl," I said. "She wants me to help break the news."

I waited as Sheila got into her Explorer and reached over to unlock the passenger door. Which was the greater tragedy for Melissa: losing her mother for the first twelve years of her life, or losing the man she loved as her father? Would mother and daughter ever be able to make up for the lost years, or re-create the bond that might have joined them? And what about Dr. Jackson? If he wasn't Melissa's father, who was he? Whatever his motivation for taking the child, whatever the joys of raising her, kidnapping is a federal crime and the penalties are severe. What would happen to him?

I got in beside Sheila and slammed the door. A mother might have found her daughter, the daughter might be restored to the mother. But there were no winners in this sad affair. Only losers, and terrible, terrible losses.

Chapter Fourteen

In the language of flowers, iris means "I have a message for you."

Flora's Dictionary
Kathleen Gips

Iris, the goddess of the rainbow, the messenger of the gods, always kept an eye out for the latest happening, which she then reported to the appropriate Olympic desk. Maybe we should christen her the goddess of private eyes.

China Bayles
China's Garden

For wheresoe're thou art in this world's globe, I'll have an Iris that shall find thee out.

Henry VI, Part II
William Shakespeare

Sheila turned on the ignition. "I just talked to Blackie," she said, putting the vehicle into reverse and backing it expertly out of the tight space at the curb. "He told me that Letty Coleman died this morning — and that *you* found her."

"Right." I flipped the visor down to keep the afternoon sun out of my eyes, took a deep breath, and shifted gears myself, mentally, refocusing my attention from Melissa and her mother to the Coleman case. "She was lying at the foot of a flight of stone stairs, behind her house. When I talked to McQuaid at lunchtime, he hadn't found any forensic evidence that would indicate foul play. However —"

I summarized the information that contradicted that assumption: the pitcher and three glasses on the patio table, Rena Burnett's sighting of a blue car in her driveway around nine-thirty, and Darla Jean McDaniels's odd behavior when Ruby tried to find out where she had been this morning. Then, realizing that Sheila was still in the dark about Coleman's various blackmail schemes, I told her what Ruby and I had dug up in our conversations with the City Council members. "I tried to get through to McQuaid to suggest that he interview Darla McDaniels again," I added, "but he was pursuing the Garza angle." I glanced at Sheila. "Did you hear that Phyllis's husband seems to have taken himself off to parts unknown?"

"Blackie told me," Sheila said, slowing to turn the corner onto River Road. "It's a complicated situation. Garza's flight certainly makes him look guilty. And he seems to have been the kind of guy who would go storming over to Coleman's house and blow him away."

"That's true," I said. "He certainly has a violent temper. But it's also possible he's running to escape the state's investigation into those phony documents he obtained, which has nothing to do with Coleman's murder." It isn't just mystery plots that are built on red herrings; life itself is full of just such odd, misleading synchronicities. Finding out what's a clue and what's a coincidence keeps cops and the courts busy. "The last I heard, McQuaid was looking for prints to compare to the one on the gun. Do you know whether he's picked anything up?"

"Not so far," Sheila said. "Blackie is giving him a couple of men to speed things up. But without a full set of Jorge's prints, it'll be tough."

"So McQuaid's investigation is still basically at square one," I said. I leaned back in the seat and stretched out my legs. "Except that now he has one gun, *two* dead bodies, and a lot more questions." I paused, thinking ahead to our conversation with Coleman's office manager. "If Iris Powell has heard about Letty's death, I don't imagine it has enhanced her sense of security."

Sheila signaled for a left, checked her mirror, and nosed into the lane. Behind us, a little man in a Honda leaned on his horn and gave us the finger, obviously offended at Sheila's audacity. She braked at the light, waiting for the traffic to clear for the turn. "You're right," she agreed. "If Iris thinks Letty was murdered and is afraid she might be next, she might be a little more willing to tell us what she knows."

I drummed my fingers on the armrest. There was another possibility I hadn't yet considered. Letty had known that Iris was involved with Edgar. What if Letty had learned that the involvement went deeper than she had thought? What if she had invited her over for a chat and had confronted her? What if the confrontation had escalated into argument, then into violence? Had Iris pushed her down the stairs, then panicked and fled? This reconstruction was entirely speculative, but possible. Briefly, I wondered what color car Iris drove.

Sheila waited for a gravel truck to clear the intersection. "Blackie told me he ran into you in the courthouse this afternoon," she said, turning left.

I put my speculations on hold and shifted my attention. "Did he tell you what we talked about?"

She moved into the right-hand lane. "Just that you didn't want McQuaid to stay on as chief. You'd rather I got the job."

"You can say that again," I said fervently. "But that's beside the point. What Blackie said to me was that you should stop worrying about politics and follow your bliss." I jammed both feet on the floor. "Shit!" The guy in the Honda had zipped out of the left lane in front of us and put on his brakes.

Sheila braked fast to avoid a rear-end collision, shifted gears, and muttered under her breath, "Boy, I wish I were a cop. A *real* cop, I mean. I'd ticket his damn ass." The driver of the Honda, obviously pleased with himself, shot us the bird again and speeded up.

"Road rage," I said. "Testosterone fury."

"Yeah," Sheila said. "I know I pulled in

front of him, but there was plenty of room." She looked at me, her eyebrows skeptical. "Blackie *really* said I should follow my bliss?"

"Words to that effect. He said it wouldn't be fair if he kept you from doing what you really wanted to do. Bottom line, go for it."

"I see," Sheila said reflectively. There was a long pause. "Follow my bliss, huh? If I only knew which way."

I glanced at her in surprise. "What's the matter? Don't you *know* what you want?"

"Being police chief is a big job."

"Well, sure. But —"

"What if I give up my university position and then find out I don't like being chief? There's a lot of stress in a job like that, you know. You can see what McQuaid is going through right now. And remember what happened to that woman chief they hired in Austin? There was so much animosity toward her in the ranks that she finally quit."

I cleared my throat. "Excuse me, Smart Cookie. I thought you wanted this job. I thought it was a job a woman law enforcement officer would die for."

"Well, maybe," Sheila said in a defensive tone, "but I might not like working with the City Council. The way you describe them, they sound like a bunch of unethical jerks with their own private agendas. And I'd have to start from scratch with the department. The entire communications system has to be overhauled, they're back in the paper-and-pencil age when it comes to computers, and the budget is below the poverty line." She smacked the steering wheel with the flat of her hand. "I don't need all that shit! I'd be working myself into an early grave."

"If you don't want to do it, don't do it," I said mildly. "You've got a good contract, cushy office, lots of job security, prestige. Nobody would blame you if you stayed where you are."

She chewed for a moment on a corner of her lip. "I didn't say I don't want the job," she said finally. "I do. It's just that —" Her mouth twisted. "Oh, hell. I don't know *what* I want."

"I can't believe this," I said, astonished. "I thought it was Blackie who was keeping you from realizing your dream of having your very own small-town police department to play with. Now you're telling me it's you!"

"I've always been my own worst enemy," she said bleakly. "You can't believe how hard it was to make up my mind to take the CTSU job. They almost gave it to somebody else before I said yes."

I shook my head. "Smart Cookie," I said, "you have a problem."

"I have a problem," she agreed, and we drove the rest of the way in silence.

The office of Coleman Enterprises occupied the left half of a one-story building at the corner of River Road and Pedernales, about a mile from the entrance to the Blessing Ranch. The place was built in the shade of a huge live oak and designed to look like an old-fashioned Texas ranch house, with a Western-style porch across the front and a tangle of honeysuckle vines growing up lattices at each end. The right half of the building was occupied by an insurance company. Neither Coleman Enterprises nor the insurance company appeared to be doing a land-office business.

Sheila parked the Explorer in front of Coleman's half, next to a new Lincoln that was the twin of the one I'd seen Letty driving — except that this one wasn't silver, it was blue. The vanity license plate read Iris I. My antennae went up. The plot, as Ruby would say, was thickening.

As I got out of the Explorer, I glanced

up at the brilliant afternoon sky. The air was hot and dry and the landscape baked under an unrelenting sun. It was hard to imagine Josephine out there in the Gulf, swirling and twirling in her scarf of wild clouds and rain. It had been a few years since a hurricane breezed into Texas, and I tried to remember the possibilities. If she headed northeast, toward Beaumont or New Orleans, we'd be on the western side of the storm and bone-dry. If she came in far to the south, around Brownsville, we'd be on the outskirts and would get a few showers, at most. But if she grew into a sizable storm and made landfall between Corpus Christi and Houston, we could get drenched. Williamson County, to the north of us, once got an entire year's worth of rainfall in two days, something like thirty-six inches, courtesy of a hurricane. As soon as I got a chance, I'd better check with the Weather Channel for an update.

I followed Sheila's yellow blazer as she climbed the steps, crossed the porch, and opened the door. Inside, the office looked more like a Houston high-rise than a Texas ranch house. It was paneled in an elegant wood and carpeted in bone-colored velvet, with ficus plants at strategic locations. Opposite the door was an elegant receptionist's desk, and on the wall behind it hung a large gold-framed landscape of an old barn in a field of bluebonnets. Off to the right was a waiting area with pale upholstered chairs and a sofa heaped with colorful cushions, all very tastefully done. The only sign of the hard sell was a jumbo topographic map of Pecan Springs and the adjoining area. The map was stuck all over with green flags, green presumably representing ecological sensitivity, the flags representing Coleman properties, of which there were a bundle. The Blessing Ranch, between the Interstate and Lookout Mountain to the south of Pecan Springs, was outlined with a green marker. I hadn't realized just how large and sprawling it was.

"Where is everybody?" Sheila asked. "Looks like the office is closed."

I turned back, noting that the top of the receptionist's desk was clean as a whistle, empty of everything except a telephone console. The chair was pushed under the desk. Operations must be shut down for a while, now that the boss was out of the picture.

A door opened to our left, and we turned. "I'm Iris Powell," a woman said. "Are you looking for me?"

She was in her late forties, dressed in belted brown slacks and a silky white blouse, open down to the second button, that showed a full, firm cleavage. Her brown hair was permed curly, and she wore tortoise-shell glasses and clip-on earrings like fat gold snails. She was holding a cigarette between the first two fingers of her left hand. Her nails and lips were an I-dare-you red and her brows were penciled into an artificial arch. She had the brash, defiant look of a woman who had come up the hard way and was proud of it.

"I'm Sheila Dawson," Smart Cookie said. "This is China Bayles." She hesitated. "Paula *did* call you, didn't she? She said you were expecting us."

Iris lifted a cigarette to her lips, pulled on it, tilted her head back and blew a cloud of smoke out of both nostrils. Almost lazily she said, "My sister oughta mind her own business." She didn't say, *so should you,* but the implication was obvious.

"Paula's worried about you," Sheila replied. "She says you're concerned that —"

Iris dropped the laziness. "Paula's a peach," she said, "but she worries too much. She heard me wrong, she got scared, and she's making a federal case out of it." From her accent, I'd guess that Iris

began life somewhere along the border between Oklahoma and Arkansas. "But hey,
it was real nice of you to listen to her, you
being her boss and all. It made her feel a
lot better. I just hate it that you had to go
to the trouble of driving out here."

"Oh, it was no trouble," Sheila said.
"However, I think it might be a good idea
if we discussed —"

"Yeah, well, as I say, thanks," Iris said,
with a dismissive toss of her head. "Now, if
you don't mind, I've got a lot of work to do.
The auditor will be coming in next week
and —"

"I gather," I said, "that the police
haven't contacted you yet."

Her eyes slid to me. A slight frown appeared between her penciled eyebrows.
She lifted her cigarette to her lips and took
another puff. "The police? Why should
they —"

"About Letty Coleman."

Her eyes flickered again, not with
amusement. Her face hardened. But the
words, when she spoke, came out in that
slow Okie drawl. "So what about Letty
Coleman? She's got nothing to do with me.
She wants to know what's going on, she
can talk to Eddie's lawyer."

"She's dead."

The words hit Iris like a fist in the stomach. Her face went ashen. She sucked in her breath and sagged against the door frame. Moving swiftly, Sheila took one arm and I took the other and we half-pulled, half-lifted her into the other room and deposited her on a leather sofa. Sheila went for water and a towel. I picked up Iris's cigarette from the carpet and dropped it in a heavy marble ashtray as I glanced around. The office was furnished with the same kind of massive pieces I had seen in Coleman's house — a heavy oak desk, upholstered executive chair, elegantly paneled walls, a plush beige carpet, leather sofa and chairs. Instead of a window, one wall sported a large lighted aquarium, with two skillet-sized goldfish and a black fish with eyes like ski goggles. Over the aquarium hung another fish, a large stuffed marlin in full fighting posture. It was a man's office — Edgar's, no doubt.

On the sofa, Iris was getting her breath. "H-h-how did it happen?" she gasped. "When?" She pulled off her glasses and pressed the backs of her hands against her eyes. "Oh, shit. Poor Letty." She began to cry, softly.

I sat down in the soft leather chair to the right of the sofa and watched her. I was sure that the news about Letty had been a surprise. I have met quite a few accomplished liars and actors in my courtroom days, and I didn't believe that this woman could have faked her physical response to the announcement of Letty's death. I also thought that Rena Burnett would have mentioned it if the blue car in her driveway that morning had been another Lincoln. But until McQuaid had checked Iris's alibi for this morning, he might consider her a suspect. It did not behoove me to feed her any detailed information about what might or might not be a crime.

Sheila returned with a damp paper towel, dabbed at Iris's face, then handed her the glass of water. Iris kept her eyes shut as she drank. Finally, she opened her eyes and put on her glasses.

"How did it happen?" she repeated.

"You'll hear the details of Letty's death when the police are ready to release them," I said, and added, "They'll also want to know where you were this morning."

"This morning?" she asked. Her eyes went from Sheila to me. Her mascara was smudged and her red lipstick was bleeding into the corners of her mouth. "Is that when she died?"

"Yes," I said.

She took the towel from Sheila and wiped her face with it again. "If you're not going to tell me how it happened, I've got to assume somebody killed her." Her voice was hoarse.

I didn't say anything.

She was getting control of herself again. She sat for a moment, chewing on her lip and thinking, but not liking her thoughts. "Christ," she muttered. She shook her head, disbelieving. "What a goddamn mess."

Sheila and I said nothing. For the next few moments, the only sound in the thickly carpeted office was the soft bubbling of the aquarium filter. "If you're thinking it might've been me," Iris said finally, "you're wrong." Her voice was stronger now, edgy and belligerent. "I spent the whole damn day — from eight until just a little while ago — with the accountant. Eddie left the books and bank accounts in a helluva mess. Not even the accountant can figure out what he was up to. The bank is calling in an auditor."

"Sounds like a good idea," Sheila said dryly.

Iris's eyes came to me. "Paula said you're a criminal attorney. What do you think . . ." She stopped, trying to formulate a question but not quite able to decide what it should be. "Forget it," she said. She reached for the cigarette case and lighter on the table, attempting nonchalance. "Doesn't matter." She flicked the lighter. Her hand was trembling and it took a couple of clicks before her Bic did its job. "I'm clean. I got nothing to worry about."

"Oh, yeah?" I asked. "You told your sister that you know too much and you're scared. Now Letty is dead and you're wondering if you could be next. So why don't you let us help you."

Iris stared at me. She drew smoke. "The police know I didn't kill Eddie," she said. "They've checked out my alibi. I flew to Phoenix for a weekend with friends, and I didn't get back to town until nearly noon on Monday. That was when I found out he'd been shot." She ran her little finger around her lips, as if smoothing her lipstick. "It was a shock, but I can't say I was surprised."

"Did you have a reason to expect it?" Sheila asked sharply.

"Let's just say he was living dangerously. I mean, you walk out in front of a train every day or two, you've got to figure on getting run over." Iris shook her head gloomily. "I won't exactly say it was a death wish, but it had to be something like that. He hated being in a rut. Nothing made him happier than lighting a fire under people."

"What did you say when the police asked you if you had any idea who *did* kill him?"

"I said I didn't know," she replied, "and that's God's truth."

She said it firmly enough, but there was something about her answer that made me think she was holding back. "No phone calls, no death threats?"

She gave a brittle laugh. "Those? Oh, hell, yes. Every week or so, somebody would storm in here, yelling and cussing. But it was all just talk. They were afraid to try anything for fear he'd come after them."

"That would include most of the City Council?" Sheila asked.

Iris's glasses had slid to the end of her nose, magnifying her eyes. She pushed them up. "What do you know about that?"

"We may have missed a few of the details, but we have the general outline," I said. "He threatened to tell the voters that he and Pauline Perkins had had a sexual relationship. He offered to blow the whistle on Winnie Hatcher's brother. He doubled

Darla McDaniels's rent. He bought a new car from Ken Bowman. He volunteered a rent-free shop location to Billie Jean Jones. He threatened to disclose that Phyllis Garza's husband had forged immigration documents. He withheld a contract from Wanda Rathbottom." I paused. "In return for his cooperation, he expected these people to vote his way when the annexation proposal came up again."

Iris's lower jaw sagged. "My God," she said. "How in *hell* did you dig up all that?"

"It's a small town. People know one another, and they talk. It's tough to keep a secret."

"No shit." She leaned forward and tapped her cigarette into the marble ashtray. "Well, I'm not going to try to defend him. Eddie had a certain way of working, a style, you might say. If a piece of useful information happened to land in his lap — and a lot of it did — he filed it away for future reference. He was always talking about leverage. Always saying he'd be a damn fool if he didn't use whatever tool came to hand."

"And sometimes he created the tool himself," I said. "Like Pauline."

Iris smiled slightly. "Yeah, she's a good example. He wasn't really involved with her, emotionally, I mean. He didn't jump in the sack with her more than once or twice." She chuckled. "Pauline isn't exactly a sex goddess. But when it was all over, she was in his pocket, so to speak. He had her right where he wanted her, you know what I mean?"

Sheila looked as if she was ready to gag. "And you approved?"

Iris lifted her shoulders, let them fall. "Pauline's a grownup, isn't she? Most of his women were like that. More than willing, I mean. Capable of making choices." She pulled on her cigarette and leaned back, blowing the smoke out to one side, speaking reminiscently. "Eddie was a real nice-looking guy, you know? A cool dresser, sexy. It was laughable, really, the way they'd beg to be had, like that real estate woman who lives down the street from his house. He just gave them what they were asking for." She frowned. "Although I've got to say that every now and then he'd come up with something downright malicious. For instance, one of his ideas involved a kid, would you believe?" She gave a snort of disgust. "I mean, a *kid*, for crissake. You'd think he'd be smarter than that, wouldn't you? Or have more heart, or something."

"You're not talking about child pornography, are you?" Sheila asked.

Iris shook her head. "Nah. He wasn't into *that*, far as I know. But it was bad, just the same. I said to him, 'Eddie, this is just gonna cause a lot of heartache. I'm telling you, Eddie, don't do it. Don't be a horse's ass.' So he backed off and I took it on myself to set things straight. But that was the worst. The rest of them, they asked for it."

As Iris leaned forward to stub out her cigarette, I thought again about Edgar Coleman's habit of using people. Had he ever been genuinely emotionally involved with anyone? Had his entire existence been a history of manipulations, exploiting people for what they could give him or bring him or do for him? Had he never done a moment's worth of good for anyone? If that was true, it was a sad waste of a human life.

Iris sat up straight, dropped her head back, and lifted her hair. She went on, half-sadly. "You know, you might not like Eddie a whole lot, but you had to admire him. He was so damn shrewd. If he wanted something, he wouldn't just go for it. He'd sit and scheme and figure out the best way to get it — and how to get something else he wanted in the bargain. Like buying those two Lincolns from Ken Bowman."

"Two?" Sheila asked.

Ah, I thought, remembering the Lincoln parked out front.

"Yeah," Iris said. "One for Letty and one for me."

Sheila's eyebrows arched. "Excuse me, but wasn't that being, well, pretty obvious?"

Iris shrugged. "Eddie was a pretty obvious kind of guy. 'If you've got it, flaunt it,' he always said." She grinned. "It was one of the things we saw eye to eye on. What's the point in having something if you can't use it to get people's attention? Anyway, he killed two birds with one stone with those Lincolns, so to speak. He got fleet price on the cars and Ken's vote into the bargain." Now that Iris had started with the details, she seemed to find a certain satisfaction in them, almost a pride. "The deal he offered to Billie Jean was the same kind of thing. He had a strip center that was in trouble — you know, the location wasn't any too hot, the utility company was digging up the road, plus he lost his anchor. He needed to get a new tenant in there fast to keep a couple of others from bailing out. So he propositioned Billie Jean. It was a good deal," Iris added thoughtfully. "I know, because I put the numbers together for him — free rent, fixtures and finish already in, plus six months' utilities. I honestly don't know why she didn't take him up on it. All she had to do was stick with her vote. It was no big deal."

"Wrong," I said. "It *is* a big deal. Didn't Eddie clue you in?"

She stared at me.

"Coleman's beyond prosecution," I said, "but it's open season on a couple of those Council members. And if I were you, I might be afraid that my employer's extortion attempts might be connected to me." I let the remark hang for a moment, and then added, "Because if that's true, things might get . . . well, a little nasty. Bribery of a public official is a third-degree felony — two to ten plus a five grand fine on each count." I heard her quick intake of breath. "By my reckoning, there are at least seven counts." I paused to let that sink in. "I'll let you do the arithmetic."

"Just a damn minute here," she said, indignant. "I didn't bribe any —"

I cut in. "The county prosecutor is a guy named Dutch Doran. Dutch is a bright guy, and very aggressive. He's coming up for reelection in the next few months, and he'd love to make a public example of a couple of corrupt Council members. Ken Bowman, for one." I grinned. "Dutch has had a grudge against Ken ever since he tried and failed to get him on the Lemon Law a couple of years ago."

Iris sounded desperate. "But that was Eddie's deal. It doesn't have anything to do with *me*."

"Oh, yes, it does," I said. "Dutch will be extremely interested in those two Lincolns. In fact, I wouldn't be a bit surprised if he impounded both of them."

"Impounded?" Iris shrilled. "But Eddie paid cash, and signed it over to me! It's *my* car, and I've got the title."

"Cash?" I chuckled. "Boy oh boy, will Dutch love *that*. And if you've done any paperwork or left a trail he can sniff out — notes you made for Coleman, messages, anything like that — Dutch will drag you into it. He won't be able to stick a bribery charge on you, but he'll probably try for accessory."

Sheila threw me a questioning look, and I gave her a brief nod. There was some truth to what I'd said. If Dutch figured he had even a glimmer of a chance at getting Ken Bowman on a charge of accepting a bribe, he'd go for it like a big bass snapping at a plastic worm.

Sheila added her weight to the argument. "Dutch won't go after you directly, Iris," she said, "but I'm afraid you stand a good chance of losing that Lincoln, at least until after the trial. He'll keep you here, too, to testify."

It took only a second for Iris to come to a similar conclusion. "Well, *shit*," she said again, definitively. "That does it." She shoved herself forward on the sofa and stood up. "I can't sit around here all day talking. I've got things to do. Plans to make."

"What sort of plans?" I asked, getting to my feet.

"Moving plans." She was emphatic. "The cops said I could leave when I felt like it, and I'm taking them up on the offer. I wasn't in a tearing hurry, but this stuff about bribery makes me nervous. And now that Letty's dead —" She gave an involuntary, visible shudder. "I don't mind telling you, I'm afraid."

"Who, Iris?" Sheila's question was urgent. "Who are you afraid of?"

"If I knew who, maybe I wouldn't be afraid," Iris said grimly. "Letty had nothing to do with Eddie's business, but now she's dead too. I don't intend to hang around and make it three."

This wasn't going quite the way I planned. "But you must have *some* idea," I protested. "Some piece of gossip, some hint, some indication that Coleman was afraid of somebody. Did a guy named Garza ever show up here?"

She frowned. "Garza? I don't think so."

"Keep thinking," I urged. "You must know —"

"If I knew," Iris said, slowly and distinctly, "I'd know what to do about it, wouldn't I? I wouldn't let some filthy son of a bitch get away with killing Eddie, would I? Quite apart from how I felt about him — which is nobody's goddamn business but mine — he was my boss. The gander that laid the golden egg, so to speak." She flashed a crooked grin. "But don't worry. I'll stop by the police station on my way home and volunteer my alibi for this morning. I sure as hell don't want the cops standing in my way when I'm ready to leave town." She reached over, picked up her cigarettes and lighter, and put them in the pocket of her slacks. Her fingers touched something else and she brought it out. A slip of paper. She studied it for a moment. "You two seem decent enough," she said finally. "Maybe you can use this." She dropped the paper into my hand. On it was handwritten three sets of numbers. 9R-11L-24R. A lock combination.

"Are you going to tell us where to look for the safe, or do we get to guess?" I asked.

"In the floor behind the desk," Iris said. "Pull out the chair mat and lift up the rug."

"What's in it?" Sheila asked.

"Just about anything you can think of and some things that would never occur to you." Iris laughed harshly. "Eddie called it his funny-business file. That's where he kept the dirt he dug up."

"Why didn't you tell the police about it?" I asked, putting the slip of paper into the pocket of my denim skirt.

Her shrug was eloquent. "I could lie and say I meant to be generous and give all that stuff to the people involved, but what the hell. Like I said, Eddie and I saw eye to eye on a lot of things. I thought I might find a use for some of the stuff. I was going to go through it this evening and see what opportunities it offered. But now that you've told me about Letty, I'm thinking that wouldn't be smart." She gave me an oblique glance. Her surprise was over, her grief for Letty and Edgar — if she'd felt any — was gone, and she was back in control. "I'm thinking maybe you'd like to take a peek, since you're so interested in Eddie's affairs. But if you'd rather hand the combination to the cops and let them paw through all that sordid stuff, be my guest."

"Thank you," I said. She was moving around the coffee table, going to the desk, picking up a large shoulder bag. "How about a key?"

"A key?"

"To the front door." I grinned. "Breaking and entering isn't my favorite sport. And we don't have time right now to inventory that safe."

"Oh, yeah. Sure." Iris pulled a key chain out of her bag, disengaged a key, and handed it to me. "Drop it through the mail slot when you leave."

"Thanks. One more thing, Iris, if you don't mind."

"What?" She slung the bag over her shoulder, opened a drawer and banged it shut, opened another. She was obviously looking for something.

"Letty said that Edgar had a relationship — she implied that it was sexual — with a woman named Jean. Does the name ring a bell?"

She looked up, rolling her eyes in mock astonishment. "When in God's name did he find time for *another* one?" But the surprise was mild and momentary. She opened another drawer and found what she was looking for, a carton of cigarettes. "The only Jeans I remember are Darla Jean McDaniels and Billie Jean Jones."

"How about an address book?" Sheila asked. "Or an appointment book?"

"The cops took his Rolodex," Iris said. "Eddie didn't keep a diary." She glanced around the office, her face betraying something close to sadness. But only for a moment. She stuck the cigarette carton under her arm, straightened her shoulders, and said gruffly, "What the hell. It was fun while it lasted."

Chapter Fifteen

It is sometimes said that the habit of dressing children in daisy chains and coronals comes from a desire to protect them from being carried off. Daisies are a sun symbol and therefore protective magic.

A Dictionary of British Folk-Tales
K. M. Briggs

"Well," Leatha said, "I wondered when you were coming home."

The scene in my kitchen did not inspire confidence in my mother's skill as a cake baker. The counter was heaped with sacks of flour and sugar, cartons of eggs, cellophane bags of coconut and walnuts, and boxes of raisins and currants and confectioners' sugar. The sink was full of dishes and on the drainboard sat three cake racks, each holding a cratered and crumbling cake layer about the color and thickness of a waffle. The table was crowded with bowls and cups and beaters and cake decorating paraphernalia, and the plastic garbage can in the corner overflowed with discarded wrapping and containers. At one point, there had clearly been an accident with an egg, and my clean kitchen floor was decorated with a delicate tracery of floury footprints.

"It looks like you're having fun," I said, avoiding the sight of the crumbling cakes.

"Oh, I *am!*" Leatha exclaimed, in her honey-and-magnolia drawl. She had changed into slacks and a red roll-sleeve shirt and had topped herself off with McQuaid's black barbecue apron, which proclaimed in red letters that she was Smokin' Hot. Her face was smudged with flour, her eyebrows and lashes were dusted with it, and her arms were white to the elbow. "It feels so *good* to be doing something useful."

"Wonderful," I said. I headed for the broom closet. If the flour wasn't swept up, it would get tracked into the rest of the house.

The door banged open and Brian came into the kitchen. "Did you see the cakes Grandma baked?" he asked excitedly, heading over to the drainboard to point them out. He was carrying a shoebox with holes punched in the lid. His shoes bore traces of dried mud, and his dirty shoe prints mingled with Leatha's floury ones.

"Next time, take your shoes off at the door," I said, taking out the broom.

The door banged again. "Did you see your wedding cakes?" Melissa asked. "Brian's grandma made them." She, too, went to admire the sad-looking layers, Howard Cosell trudging behind. Now there were two pairs of smudgy shoe prints, plus a quartet of doggie paw prints. "But she's making a couple more, just in case," Melissa added. She turned to grin at me and in her face I saw the unmistakable likeness of the woman I had met this afternoon, the woman who claimed to have given birth to Melissa — to Elena — in prison.

Leatha wiped her hands on McQuaid's apron and frowned at the box. "What have you got in there? Nothing that *hops,* I hope."

"It's only a little green snake," Brian said. "We found it in the garden. Want to see?" He began lifting the lid off the shoebox.

"Heavens, no!" Leatha backed up, making a face. "Get that slimy creature out of my kitchen!"

Her kitchen?

"But he's not slimy," Brian said earnestly. He opened the box lid. "Here. Feel, Grandma. Snakes are really very dry."

Leatha put both hands behind her back. "Put that lid on," she commanded, "or you won't get any of the extra cake."

"If you don't mind my asking," I said, "why are you baking multiples? In case of what?"

Leatha made an effort at nonchalance. "My first effort wasn't . . . that is, it didn't . . ." She sniffed. "I think I left out the baking powder. And your oven is terribly tricky, China. I don't know why you don't buy yourself a new stove."

"Because I like the one I have," I said. "*I* know how to manage it."

"But there's plenty of time," Leatha went on, as if I hadn't spoken. "I thought I'd just keep practicing until I get it right. The children will be happy to eat the extra, or I can take it home to the ranch." She gave me a defiant look. "Now, don't scowl, China. The cake will be fine. I *promise*." She paused, and a furrow appeared between her brows. "I wonder, though, if you've heard about the storm."

"Yeah," Brian said enthusiastically. "We're going to have a hurricane. Her name is Josephine."

I sighed. "Yes, I've heard. We're making

contingency plans in case it rains." I began sweeping. "Speaking of plans, shouldn't we give some thought to dinner?"

"Dinner?" Leatha asked innocently. She looked at the clock, which showed half past six. "Oh, for heaven's sake. Just look how late it's gotten! I've been so involved and busy, I didn't even think about dinner. Well, let's see. Who's going to be eating?" She gave me a bright smile. "Why don't we call up and get something delivered?"

"That would work," I said, "if you want pizza. This is Pecan Springs, remember? We don't have much in the way of gourmet takeout." I pushed the broom under the stove — my old green Home Comfort stands up on legs — and swept out a dead mouse.

"Hey, look!" Melissa nudged Brian. "It's the one that got away!"

Howard Cosell hurried over to see whether the escapee was something he should personally take responsibility for. I scooted it onto the dustpan and tossed it into the trash. "Cancel one mouse," I said, firmly. "Howard, you need to stick to dog food and milk thistle seeds."

"Milk thistle?" Melissa asked.

"It's an herb," I said. "Howard is taking it for his liver."

"You don't have to order any pizza for me," Brian announced. "I'm going to Melissa's house."

"*May* I go to Melissa's house," I said.

"Oh, sure," Melissa said, grinning wide enough to show all her braces. "Dad is cooking hamburgers on the grill tonight. I bet there's enough." She looked at Leatha and asked, politely, "Would you like to come too?"

"I'm sorry," I said, and put my hand on her shoulder. "I was just correcting Brian. He needs to ask permission before he makes dinner plans."

"Oh," Melissa said, disappointed. "If you came, we could look at where I want to dig Jennie's herb garden, and give me some ideas about how big it should be."

"*May* I?" Brian asked.

"Yes, you may," I said. I gave Melissa a quick hug. "Ask me again soon, okay? I'd love to look at your garden site." If Rachel Lang's assertion checked out, Melissa's world would soon be rocked by a major earthquake. She'd need all the friends she could get.

"I forgot to mention that Mike called a little while ago," Leatha said, as Brian and Melissa left with their snake and Howard settled down under the window, chin on paws, to brood over the mouse that got away. "He won't be coming home for dinner. He said something about a murder investigation." She dusted her hands, sifting more flour onto the floor. "After everything that happened this spring, his getting shot and all, I hope he's not planning to go back to police work, permanently, I mean. I thought he was so well settled at the university, with a good salary and job security. Really, China, at your ages, I should think you'd be —"

I cut in sharply. "Whatever McQuaid decides to do is fine with me. People have to follow their bliss." I swept up the pile of flour and bits of mud I had gathered and dumped it on top of the dead mouse. "Did he say where they were with the investigation?"

"Not really," she replied vaguely. "Oh, wait. He said to tell you something about a fingerprint."

My head snapped up. "What about the fingerprint? *Whose* fingerprint? Did he say they'd found a match?" Was Jorge the killer, after all? "Did he say whether they've located Garza?"

"My goodness, China." Leatha took off the apron. "You can't expect me to keep track of things like that. If you want to know all the gory details, you'll have to call Mike and ask him to tell you. But it did sound as if he had his hands full." She put a carton of cream and a bowl of eggs back into the refrigerator. "Since it's just us, let's run out for a quick bite. I want to make another practice cake tonight, and it takes an hour and a half to bake."

Another practice cake? If it were me, I'd give it up as a bad job and go look for a baker in Austin. But I had to admire Leatha's resilience in the face of adversity. And it's the thought that counts — right?

"How about having a sandwich here instead?" I asked, putting the broom away. "We've got the makings for subs left over from last night, and I need to see somebody at seven this evening."

To tell the truth, a quick sandwich was about all I had time for. I still had the combination to Coleman's floor safe, and I had to decide what to do with it. I could hand it over to McQuaid, who would then have to spend valuable time sorting a batch of stuff that might not amount to a hill of beans. Or I could go over there and poke through the safe myself, with the same outcome. Either way, it was probably a waste of a good hour. But I'm only human, with as much healthy (or unhealthy) curiosity as the next person, and I couldn't help wondering what sort of dirt Edgar had dug up. Quite apart from its potential relevance to his murder — and perhaps to the death of his wife, as well — whatever was in that safe might have a certain tawdry entertainment value. So I thought I'd squeeze in a trip to Coleman's office later in the evening.

Before I did that, though, I needed to get out of the clothes I'd been wearing all day and into jeans. Then I had to stop by the Pack Saddle Inn and find out for myself whether Rachel Lang was who she claimed to be, and, if so, what was ahead for Melissa. And sometime this evening or tomorrow, I *had* to go to Ruby's house and see exactly what she intended to wear to the wedding. Between Leatha's experimental wedding cake and Josephine doing pirouettes in the Gulf, I had enough anxiety for three or four brides. I didn't need to be fretting over whether my matron of honor was going to remind people of something out of a Cecil B. DeMille extravaganza.

If you find yourself in Pecan Springs overnight, you might consider staying at the Pack Saddle Inn, on River Road, or at least dropping by for dinner. (You won't be sorry if you order the asparagus with hollandaise and potatoes roasted in olive oil and herbs to go with your medium-rare rib eye.) Bring your camera and plan to make time for a leisurely stroll along the crystal clear Pecan River, which loops through the landscaped grounds, wide swaths of native wildflowers and ferns growing lush along each bank. It's an idyllic spot.

My first stop was the reception desk, where I had better luck than I deserved. Linda Davis is the Pack Saddle's manager and a longtime friend. She was behind the registration desk, giving the harried desk clerk a hand with last-minute check-ins. As I came into the lobby, the last person in line was getting her key and Linda was switching on the No Vacancy sign beside the lobby door.

"Looks like you've got a full house," I said, after we traded greetings.

"There's a conference at the university," Linda replied, going back behind the counter. "We get the overflow when they can't handle it."

Linda Davis has a bright, alert face, snappy dark eyes, and a quick smile. She's a little over five feet tall, and beautifully trim — one of those tiny dynamos that never seem to stop. She attributes her mile-a-minute energy to a combination of daily workouts at the new health club, the ginkgo biloba she buys at Thyme and Seasons, and the meditation classes she takes from Ruby. Whatever the source of her vitality, Linda is an adventurer. In her belted khaki suit, neat white camp shirt, and zebra-striped silk scarf, she looked as if she were about to set off on safari.

She flipped her hands through her brown, curly hair, tossed me that quick smile, and said briskly, "Hey, China, how're things? I see we've got you down for Friday night, wedding party of fifteen, with a mariachi band. Your big day must be right around the corner."

"That's right," I said. "Sunday. Outdoors in the garden at Thyme and Seasons."

She moved the vase of wildflowers to the end of the counter and squared a stack of untidy promotional flyers. "Sunday, huh? Have you been watching the weather? Do you know about Josephine?" She lined up the plastic display racks so they faced out, and straightened the brochures. "They're saying it could come ashore around Corpus Christi, which means rain for us."

"Yeah," I said. I made a face. "If it happens, I guess we'll move the wedding into the shop."

"Into the shop?" Linda raised an eyebrow. "That'd be a little crowded, wouldn't it? How many people are you having?"

"Only forty or so," I said. "It isn't a very big wedding."

"If you need more room, you might think of moving it here. The Garden Room isn't booked. We've had several weddings there, and it works fine. The room opens onto the river, which is just a few yards away from the windows. There's a pair of resident swans and quite a few geese and ducks. Serene and romantic."

"Yes, I know," I said. "I was a guest at Maureen Rodman's wedding, and it was lovely. I'll think about it and let you know. One way or other, we'll manage."

"Right," Linda said cheerfully. "Life's a blast. If it isn't one damn thing, it's another. You've just got to take it as it comes and be flexible — that's my motto." She picked up a stack of registration cards and began to riffle through them. "How can I help? Want to go over the menu for Friday night, or is Mrs. McQuaid taking care of everything? Do you need to make some reservations for out-of-town guests?"

"No," I said, "I need to ask you to do something mildly illegal."

She stopped riffling and looked at me with interest. "Oh, yeah?"

"Yeah. You've got a guest named Rachel Lang. At least, that's the name she gave me. I'd like to see her registration card." I spoke half-apologetically, not knowing how squeamish Linda was about breaking the law.

She went back to the cards. "Care to tell me why?"

"The woman came to see me today. She says she's the biological mother of one of Brian's friends. She claims that her daughter was abducted by the child's father nearly ten years ago. I need to verify her story, if I can. I know that you check driver's licenses at registration. If she's registered with you as Rachel Lang, I'm safe in assuming that's the name on her license." The Pack Saddle is old-fashioned that way, checking IDs on all their guests. The practice only antagonizes drug traffickers and other villainous types; honest people don't mind proving they are who they claim to be.

"Mm-mm-mm," Linda said, frowning. "A parental kidnapping? Nasty stuff. Very bad. My cousin's twin boys disappeared a few years ago. Their father drove them from Little Rock to San Diego, where he was shacked up with his girlfriend, would you believe?"

"Yeah, I'd believe. What did your cousin do?"

"Well, first she tried the Little Rock cops, which got her exactly nowhere. The kids were gone and out of their jurisdiction, and at that point, she didn't have a clue where they were. Then she hired a private eye from Dallas, but still no dice. Finally she got connected with an outfit called the Center for Missing and Exploited Children, and they located the kids in less than a month. Put their pictures on a Web site, and a day-care worker out there in San Diego spotted them and made a phone call." She shook her head. "You know, I used to worry about privacy and computers and the web and all that stuff, but not anymore. You got people stealing kids, they've given up their right to privacy, far as I'm concerned."

"This woman says she's working with the Center," I said. "That's how she located her daughter." I pulled out the card Rachel Lang had given me. It had the Center's address on it, and the case worker's name and phone number. "I intend to give them a call before I talk to her."

"Well, if that part of the story checks out, you can believe the rest," Linda said decidedly. "The case workers review everything to make sure it's a legit claim. My cousin had to give them copies of her custody papers and the police reports and everything, before they'd even talk about working with her." She shuffled the deck of registration cards once more, and dropped one on the counter in front of me. "Excuse me," she said, turning away. "I've got to go to the dining room for a coupla minutes. We've got a new kid waiting tables, and I want to make sure he knows what he's supposed to be doing." She heaved an exasperated sigh. "The last one we hired, turned out she couldn't read the menu. Took us a month to get her trained, and then she ran off to New Orleans with the dishwasher. Sometimes I think I could have found an easier career path."

The card on the counter was Rachel Lang's. I copied down the automobile license plate — a rental, most likely — and the Orlando home address and phone number, then stuck the card under the vase of flowers where Linda could find it when she got back from the dining room. I stopped at the pay phone in the outer lobby, where a long-distance conversation confirmed that Rachel Lang had first requested the Center's services two years before to institute a search for her missing daughter, Elena, and that she was now in Texas, following a lead. The story Lang had told me was checking out — as if I had needed any additional verification, after seeing the age-progressed photo and comparing mother-daughter noses.

The Pack Saddle's main building, brown-cedar-shingled and with a red tile roof, is constructed like a large ranch house, with a half-dozen wings angling off in various directions. Rachel Lang's second-floor west-wing room was large and comfortable, with chairs on the small balcony overlooking the river and a sweep of lawn, khaki-colored from the summer's heat. I accepted the offer of a soft drink over ice and we sat outside on the balcony.

The sun had slipped below the western horizon and a flock of mallards was settling down for the night in the ferns along the riverbank. Nighthawks zipped across the lawn in search of winged snacks, and the tree frogs practiced their metallic call. Ms. Lang — Rachel, as she asked me to call her — began to tell her story, and I spent the next half hour listening and learning and asking questions, not just about Rachel's experience but about parental kidnapping, a painfully tragic crime that destroys lives as surely as murder but is rarely sensational enough to hit the headlines.

Rachel's tale wasn't sensational by tabloid standards, and she told it in a quiet, steady, reportorial voice that underplayed its human drama. But even so, her story was terrifyingly, horribly *real*. While she was getting her accounting degree, Rachel worked as a bookkeeper in a large Orlando furniture store owned by her uncle. Following a complicated series of events that she didn't explain, Rachel and her uncle were charged with tax fraud. (Although she didn't directly accuse her uncle, I got the idea that he had set her up, and I wondered if a smart defense attorney could have gotten her off.) Both went to federal prison, he for ten years, she for six. At the time of her trial, Rachel was pregnant — the child had been conceived during a brief sexual relationship with a longtime friend — and a few months after she went to jail, she gave birth to Elena.

The child's father, whose name was Jim Carlson, tried numerous times to persuade Rachel to marry him. She kept refusing him, and he angrily demanded that she surrender Elena to him. He sued for custody, but the court considered his history of intermittent unemployment and awarded temporary custody to Rachel's mother, who had been caring for Elena since the child's birth. Carlson was granted regular visitation rights. Rachel intended to go back to court to seek permanent custody as soon as she was released. But shortly before Elena's second birthday, Carlson took the little girl to Disneyworld on a regular weekend visit and failed to bring her back. Father and daughter disappeared without a trace.

The child's grandmother was devastated by Elena's loss and held herself responsible. For Rachel, still in federal prison and unable to do anything to help her frantic mother, the pain was excruciating. Even though she had rejected Carlson's repeated offers of marriage, Rachel had considered him a friend, and she felt betrayal and a racking grief, as well as anger both at herself and at him. If she hadn't let her uncle manipulate her, she would be at home with her daughter now. If she had agreed to marry Carlson, she might somehow have prevented the abduction. The only thing that kept her going was her mother's support and her academic work: She had enrolled as a graduate student in a prison program in psychology and was hoping to be certified as a therapist upon her release.

But Rachel had plenty of trauma of her own to work on. Obsessed with recovering Elena, her mother searched endlessly and tirelessly, far beyond the limits of her failing strength. Within the year, she was dead of a massive heart attack. Now there were three victims of the kidnapper's crime, and Rachel was left to mourn both her daughter and her mother.

When Rachel was released from prison, she began her own efforts to recover Elena. "I was absolutely driven that summer," she said quietly. "I finally figured out that when somebody steals your child, *you've* got to take charge of the search. There are too many missing kids and the authorities just don't have enough people to do what has to be done. But I let the search swallow up my life. It was all I lived for, and that wasn't healthy." She touched her scarred face ruefully. "Then the accident happened, and I was left facing several years of rehabilitation and plastic surgery, and lots of thinking about who I was and what I needed to do. I had to accept the fact that finding Elena was my second priority. Getting well, putting my life back together, finding my right livelihood — all that had to come first." She had just begun to heal and find some balance, when she learned, quite by accident, that Jim Carlson had died in a house fire in Miami only a few months after he abducted Elena.

Rachel's face clouded and she shuddered. "I went into another tailspin, thinking that Elena might have burned to death with him. The Miami police and fire officials said they had recovered only one body — but the house had been completely destroyed. She was so small, just a little over two years old. What if her body had been buried in the rubble and carted off by the heavy machinery they brought in to clear the burned-out site? What if they hadn't found her because they hadn't known to look for a little girl?"

"Dear God," I whispered. I was awed by the pain this woman had suffered, by the terrifying weight of the tragedies that had been heaped on her.

"I prayed a lot, too," Rachel said matter-of-factly. "Then I learned from a family friend that Jim Carlson's father had been seen in Atlanta some time before. With him had been a little girl who might have been Elena. The friend tried to talk to him, but Dr. Carlson walked away."

Rachel attempted to trace the senior Carlson, who had lived in Miami, and discovered that he had sold his house and left his work — a successful dental practice — just after his son died. Convinced now that her daughter was still alive and with her grandfather, Rachel contacted the Center for Missing and Exploited Children and began searching in earnest: not just for Elena, but for Dr. Jack Carlson.

"Jack Carlson?" I asked, and then, incredulously, put it all together. "Jack Carlson, Carl Jackson! Dr. Carl Jackson, my dentist!"

"You'd think it would be easy to find a professional man, wouldn't you," Rachel said with a wry twist to her mouth. "After all, doctors and dentists are only supposed to practice under their own names and after they've legally met the state's requirements for licensure. But it turns out that it isn't all that difficult for a dentist to establish a practice under an assumed name, especially in rural areas or in big-city dental clinics. Clinic directors don't always check references or medical credentials, and if an out-of-state dentist doesn't voluntarily register with the state board of dentistry when he goes into practice, he probably won't be discovered unless he somehow calls attention to himself."

This information wasn't particularly new or startling. I'd been involved in a distasteful case ten years or so before in which the defendant — our firm's client — was a self-styled doctor who had practiced for nearly a dozen years in a Houston clinic under his dead brother's name and credentials. He wasn't found out until he was charged with embezzling the clinic's funds. But still, this was Dr. Jackson we were talking about — excuse me, Dr. Carlson — whose hands had been in my mouth as recently as Monday. And he owed me a permanent crown.

Rachel drained her drink and set down the glass. "As I found out, Jack Carlson had taken Elena to Atlanta, where he got a job in a dental clinic. He left when my friend recognized him and moved to Syracuse. They were there for only about six months; then he took Elena to Boise, Montana, and finally to Seattle, working in dental clinics along the way."

"Did you do your own detective work?" I asked.

She shook her head. "I hired a guy who traced Carlson to Syracuse, then to Boise. But private detectives are expensive, and I ran out of money. I got lucky, though. The Center got a tip that he was in Seattle, where he married one of his patients, a widow whose husband had recently committed suicide, leaving her very well fixed. Carlson apparently used her money to buy a practice from a retiring dentist here in Pecan Springs and relocated once again. He must have thought that the trail was so cold by now that it was safe to settle down. He and his wife — Jennie, her name is — have even purchased a large piece of land and are preparing to build a house."

I frowned. "But I thought you said you caught up with him in Seattle."

"I did." She sighed. "I flew there, but missed him by a couple of days. When Carlson and his wife took Elena and left town, they didn't tell anybody where they were going. I couldn't find a single clue to where they were headed."

"How did you trace them to Pecan Springs?"

"A woman from this area e-mailed a tip to the Center. She said she'd seen Elena's age-progressed photo on the Center's Web site and recognized her. She also sent the Carlsons' address, so when I got to Pecan Springs, I drove by their house. Elena and your son were out in the yard. I watched

them, and after a while they rode their bi-
cycles to your shop to work in the garden.
It wasn't hard to follow them there. I
strolled around, pretending to look at your
plants, but I was really eavesdropping on
the children." Her smile was crooked. "I
liked what I heard, very much. Whatever
else he's done, Jack Carlson has brought
up a bright, healthy little girl with a great
deal of self-confidence and a strong self-
esteem. I would give anything to have had
Elena during her growing-up years, but I
don't think she has been badly damaged."

"She thinks her mother died when she
was born," I said. "She says she dreams
about her." I left out the part about Melissa's dream mother being blond-haired
and blue-eyed and as beautiful as Princess
Di. Children can be unintentionally cruel,
expecting their mothers to be like the
moms they see on television. Uncomfortably, I wondered if there wasn't a lesson
for me in this. If I had accepted Leatha as
she was, rather than wanting her to be another Donna Reed —

"I'm glad I'm still alive for her," Rachel
said, "if only in her dreams." She tilted her
head, watching a young couple drifting lazily down the river in a red canoe. "I want
to meet her. I want to tell her who I am,

and that I've been searching for her for almost ten years. I need to tell her that I love her, that I want her to come and live with me and grow up as my daughter." She turned to face me, and her voice became more urgent. "But I need to do all of that without traumatizing her, China. That's where you can help. Elena likes and respects you. She trusts you. I believe she'll accept what you say about me, about this situation. Will you help?"

I turned answers over in my mind. I had plenty of reasons to stay out of this complicated affair. The wedding, of course, and after that, the honeymoon. And there was all that sad business about Edgar Coleman, and Letty. But the Colemans were McQuaid's problem, not mine. Most of the work for the wedding was done — and what was there to a honeymoon, except throwing a few clothes in a suitcase and boarding a plane? Anyway, it didn't sound like Rachel needed me to do much more than talk to Melissa and intercede with Dr. Jackson and his wife. If it looked as if there were serious legal questions or the negotiations threatened to blow up, I could always call the Whiz. In fact, I should call her anyway. Chances were that she'd been involved in this sort of thing before and would have some suggestions on how to proceed. But the most important thing was my feeling for Melissa, who was a very special young woman. I owed it to her to help her learn the truth about her past, in as gentle and supportive a way as possible.

"Okay," I said. "I'll do what I can."

"Thank you, China," Rachel said simply, and put her hand on my arm. Tears were glistening in her eyes. "Thank you, for Elena, and for me."

I was silent for a moment. Thinking about the Jacksons had brought another question to mind. "What are you going to do about Dr. Jackson?" I frowned. "Sorry. That's the name I know him by."

"I understand. I need to learn to call my daughter Melissa. I'm afraid she'll never be Elena to anyone else but me." Rachel's face was troubled, her voice low and tense. "Dealing with her grandfather is terribly tricky, don't you think? My mother was Elena's temporary guardian, and she's dead. I was never Elena's custodial parent. Dr. Carlson has raised her, and he's done a first-rate job under difficult circumstances. She clearly loves him very much, and it would be dangerous to wrench her away." She passed a hand over her forehead wearily. "I don't see how it would help to get the authorities involved, or try to press kidnapping charges against him. In fact, I don't think there's anything that would stick."

I wasn't sure I agreed. Carlson might try to argue that he didn't know the whereabouts of Melissa's mother and that when his son died, he simply assumed custody of his fatherless granddaughter. But how would he explain the fact that he had taken the child to Atlanta and begun practicing under an assumed name — and then repeated the process in the states of New York, Idaho, Washington, and Texas? Under oath, he would be forced to admit that he had fled from city to city to prevent discovery of his granddaughter's whereabouts. What's more, I seriously doubted that the Texas State Board of Dentists would approve of his behavior. They take a dim view of dentists who practice without a state license. But there was no point in introducing these issues just now. They might come in handy later, though, if Rachel needed some leverage.

I went back to the subject. "It's your call, Rachel. If Melissa's situation can be resolved without a custody battle, so much the better."

Rachel shifted in her chair. "I'm hoping

I can convince Elena's grandfather — and his wife, too, now that he's married — to let me become a part of my daughter's life. Legally, I suppose, that means assuming some sort of joint custody. I'd be willing to move here, if that's the only way we can work it out."

I was still thinking of leverage. Rachel and I weren't the only ones in Pecan Springs who were aware that there was something unusual about Dr. Carlson and his granddaughter and cared enough to do something about it. "The woman who sent in the tip," I said. "Do you know her name?"

"I have it in my notes somewhere." Rachel gave me a quizzical glance. "Why? Do you think it's important?"

"I don't know," I said. "It might be, especially if you're hoping to keep a lid on this. She might feel she has some sort of stake in seeing the matter resolved and begin making inquiries." I paused. "Or maybe I'm just irredeemably curious."

"I'll see if I can find it." Rachel got up and went through the balcony doors into her room, while I sat and thought about what I had just heard, reflecting that life offers more complications and complexities than we can ever imagine. After listening to the catastrophes Rachel had lived through, all I could think of was a get-well card that a cop friend sent to McQuaid after he got shot: *Don't Sweat the Small Stuff*, it read. In light of Rachel's loss of her daughter, everything — including Leatha's experimental wedding cake and the menace of Hurricane Josephine — seemed like pretty small potatoes. Another lesson?

After a few minutes, Rachel came back out on the balcony. "Your question started me thinking, China. In her E-mail, the woman said something to the effect that it might be a good idea to get somebody out here right away. The case worker who got the tip thought Carlson was getting ready to flee again — although when I got here and saw the situation, I decided that wasn't the case. I don't know what the tip-ster meant to convey. Anyway, here's the name, for whatever it's worth." She handed me a slip of paper.

I glanced at it, then looked again.

The name was Iris Powell.

Chapter Sixteen

The use of lavender to calm fits of madness in some forms of mental disease is at least 2000 years old.

Lavender, Sweet Lavender
Judyth A. McLeod

I judge that the flowers of lavender, quilted into a cap and worn daily, are good for all diseases of the head . . . and that they comfort the brain very well.

Herbal
William Turner, 1568

The first thing I had to do, of course, was to call Iris. Was it just a coincidence that she had happened to see the Center's Web site and Melissa's picture? Or had she come by the information about the abduction by a different route, via Edgar Coleman, say? But I didn't want to think about that just now. If Iris was planning to leave town — and that seemed to be a strong possibility, given what she'd said that afternoon — I needed to talk to her.

I used the telephone book in Rachel's room to locate Iris's number. I dialed and let the phone ring, but there wasn't any answer. I copied the address out of the phone book, promised to call Rachel in the morning to discuss how we were going to approach Melissa and the Jacksons, and drove to Iris's upscale condo complex on the north side of town. There was no response to my knock, but the front drapes were open just enough so that I could see she hadn't moved out yet. The living room was furnished in *Better Homes and Gardens*-modern, with a large gold-framed landscape over the fireplace and a beige carpet on the floor. The expensive sofa and chairs were strewn with clothing and magazines. The remains of a takeout pizza had been dragged from the coffee table to the floor and across the room to a plush dog bed in the corner, leaving an interesting trail of tomato sauce and bits of pepperoni. A yappy dog on the other side of the door was announcing that I should leave immediately or he would come out and sink his vicious, sharklike teeth into my leg. Ignoring his threats, I scribbled a "Call me, Urgent" note on a business card, added my home phone number, and stuck it in the door. Then I paused. I hated to depend on Iris to get in touch with me. Maybe I should just hang out in my car and watch the condo until she came home from wherever she was spending the evening.

But I'm too impatient to be much good at surveillance. When I wait for people, I tend to mutter swear words under my breath and worry my cuticles into little rags. Maybe I should go away and come back later. Maybe I should go over to Ruby's and get a look at that dress. No, maybe I should go to Coleman's office and search his floor safe. Yes, that was it. There might be something in the safe that would give me an idea where Iris learned about Melissa — and what Coleman had done with the information.

I looked at my watch. I had a key to Coleman's office, but it was getting dark and something told me I should have company on this errand. Smart Cookie lived only a couple of blocks away. I could swing by her house and pick her up.

I was standing there, thinking about this and staring at the claw marks on the bottom half of the door where the yappy dog had tried to scratch his way in, when another thought occurred to me. Iris had actually spoken about Melissa this afternoon, although she hadn't come right out and called her by name. What was it she'd said, exactly? I shut out the dog's clamor, sent my mind back to the afternoon's conversation, and came up with it — not verbatim, the way I used to do when I was doing it for a living, but close enough.

The way I remembered it, Iris had remarked that one of Coleman's malicious schemes involved a kid. She said she'd told him he was going too far. She'd made him back off, then taken it upon herself to set things straight. Presumably, that was when she e-mailed the Center and told them to send somebody out right away to check into the matter. Iris figured that took care of things. She had told Coleman off and done a good deed, to boot. End of story.

The dog had gone into major-attack mode, flinging himself against the door so hard it shook. Tired of his insults, I stuck my hands in the pockets of my jeans and began to walk toward my Datsun, still thinking. What if that hadn't been the end of the story? Maybe Coleman hadn't backed off, after all. Maybe he'd gone to Dr. Jackson — excuse me, to Jack Carlson — and accused him of abducting Melissa and practicing dentistry under an assumed name. Maybe he'd told Carlson that in return for a certain sum of money or for some other important consideration, he would keep his mouth shut about what he knew. Maybe —

I shooed away a couple of grackles roosting on the hood of my car, opened the door, and got in. Okay, so assume all those maybes, just for the hell of it. So how would Carlson respond when Coleman threatened to blow the whistle? In other instances when he felt threatened, he left the clinic he was practicing in, packed up the girl, and hauled ass for another state. But not this time. This time, it seemed, he had stayed put, which might mean that Iris was right after all and that Coleman had backed off. Or maybe it meant something else entirely. Maybe —

I put the key in the ignition and started the engine. The air conditioner burped a bubble of stale air that smelled like sour milk — a leftover from the week before, when I'd forgotten a plastic half-gallon of milk in the trunk and only discovered it when it had burst in a puddle of sour yucky. Maybe *what*, for Pete's sake?

Well, maybe this time, Jack Carlson decided he was getting too old to run. He was tired of hiding out, and he didn't want to start over again in a new place. After all, he stood to lose a bundle if he was forced to leave Pecan Springs. He'd take Melissa, of course, but he'd forfeit his practice and the land that he and his wife had bought. I rolled down the window for some fresh air and sat for a moment with the engine running, thinking. Carlson might also forfeit his wife, especially if she didn't know the full story behind his travels during the last decade. In fact, having met the lady myself, I seriously doubted that he had filled her in on his past, or Melissa's. Jennie Carlson struck me as an exacting, fastidious woman. She might act out of passion — sometimes a cool and polished exterior conceals a passionate heart — but I didn't think she would have married Dr. Carlson if she'd known that he was involved in something as messy as abduction and criminal flight.

As I put the car in gear and drove out of the parking lot, heading in the direction of Sheila's house, a memory nagged at the corner of my consciousness. The memory of Dr. Jackson — Dr. Carlson — standing at the window of his office, watching through the blind while Melissa — Elena — climbed into his wife's Taurus. I had remarked on what a wonderful girl Melissa was, and he had agreed. "I would do any-thing for that child," he had said with an intensity that, thinking about it now, seemed almost frightening.

The words echoed in my mind. *I would do anything for that child. Anything. Any-thing. Any—*

I suddenly felt cold. What if . . . what if he had *killed* for her? What if those skilled professional hands, which on Monday morning had been in my mouth, adjusting my temporary crown, had picked up that wicked little silvery gun and —

The gun. Another memory surfaced, this one from my noontime lunch with Mc-Quaid. According to McQuaid, the murder weapon had been purchased in Miami about ten years ago. Miami, where Jim Carlson died shortly after he abducted his daughter some ten years ago. Miami, where Dr. Jack Carlson had once had a flourishing dental practice. Was it a coinci-dence? Or had one of the Carlsons, father or son, been the original purchaser of the gun that killed Edgar Coleman on Sunday night?

But my speculations were ranging far ahead of what I knew of the facts. I needed to talk to McQuaid and find out the name of the original firearm purchaser. If it was

Carlson, of course, that just about sewed it up. Even if it wasn't, McQuaid would want to get the man's prints and have a talk with him before the night got any older.

Which brought up a separate but equally perplexing and urgent problem. The minute McQuaid brought in Carlson for questioning, Melissa's situation would be exposed and Rachel's hope of working gently with the little girl would be destroyed. Melissa was a smart kid — she'd find out what was happening to her grandfather and why, and she'd be devastated. She might blame herself for her grandfather's actions. She might blame her mother. Either way, there was nothing but losers and losses.

It was time to have a look in that safe to see if I could find any evidence that Coleman had attempted to blackmail Jack Carlson. I reached for my cell phone. It was also time to call McQuaid and find out who had purchased the gun. But instead of McQuaid, I got Viney Spry, the evening dispatcher, who is the best of McQuaid's new hires. Viney is a tall, skinny, black woman who wears a regulation uniform and handsome nonregulation hair, braided in about a thousand tiny braids close to her head, all tied with red thread.

"Sorry, Miz Bayles. The chief i'n't here. Him and the Ranger are in the jail questionin' somebody they just hauled in."

"Jorge Garza?" I asked uneasily.

"Yeah. That'ud be him," Viney said. She made little clucks with her tongue against her teeth, and I could picture her shaking her braids. "Bad customer, ya ast me. Dang'rous. They had theyselves quite a time wit 'im. Kickin' an' bitin' an' stuff."

I could imagine. Jorge saw himself in a tight spot, and he probably had no idea how to get out of it. I'd better get in touch with Phyllis and see if she needed any help locating a lawyer.

"I'd appreciate it if you could get a message to the chief," I said. "Tell him I need to know the name of the person who purchased the Coleman murder weapon. Tell him I suspect that the purchaser is living here in Pecan Springs, under a different name. Ask him to call my cell phone number when he's got the information."

"Where you gonna be, case he wants t' talk t'ya in the flesh, so to speak?"

"Iris Powell gave me a key to Edgar Coleman's office and the combination to Coleman's safe. Tell the chief I'm about to dig up a little dirt."

"Hunh," Viney grunted. "Thought you got enough down and dirty durin' daylight hours, 'thout diggin' in the dark too." She paused. "Say, you bin keepin' a eye on that ol' hurricane out there? Hope it don't interfere none with your weddin' plans, you gettin' married outdoors an' all."

"So do I," I said fervently.

"Well, if ya'll need to get dry, my cousin runs PeeJay's Dance Hall out on the old Austin highway. People get married out there a lot, so's they kin dance after. Tell PeeJay I sent you an' he'll give you a break."

"Thanks, Viney," I said. "We might have to take you up on it. Don't forget about that message. Okay?"

"On my way," Viney said cheerfully, and hung up.

The last of the twilight was fading when I got to Sheila's, just in time to catch her locking her bicycle in the private courtyard outside her apartment. Biking is Smart Cookie's way of keeping in shape, although her shape is already so shapely that she could skip a couple of weeks in the saddle and it wouldn't matter more than a quarter-inch or so. She was wearing black spandex shorts, a sweaty orange Hook 'Em Horns

T-shirt, and orange knee socks. Her usually sleek blond hair was damp and stringy. It was the first time I had ever seen her looking less than absolutely perfect.

"What are you doing here?" she asked, wiping her face with the towel she had slung around her neck. "I thought you and Ruby would be working on wedding stuff. Although —" She paused, frowning. "I think we need to have a game plan in case we get rained out. I saw a radar picture of Josephine, and she's looking pretty mean. The winds are up to fifty-five already, although she doesn't seem to have much of a sense of direction. Nobody knows whether she'll make landfall in Louisiana or Texas."

"I need to put the wedding stuff on hold for tonight," I said. "There's a different game to plan for. I think maybe you and I ought to go to Coleman's office and have a look at the stuff in that safe."

"Tonight?" Sheila looked at her watch, one of those fancy sport models about the size of a hub cap. "I've got a couple of loads of laundry to do. Can it wait?"

"See what you think," I said. Rachel's story was complicated and it took three or four minutes to sketch it out. When I got to the part about Miami and the gun that Jack Carlson — Dr. Carl Jackson — might or might not have purchased, Sheila's jaw dropped.

"Dr. Jackson? My *dentist?*"

"The very one," I said. "My dentist too."

She shot me an incredulous look. "You're saying that he's a child abductor and possible killer? Unbelievable!"

"*Who* is a child abductor and possible killer?" Ruby asked. Sheila and I had been so intent on our conversation that neither of us had heard her come into the court-yard.

"You're not going to believe me either," I said with a sigh, and launched into the story for the second time.

"Jack Carlson. Carl *Jackson?*" Ruby gulped, her eyes big.

"Everybody's favorite dentist," I said dryly. "Hard to believe, huh? But I have to tell you that Rachel Lang's story checks out with the Center for Missing Children, and she's shown me enough documenta-tion to persuade me that she's Melissa's real mother."

"What are you going to do about it?" Ruby asked.

"It depends," I said, "on McQuaid's in-formation about the gun."

Ruby frowned. "The gun?"

"McQuaid has the name of the gun's

original buyer. If it was purchased by Jack Carlson or his son, we have a strong supposition of guilt, and McQuaid will try for a print match."

"What are we waiting for?" Sheila flung the towel over the handlebars of her bike and began fishing her car keys out of her fanny pack. "Let's take the Explorer."

"There's time, if you want to dump your laundry in the machine or change your clothes," I said. "I don't suppose that stuff will walk off."

"Laundry, hell," Sheila said. "I want to see what's in that safe. Come on." She opened the gate and headed toward the parking lot.

"What safe?" Ruby asked. "What stuff?" Looking confused, she hiked her purse over her shoulder. She was wearing a garnet broomstick skirt and matching push-sleeved tunic, with a garnet crushed velvet hat pinned sideways on her head. "I'm supposed to have dinner with Hark," she said indecisively. "Where are you two going?"

I started after Sheila. "Coleman's office," I said over my shoulder. "Iris gave us the combination to his safe, where he kept his funny papers. If you want to come, come."

Ruby ran to catch up. "Funny papers?"

"Blackmail backup," I said.

"Oh, wow," Ruby said, holding on to her hat with one hand and her shoulder bag with the other. "Wait for me, China. I'm coming too."

In the parking lot, I stopped at my car and took out the flashlight I keep under the seat in case the Datsun decides to give up the ghost on a dark and stormy night. I also picked up my cell phone and checked to see if I had a call waiting. Nothing — which meant that McQuaid hadn't yet tried to get back to me about the gun.

"May I use the phone?" Ruby asked breathlessly. "I need to call Hark and tell him I can't have dinner with him."

Sheila was already in the Explorer, revving the engine. Ruby climbed in the back and started to punch in Hark's number. I got in front beside Sheila.

"Git along, little dogies," I said, and Sheila put the Explorer in gear.

"Hark?" Ruby said, as we pulled out into the street. She raised her voice over the noise of the engine. "Listen, Hark, I'm afraid I can't make it tonight, after all." There was a silence. "Yes, I know you're hungry, and I'm sorry. But I ran into China. She's breaking into —"

"Ruby!" Exasperated, I turned around in the seat.

Ruby covered the mouthpiece. "But Hark and I made a promise never to lie to one another. Relationships are built on trust, and every lie destroys —"

"There are lies," I said fiercely, "and there are lies. Hark is a shark when he's after a story. Do you want the *Enterprise* breathing down our necks while we dig through that safe? Do you want Melissa's predicament plastered all over the paper?"

Ruby frowned. "Sorry, Hark. Did I say breaking into? I meant breaking *down*. China is having some sort of emotional crisis. I need to stay with her. I think I can help."

"Ruby!" I cried, flinging my arms into the air. "Think what you're saying!"

"Did you hear that, Hark?" Ruby asked. She looked up at me, nodding, and mouthed *He heard that.* She spoke into the phone again. "I know," she said sadly. "Right. Crazy, as in violent. A fit of madness. Her eyes are rolling back in her head and she's throwing herself around." She sighed. "And so close to the wedding, too. Do you think it might be the weather? Josephine, I mean. Sometimes storms interfere with the electrical system in the brain." There was a brief pause. "Yes, well, I'm sorry about standing you up, but China needs me." Another pause. "I'll tell her. Thanks."

She flicked the Off button and handed me the phone. "Hark says weddings affect him that way, too. But he's ready for Hawaii anytime you are." She frowned. "What's with Hawaii?"

"Hula hula," I growled. The phone rang in my hand. "Yeah?" I snapped into it. "What do you want?"

"You okay, hon?" McQuaid asked, surprised.

Hon. Ever since I was a child and heard Ozzie call Harriet "Hon," I have vowed that I would never be one. I gritted my teeth. "I'm having a breakdown," I said, "and Ruby is telling the newspaper about it. Don't be surprised to read that I've been hospitalized for emotional instability."

"Lavender," Ruby said. "Lavender's supposed to be good if your mind's going."

Sheila turned a corner fast, and a woman jogger wearing a pastel blue running suit hopped back up on the curb. "Are you talking to McQuaid?" she asked. "Did he get the name of that guy?"

"Hark would never print that," McQuaid

said reassuringly. "He's a friend."

"You wait. Did you get the name of the guy who bought the gun?"

"Carlson," McQuaid said. "Does that ring a bell?"

I looked from Sheila to Ruby. "He wants to know if the name Carlson rings a bell."

"Ding dong!" Ruby cried.

"Excuse me?" McQuaid said. "Is that Ruby making that noise?"

"It's a long story," I said. "The bottom line is that Jack Carlson is the real name of our dentist, Carl Jackson."

There was a moment of stunned silence. "Melissa's father?"

"Melissa's grandfather." I sighed. "It's a very long story."

"Good Lord," McQuaid said. "You're saying that Dr. Jackson owns the gun that shot Coleman? But if he did it, *why?*"

"Because Coleman found out that Jack had abducted Melissa and threatened to let her biological mother know their whereabouts. Something like that. Or maybe nothing like that. While you're printing Jackson, maybe you can get him to tell about it." I snapped my fingers. "Wait. Remember what Lila said at lunch today about Dr. Jackson having breakfast with Letty at seven this morning? What if he followed her home? What if he —"

"I'll get right on it," McQuaid said crisply. "Thanks for the tip, China. Thanks a lot."

"Yeah," I said. "You're welcome." The words tasted bitter.

The parking lot in front of Coleman's office building was empty. Sheila parked in the farthest, darkest corner. A mercury vapor light high on a pole cast a watery blue glow over the asphalt. We all got out and stood beside the vehicle.

The insurance office that occupied the right half of the building sported an orange neon sign that spelled out the words WE TAKE ALL THE RISK. It flickered erratically, as if it had a bad case of the hiccups. The live oak at Coleman's end of the building was a brooding black shadow against the early night sky, and the porch light beside the entrance door didn't do much to dispel its darkness. There was no sign of a rent-a-cop hanging around. A drive-by security guard might show up, however, in which case I would be glad to have Sheila along. As CTSU's chief of security, she lent a certain legitimacy to our clandestine visit. And of course, we weren't breaking and entering. Having a key in your hand makes a big difference when you're faced by a security guard with a gun on his hip and a chip on his shoulder.

"So," Sheila said, "what's the plan, Sherlock?"

I held up the key. "Very simple," I said. "We walk across the lot and go up to the front door. We put the key in the lock, and turn it. Once inside, we go into Coleman's office, open the safe, and see what's in it. This is a piece of cake."

"Right," Sheila said. "Piece of cake."

"Yeah," Ruby said. "Who'd suspect three women of being burglars?"

I grinned at Ruby. "Especially not us." I was dressed in a bright white shirt, Sheila a flamboyant orange T-shirt, and Ruby in eye-catching dinner-date finery. "We're not dressed for burgling somebody's building. We don't exactly blend into the background."

A large truck rumbled past. Sheila jerked her head. "Come on, gang, let's go. I can hear my laundry calling." She started toward the building.

"Wait," Ruby cried softly, putting out a hand. "Somebody's pulling in!"

We had just moved out of the shadow of the tree. We danced back behind Sheila's Explorer and watched as the lights of a car swung in a wide arc across the lot and out of sight around Coleman's half of the building. In the quiet dark, we heard the engine stop. A car door slammed softly.

"Damn," Sheila muttered.

"Probably Security," I said. "He'll check the door and be on his way."

"Yeah, Security," Ruby said. "We'll just wait. No sweat." She began to hum under her breath.

A flashlight made intermittent stabs into the dark as the security man — a slender, silhouetted figure — walked around the left end of the building, up the steps, and onto the porch. He paused in the weak spill of porch light and put his hand to the door. But instead of trying the lock, it looked as if he was inserting a key. He paused and looked over his shoulder, making sure that nobody was watching. Then he pushed the door open and went in.

"Hell," I said disgustedly.

"Why?" Ruby asked, puzzled. "I mean, why should a security guy go inside an office?"

"How should I know?" I said. "Maybe he wants to pick up a Blessing Ranch brochure." I stepped forward. "You guys wait here. I'll go see who it is."

"Stop," Sheila hissed. "You can't go up there alone."

"Why not? I have a key, don't I? Anyway, maybe this isn't a security guy after all. Maybe it's Iris." As I spoke, I realized that this made good sense. The figure was slender, and moved more like a woman than a man. Maybe Iris had decided that there was something in that safe she really wanted to have a look at, or have for her very own, before we had a chance to inventory and evaluate the lot. If so, it would be smart to let her know that this wasn't an option.

"I don't like this," Sheila said, shaking her head. "You don't know it's Iris. Hell, it might even be Jackson — and he could be armed. Stay where you are." She dove back into the Explorer and came up with a holster. She began to strap it on her hip.

"What *are* you doing?" Ruby asked nervously.

"What does it look like I'm doing?" Sheila reached under the seat and took out a .357 Magnum, checked the cylinder, and holstered it. "I'm putting on my gun."

Ruby tilted her head critically. "It looks a little . . . well, weird," she said. "With your biker shorts, I mean."

"Who cares how it looks," Sheila said,

adjusting the holster so that it rode low across her hips. "It's how it shoots that counts."

I cleared my throat. "I really don't think a gun is necessary, Smart Cookie. It's probably just Iris. If we go in with a gun, she'll have a heart attack."

"Don't tell *me* when to wear my gun," Sheila snapped. "Who's the cop here, anyway?"

I blew out a breath. "All right, all right. Ruby, Sheila and her gun are going with me. You stay and guard the car."

"I'm not standing here in the dark by myself," Ruby declared flatly. "I'm coming with you guys."

When Ruby makes up her mind, there's no reasoning with her. So the three of us made our way across the dark parking lot to the porch, tiptoed up the steps, and stopped at the door. I pushed gently but it didn't open. I took the key out of my pocket, put it into the lock, and turned. It stuck. I gave it a little jiggle and turned again. This time, the lock clicked. I pocketed the key and pushed the door open. With Sheila just behind me, right hand on her gun, and Ruby bringing up the rear, I crossed the threshold into the reception area.

The room was dark, but there was enough light coming through the window onto the porch to see that it was empty. I turned to my left. A splinter of light was showing under the door — the only door to Coleman's windowless office. The intruder was trapped.

"Stay back." Sheila stepped around me, pulling her gun, and went to stand beside the closed door, back against the wall. "I'll kick the door open," she whispered. "If this is a thief, he's probably armed. The opening door will startle him, and he'll fire. Then I'll step through and get the drop on him."

Ruby opened her purse. "I've got some handcuffs in here somewhere," she said, rummaging around.

"Handcuffs?" Sheila asked, startled.

"I found them when I was cleaning out some Halloween stuff at the store," Ruby said. "They're just toys, but they'd probably work. I was taking them home, so I'd have them in case somebody tried to burgle me." Triumphantly, she pulled them out and dangled them in front of us. "*Here* they are!"

Sheila rolled her eyes. "Here we go with the door. Stand back. One, two —"

"Wait," I said. "Let's do it my way first,

huh? I'll open the door a crack and try to get a peek at who's in there — without getting shot at."

Sheila hesitated. "Okay," she said finally. "Be careful, though. I don't want to see you get shot just before your wedding."

"I don't want me to get shot *period*," I said. "It is not part of my life plan."

I went to the door, put my hand on the knob, and turned it, trying not to make any noise. The door opened a fraction of an inch, but all I could see was one end of the sofa that stood against the opposite wall, and the back of the chair facing it. The room was lit only by the light in the burbling aquarium and a light at the far end, probably Coleman's desk lamp. I opened the door another fraction, then another, hoping that the intruder was too engrossed to notice. So far, not a sign of anybody. Then, suddenly, I realized where the intruder was: crouched on the floor behind Coleman's massive desk, at the far end of the room. I pulled the door shut and stepped back.

"Whoever is in there is down on hands and knees, busy with the safe," I said quietly. "Let's just walk up and say 'hi.' We'll have the advantage of surprise."

"Well," Sheila said.

"I don't know," Ruby began.

"Good," I said. "Come on." I opened the door and went into the room, Sheila and Ruby close behind. We walked silently across the velvety carpet until we reached the desk. Sheila moved to my right, her gun at the ready. I put both hands on the desk, leaned over it, and said, very pleasantly, "Hi. Can we help you find something?"

There was a yelp of surprise, a scramble of hands and feet, and a flurry of papers. The woman crouching behind the desk turned her pale, startled face up to me, lips parted, eyes wide with fear.

"Oh, God," she cried. Her head went down, her hands came up to cover her face, and she burst into wild weeping.

The woman was Melissa's stepgrandmother. Mrs. Carl Jackson.

Jennie.

And then the whole muddy, murky mess became suddenly very clear.

Chapter Seventeen

By Tudor times, lavender seemed to have established a hot line to Cupid. If a maiden wanted to know the identity of her true love, she would sip a brew of lavender on St. Luke's Day while murmuring:

St. Luke, St. Luke, be kind to me,
In my dreams, let me my true love see.

"The Meaning of Lavender,"
by China Bayles
The Pecan Springs *Enterprise*
Home and Garden Section

Ruby's Lemonade with Lavender and Rosemary

1 can frozen lemonade concentrate
2 cans water
2 cups lavender-rosemary tea
Sugar or honey to taste

To make lavender-rosemary tea, pour just-boiling water over 2 tablespoons lavender blossoms and 2 tablespoons dried rosemary. Let steep for 5-7 minutes, strain. Prepare lemonade, diluting with 2 cans of water. Add the lavender-rosemary tea and serve over ice.

"Jean," Ruby said. "I still can't believe that Jennie Jackson is the *Jean* we were looking for."

"Jennie, Jean — it was a natural mistake," I said. I glanced up at the schoolhouse clock that hangs over the refrigerator in my kitchen. The hands pointed to midnight, and McQuaid wasn't home yet. "Letty told Rena Burnett that she'd gotten the name off the answering machine, and that maybe she hadn't heard it right." Darla Jean and Bobbie Jean were home free, after all.

"So Jennie Jackson was having an affair with Edgar Coleman," Ruby mused.

"That's what it looks like," I said. "She must have found herself in a situation that was getting increasingly out of control, and it frightened her into doing something dramatic. But we'll have to wait until McQuaid gets home to hear the rest of the story."

After we had caught Jennie in the act of rifling the safe, we parked her on the sofa with a large supply of tissues. I offered the phone to Sheila. "Call McQuaid."

"You call him," Sheila said. "You thought this up."

"Nobody knows that but you, me, and Ruby," I said. "The City Council will be impressed when they hear that their future police chief has already solved the crime of the year."

"But that's not fair," Sheila protested.

"The truth won't sell one extra ounce of potpourri," I said, "whereas you can use the brownie points." I thrust the phone into her hands. "Call."

"If it'll make you happy," Sheila said, and dialed. While we waited for McQuaid, I took the opportunity to glance through the documents Jennie Jackson had pulled out of the safe — a picture of Melissa, a print copy of a listing from the Missing Children's Web site, and a couple of highly incriminating letters Jennie had written to Coleman while they were lovers, before they had their fatal falling-out. When McQuaid got there, he took custody of Jennie, detailing Sheila and another cop to collect all the materials from the safe and seal the office.

"I'm sure you'll say I'm being irrational to pity a murderer," Ruby said sadly, "but I felt sorry for Mrs. Jackson. She looked so forlorn, sitting there on the sofa, crying her heart out. I can't help feeling that she got caught in Coleman's web, and it wasn't her fault. She couldn't have guessed how this was all going to turn out."

"Maybe she should have given the matter some thought before the two of them fell into bed," I said tartly. "Anyway, she's a grownup and presumably mature enough to be held accountable for her actions. If you really want to feel sorry for somebody, feel sorry for Melissa."

As Jennie was being hustled into the police car, she turned her tear-stained face to me and asked me to tell her husband what was going on. So Ruby and I drove Sheila's Explorer back to the apartment, where I left Ruby and picked up my car. Dr. Jackson was watching TV in his bathrobe when I knocked on his door shortly after ten. He was stunned when he heard that Jennie was about to be charged with Edgar Coleman's murder, and utterly dazed when he learned that Rachel Lang was in town and that she knew he had Melissa.

"It's like the roof has suddenly caved in," he whispered, his face ashen. "What am I going to do? What's going to happen to Jen? Is Rachel going to take Melissa away from me?"

Looking at him, at the tears welling in his eyes and the defeated slump of his shoulders, I judged that flight was a very remote possibility. And now certainly wasn't the time to discuss any criminal charges that might be filed against him, or whether he had learned, after the fact, about what Jennie had done. Now was the time to face up to what had happened and make sure that everyone's rights were protected.

"Go talk to your wife, if they'll let you," I said gently. "Get her a good criminal lawyer and ask him to represent you, too. Sit down with him and make a clean breast of the last ten years with Melissa so he — or she — knows how best to defend you, if it comes to that. Make sure that Jennie does the same thing. You'll both need all the help you can get." I looked around. "Is Melissa asleep?"

"She's finishing a book report," he said. "On the computer upstairs."

"Why don't we tell her that you've been called out on a patient emergency," I said. "Since your wife isn't here, you'd like her to go home with me."

"Melissa," he groaned, rubbing his hands over his eyes. "Melissa, Melissa. How am I ever going to tell her what's happened?"

"Rachel Lang has already asked me to talk to her," I said. "She has to know the truth about herself and her mother, and you, too. She has to build a new life, and tomorrow is the best time to begin."

He gave me a despairing look. "I did it for her," he said. "Only for her. All the running and the hiding, all the times we had to move to a new place and start over again — it was all for Melissa, to keep her from finding out who she was, who her parents were. I *had* to, don't you see? I was afraid the courts would give Melissa back to her mother, in spite of the fact that she was unmarried and an ex-con and certainly not fit to raise a child. And my son . . ." He closed his eyes, then opened them again. "You know about Jim?"

"I was told that he died in a fire in Miami," I said.

Jackson nodded. "It was all about drugs." He rubbed his forehead. "If Rachel had married him, he might have been able to straighten himself out, and things would've been different. But when she turned him down, he began to slide." His voice was bleak. "In the end, he wasn't a fit parent, either." There was a long silence; then Jackson said, very softly, "It wasn't his fault, though. I want you to understand that. It was the drugs. And it wasn't malice that made me take Melissa away from her mother. I did it because I *loved* her."

"Even addicts are accountable for their actions," I replied. "And it was up to the court — not you — to decide whether your granddaughter should be with you or go to her mother." Our judicial system is deeply flawed, but that doesn't change our moral obligation to live by the law and fulfill our obligations to one another — especially the children.

He turned away with a choked sob. "Tell Melissa I love her," he said. "Ask her not to . . . to blame me too much."

He got dressed and left for police headquarters. Melissa packed an overnight bag and came with me without question, and I put her to sleep in the other bed in Leatha's room. My mother sat up when we came in.

"Wazzat?" she asked. "Whosis?"

"It's Melissa," I said. "She's spending the night. Okay?"

"S'fine," Leatha said. "No snakes." She fell asleep before I finished tucking Melissa in, her mouth open, snoring gently, foam curlers like fat pink butterfly larvae clustered all over her head.

I went downstairs to wait for McQuaid

and found Ruby in the kitchen, making sandwiches and pouring lemonade. "What are you doing here?" I asked, surprised. "It's after eleven."

"What does it look like I'm doing?" Ruby said. "I'm making us some sustenance. We've *got* to come up with a contingency plan." She poured me a glass of lemonade. "The Weather Channel says that Josephine is going to dump a ton of rain from Corpus to Beaumont, and miles inland."

"The Garden Room at the Pack Saddle Inn," I said. "It's got a great view of the river, very scenic, with swans, ducks, and plenty of room for the reception. And Linda Davis, the manager, says it's available. I'll call her first thing in the morning and confirm." I sipped my lemonade.

Ruby gave a windy sigh of relief. "Good," she said. "Wonderful. I can stop worrying about whether we can all crowd into the tearoom. Now, about the cake." With a rueful grin, she gestured in the direction of a half-dozen brown waffle-like layers stacked on the rack. While we were out playing crime stoppers, my mother had been practicing. "Leatha's heart is in the right place, but baking obviously isn't the best use of her talents. If we put something like that on the table, we'll all be embarrassed. Tomorrow, I'll call Lucy's Cakes in Austin and order a regular wedding cake. Maureen Rodman got hers there last year, and it was gorgeous."

I sipped my lemonade. Ruby certainly had a point. But suddenly Leatha's cake-baking didn't seem funny anymore, or embarrassing, or annoying. It seemed sweet and caring. It seemed like the sort of thing a mother would do for a daughter she loved.

I put down my glass. "No, don't order anything, Ruby," I said. "Bertha and Betsy will be here tomorrow, and Bertha will be glad to help Mom with the cake. Maybe I'll have time to help her, too."

Ruby arched her eyebrows. *"Mom?"*

Howard Cosell stumped over and flopped down beside me, his great sad eyes asking for the last bite of my sandwich so he wouldn't starve during the night, alone and abandoned in his doggie bed. I got up, sprinkled a few milk thistle seeds on what was left of my bread and bologna, and dropped it into Howard's bowl.

"Yeah, *Mom*," I said. "Nobody's got a corner on perfect. I've lived with hard feelings and anger long enough, and I'm tired of hanging on to pain. It's time to get past that stuff."

"Well, good," Ruby said. She reached under the table, pulled out a box, and put it in front of me. With a secret smile, she said, "Here. Tell me what you think of this."

I looked down at the box. The label said Sexy Secrets. Ruby's mail-order wedding costume. I opened the lid apprehensively, unfolded the tissue paper, and peeked. Sure enough. Laurel had been right. It was a nightgown, fine, filmy, and utterly transparent.

"Damn it, Ruby," I said, "you can't wear this out in public!"

Ruby looked shocked. "I'm not going to wear it anywhere. Much less in public. It's for you, silly."

"For me?"

"Sure. What do I want a nightgown for? I always sleep naked."

"But —"

"It's *your* nightgown. For your wedding night. How can you go on a honeymoon without a sexy nightgown?" She rolled her eyes. "Don't answer that. You were probably planning to sleep in one of McQuaid's old T-shirts. Or you were going to run out to Walmart at the last minute."

She was right. It was either the T-shirt or Walmart. "Thank you," I said humbly.

"You're a good friend, Ruby."

"You're welcome," she said. "Oh, by the way. Your machine is blinking."

I went to the answering machine and punched the button. It was Harold Tucker. "I just want to make sure you received our letter," he said. "As we said there, I've accepted an offer to teach at Indiana State, and we hope to put the house up for sale as soon as possible. Of course, we'll be glad to consider any offer you would care to make before we list the house with a real estate broker. Please get back to us as soon as you can and let us know if you're interested in buying it." He left a phone number and rang off.

"Oh wow!" Ruby exclaimed. She threw up her hands. "This wonderful house is for sale, China! What fantastic, marvelous, incredible news! Why, it's every bit as good as winning the lottery!"

"Our house is for sale?" I asked, dazed. "We can buy it and live here forever? I don't believe it!"

The kitchen door opened and McQuaid hobbled wearily in, leaning on his canes. He had a day's worth of black beard stubble, and the front of his shirt displayed a coffee stain the size and shape of a necktie. Sheila came behind him carrying his briefcase, her holster slung over her shoulder like a *bandido*. She was still wearing biker shorts and the orange T-shirt, and she hadn't combed her stringy blond hair. Both of them looked tired.

"Where's Marvin?" I asked, looking over Sheila's shoulder. "Isn't he with you?"

"He's on his way back to Austin," McQuaid said. "The case is closed, as far as he's concerned."

Which was exactly the way it should be, as far as *I* was concerned. "You'd better sit down," I said. "I want you to listen to something." As McQuaid dropped into a chair, I hit the replay button and Harold Tucker made his astonishing offer for the second time in five minutes.

"Sold," McQuaid said. "I'll call him tomorrow."

"Just like that?" I asked, surprised. "But —"

"Just like that," McQuaid said firmly. "Don't look a gift horse in the mouth."

"But where will we get the money for the down payment?"

"I can loan —" Ruby began.

"Hush, Ruby," McQuaid said. He patted my hand. "Don't worry, China. We'll get the money. This is *our* house, and that's all there is to it."

"The boss has spoken," Sheila said. "Ours is not to wonder why." She glanced at Ruby. "It's late. How come you're here?"

"I'm waiting for you," Ruby said. "I couldn't go to sleep without knowing what happened." She stood up. "You guys want some lemonade? How about a sandwich?"

"Yes to both." McQuaid looked at me. "Jackson showed up at the jail, so I guess you talked to him." His grin was lopsided. "Thanks, hon. Sorry to shovel that messy job onto your plate."

Hon. Oh, well. Some things you have to live with. "It had to be done," I said. "How's Jennie? What happened?"

"Long story," McQuaid said wearily, lowering himself into a chair.

Ruby poured the last of the lemonade and put the glasses on the table.

"Thanks," Sheila said. She drank half of hers in one long thirsty swallow. "Lovely."

"You're welcome," Ruby said, returning to the counter for the sandwiches. "I did your laundry," she added.

"You did my laundry?" Sheila asked in surprise. "Gosh, that was nice."

"It was the least I could do for our next chief of police," Ruby said. She put the plate on the table and went back for cookies. "Remind me to ask you about that funny little lacy thing, though." She put a hand on McQuaid's shoulder as she put the cookies on the table. "Did Jennie confess?"

"It doesn't work that way, Ruby," I said. "First McQuaid reads her rights, then she gets a lawyer, who tells her not to say anything until —"

"She confessed," Sheila said, and reached for a sandwich. "What funny little lacy thing? Are you talking about my new camisole?"

"Oh, is that what it was?" Ruby asked. She sat down. "There's milk in the refrigerator, if you want some."

I turned to McQuaid. "She *confessed?* Where the hell was her lawyer? Who coerced her into —"

"Hold on, China," McQuaid said, raising his hand. "Nobody coerced her. We couldn't keep her from telling us what happened, Miranda or no Miranda." He bent over to rub his bad leg. "She was so anxious to get it off her chest that she just spilled it all. She killed Coleman, and she fully intends to plead guilty. The Letty business is a little more complicated."

"She intends to plead guilty *now,*" I said. "But wait until her husband gets her a good defense lawyer. Heck, not even a good one — a mediocre one will do the same thing. He'll get the confession thrown out and you'll have to make a case on whatever flimsy —"

"It's her right index fingerprint on her husband's gun," Sheila said. "And she knows some details of the crime scene that didn't make it into the newspaper. It's a tight case, China. Not even you could get her off."

"What about Letty?" Ruby asked.

"Jennie says she went to the Coleman house after Letty called and invited her," McQuaid said. "There must have been something in that breakfast conversation at the diner with Dr. Jackson that made the connection in Letty's mind. Anyway, Letty accused Jennie of having an affair with Coleman and asked her, point blank, whether she had killed him. Jennie said she went to pieces and told Letty the truth. At that point, Letty tried to shove her down the stairs, but fell herself, instead."

"Self-defense," I said.

"Manslaughter," McQuaid said.

"Accidental death, maybe," Sheila said. She went to the refrigerator and came back with the milk. "If the county attorney gets a guilty plea in Coleman's murder, he might decide not to prosecute her for Letty's death."

Ruby reached for a cookie and sat back. "So why did she kill Coleman? She was pissed about the other women? He threatened to blow the whistle on their affair?"

"Nope," McQuaid said. "He threatened to blow the whistle on Dr. Carlson. Jennie killed Coleman to keep him from revealing that her husband had kidnapped his granddaughter and was practicing dentistry under an assumed name. Coleman had happened to see Melissa's picture somewhere, and looked her up on the Missing Children's Web site. He put two and two together and came to the conclusion that Jack Carlson and Carl Jackson were the same man, and that the good doctor's Texas dentistry registration was phony."

"Pretty juicy blackmail stuff," Sheila said, around a mouthful of sandwich. "Especially for Jennie. Listening to her talk, I'd say that above anything else, she values her husband's status in the community. She loves Melissa and doesn't want to lose her, but mostly, she wanted to keep Coleman quiet about who Jackson was and what he had done. She wanted to go on joining clubs, wearing nice clothes, and playing the dentist's wife."

"But what was Coleman after?" I asked, frowning. "What did Jennie have that he wanted? Neither of the Jacksons is on the City Council, so he wasn't after a vote. Was it more sex? Money? What?"

Sheila poured herself a glass of milk. "A piece of land."

"Land!" Ruby exclaimed. "Good Lord, didn't he have enough of *that?*"

"Rachel Lang told me the Jacksons had bought some residential property here," I said. "She thought they were planning to build a house."

"Who the hell is Rachel Lang?" McQuaid demanded irritably. "Why do I feel as if I'm the last to know any of this stuff?"

"She's Melissa's real mother," I said. I grinned at him. "Don't be impatient, hon. All will be revealed in good time."

"About the land," Sheila said. "The Carlsons — it sounded as if Jennie was the major player here — had snapped up a piece of real estate that Coleman needed in order to have access to the most scenic section of the Blessing. Without that land, he'd have to build a road across a ravine, at a cost of something like a half million dollars. He asked the Jacksons for an easement, but they refused."

"Ah," I said, "Coleman would keep quiet about Melissa if the Jacksons would sell him their land — at bargain basement prices, no doubt."

"Yup," McQuaid said. "But Jennie didn't trust him to keep quiet. She was afraid he'd keep upping the ante."

"And if he blew the whistle, it would mean the end of the practice, the end of their comfortable life in Pecan Springs — the end of everything, really," Sheila said.

"So she killed him," Ruby said reflectively.

"She killed him," McQuaid said. "Murder."

"But not just like *that*," Sheila said. "She pulled out the gun, he tried to take it away from her, there was a struggle, it went off, blah blah blah."

"Manslaughter," I said. "You wait. That confession isn't worth the time it took to write it down."

McQuaid shrugged. Ruby sighed. Sheila looked off into space. Nobody seemed to feel like arguing with me. Finally, after a long silence, Sheila said, "Well, one good thing came out of all that stuff tonight."

"Yeah?" I asked glumly. "What?"

"This case has reminded me of the things I like about police work. I'm going to make a run for police chief."

"Way cool!" Ruby exclaimed. "Just think of it — a female police chief in Pecan Springs! That ought to make the good old boys choke on their chewing tobacco."

I looked at McQuaid. "How do you feel about Sheila's running for your job?"

"More power to her." He stretched wearily. "After the week I've had, I'm ready to turn in my badge and let Marvin finish filling out the paperwork. This case has reminded me of all the things I *don't* like about police work." He gave me a narrow look. "Which is not to say that I wouldn't take an investigative assignment or two, as opportunity knocks."

"I don't think I want to hear any more knocking," I said firmly. "I'm more interested in hearing you say that you're quitting — if that's what you really want to do."

"Well, listen up, babe." He leaned forward and said, loudly and distinctly, "I quit." He leaned back and gave me a crooked grin. "How's that?"

"Way cool," I said. Now, the only problem I had to solve was finding another dentist.

Chapter Eighteen

The herb of fidelity, rosemary was dipped into scented water and woven into chaplets for brides. Bridesmaids gave a sprig of it to the bridgegroom on his wedding day to carry as an emblem of love and loyalty. Wedding guests received gilded branches of it tied with silk of many colors.

Herbcraft
Violet Schafer

Newlyweds would put bunches of dried lavender under their mattresses to ensure marital passion.

Lavender
Tessa Evelegh

It was late when we got to bed that night, and while I was very happy that McQuaid would soon be out of a job, I was already rehearsing what I had to tell Melissa when she got up the next morning. But she's a tough, resilient young woman, and I was confident that with the right support and lots of love, she'd come through, and that she and her mother would work things out. I was also relieved that McQuaid's investigation was over, except for a few loose ends and the inevitable paperwork. I could stop worrying about being stranded at the altar or forced to go on my honeymoon with Hark. None of which meant that I was easier in my mind about the marriage. I don't have any personal experience to go by, but I suspect that weddings and honeymoons are a lot easier to orchestrate than the long haul.

If all you're interested in is the mystery, you've come to the end of the story, more or less, and you can put this down and go on about your other business. But there's one more chapter, and if romance is your cup of tea, settle back in your chair and I'll tell you about the wedding.

On Friday, Bertha Reppert and Betsy Williams appeared at the shop around nine, full of their usual enthusiasm, irrepressible good humor, and boundless wealth of herbal ideas. We hugged, sat down for tea, caught up on all the gossip, and then got serious about what needed to be done.

"It doesn't look like a problem," Betsy assured me, when we had glanced over the list of gardens we'd been given permission to pillage. "As long as there are plenty of willing pickers."

"The Merryweathers are glad to oblige," I said. "It's Josephine that's kicking up the fuss." The storm had wobbled into the western Gulf of Mexico, and bands of showers would soon be moving in from the east. The Weather Channel was predicting severe tidal flooding, the police had closed the JFK Causeway to South Padre Island, and Galveston was filling sandbags. It wasn't clear just how bad things might get in Pecan Springs, but it was beginning to look like a wet and wild weekend.

"So what's a little rain?" Betsy said confidently, tossing her brown hair. "We'll wear boots and ponchos. Anyway, we need to get the flowers this afternoon and evening, if possible. It takes twenty-four hours to condition them before we start to arrange."

Bertha didn't bat an eye when I told her about my mother's cake catastrophes. She pushed her big owly glasses up on her nose and said, "Listen, China, I've been in worse situations. Have I ever told you about the time we planned to feed lunch to a hundred and fifty and —" We were off on one of Bertha's amazing hair-raising herbal adventures.

Ruby drove Bertha to my house to bail my mother out of her cake-baking jail, while Betsy rolled up her sleeves, assembled the available Merryweathers, and put them to work gathering flowers and herbs before Josephine got serious. She reminded the pickers to cut the stems on a long slant, remove the lower leaves, and plunge the plant materials in warm water as soon as they were cut. As the buckets were brought in and stored in the kitchen of our tearoom, she misted the flowers, then closed the door so they could rest quietly in the dark until the next day.

If you've ever done flowers for a wedding, you know how much work it is, and Betsy is a perfectionist. In her hands, everything is done with exquisite attention to detail, and the result is elegant and sophisticated. Late Saturday morning, as Josephine (now a full-bodied, self-willed hurricane) lashed the windows with sheets of rain, we cleared the tables in the tearoom and Betsy and her flower arrangers settled down to work. They started with the boutonnieres for the men and then went on to the bridal chaplets of ivy, rosemary, and white roses. When those were finished, they turned to the tussie-mussies — handheld herbal nosegays in which each plant has a special significance — for the women guests. As each piece was completed, it was misted, bagged in plastic, and refrigerated. Then they worked on the large floral arrangements for the altar and the smaller aisle markers, using boxwood and myrtle, mint, mugwort, ivy, roses, ferns, and lilies. I provided a dozen rosemary topiaries I'd been saving for the occasion, and those were decorated with pinks and lavender and tied with white ribbons.

Then Betsy put her arrangers to work making wonderful tussie-mussie style herbal bouquets for Ruby and me, following the traditional language of flowers. Each one was centered with a single perfect white rose from Winnie's garden, symbolizing love and desire, and surrounded with mint for joy, myrtle for passion, lavender for devotion, sage for health and long life, southernwood for constancy, rue for vision, thyme for courage, ivy for faithfulness, and of course, rosemary — the marriage herb — for love, remembrance, and fidelity. Finally, they fashioned the groom's flowers: sprigs of rosemary and sage, a ruffle of parsley, and a tiny white rosebud. If the flowers spoke truly, McQuaid would live long and be healthy, be constant and loving, and not talk back to the boss.

While all this was going on, Bertha and my mother had shifted into high gear. By early Saturday evening, before we left for the party at the Pack Saddle Inn, they had produced not only the bride's cake — a three-tiered beauty decorated with lavender, rosemary, and tiny rosebuds — but the groom's cake as well, dark and rich and nutty. We'd already agreed on a menu centered around a sandwich loaf that could be easily sliced, a delicate tuna–cream-cheese mousse, a tomato–rose-hip aspic, herbed fruit skewers, and plates of herbal goodies supplied by volunteer Merryweathers. On Sunday, when it came time to lay out the food table in a room adjacent to the Garden Room, Bertha put down a snowy white tablecloth, then arranged cloth-draped boxes of different heights to display the food and flowers. One of her favorite expressions is "and just one more!" so when everything was finished, the reception table was delightfully crowded with an abundance of food and flowers, candles and crystal and mirrors, and fruit and flowers and herbs tucked into folds of the cloth.

That was the good news. The bad news was that Josephine made landfall on Saturday night just south of Corpus Christi, moved inland toward San Antonio, and then showed no inclination to go anywhere else very soon. Which meant that here in Pecan Springs, the flash-flood warnings were posted on Saturday night and the rain bucketed down at the rate of an inch an hour for most of Sunday — a bad-hair day to end all bad-hair days. Embedded in the bands of rain were thunder showers as well, which meant even heavier rain and a display of pyrotechnics now and again. The road to New Braunfels was closed by noon and the road to Gruene shortly thereafter, and the Pecan River began to show signs of rising over its banks and flooding the park. By the time we loaded the food and flowers into the vans and out of the vans and through the downpour to the Garden Room, we were drenched and ragged-looking.

And yes, the work party included the bride, and the groom too. We couldn't let our friends have all the fun, could we? McQuaid drove one of the vans and Blackie drove the other, while Ruby, Sheila, Leatha, and I toted and hauled. We were finished by two, which gave me barely two hours to throw Ruby's nightgown and a few other things into my honeymoon suitcase (a gift from my mother), then shower and change and make myself pretty. It's a good thing I didn't let Bobbie Rae talk me into the Bride's Getaway, though. All that beauty would have washed off while I was slogging through ankle-deep water with my arms full of boxes, half of my fingernails broken off, the other half chipped, and my hair draped like a wet floor mop over my head. It took Ruby's and Leatha's combined efforts to make me halfway presentable.

And the wedding itself? Well, it was quite an experience. The herbs and flowers filled the room with a rich fragrance, and hundreds of votive candles flickered softly against the gray rain sheeting down the windows. As people gathered, Sheila played "Lavender's Blue" and "Greensleeves" on her CD player. Ruby wore a simple blue ankle-length tunic, and Leatha, whom I had asked at the last moment to give me away, was dressed in soft mauve silk. I stepped down the aisle to the measured beat of the *Bridal Chorus*. Maude Porterfield, the oldest Justice of the Peace in the state of Texas, remembered to turn up her hearing aid for the occasion but forgot to take "obey" out of the ceremony. Wearing his Mexican wedding shirt, McQuaid stood firm and solid without his canes throughout the ceremony.

417

I took my place beside him, feeling as brides have always felt at such moments, full of an unruly joy slightly dampened by a clammy stage fright.

But all the anxiety vanished when he bent to kiss me, wrapping both arms around me and pulling me close, kissing my lips, then burying his face in my shoulder. My arms went around his neck and we stood, eyes closed, forgetting everyone else, finding shelter in each other. It wasn't the embrace of passionate lovers (that would come later) but of beloved friends, grateful that they had at last found sweet sanctuary after the harrowing journey of the past few months. We held one another until Brian, sitting in the front row beside Melissa and her mother, said plaintively, "When are they gonna *quit?* I want some cake!"

That brought down the house. A ripple of laughter went across the room, echoed by a clap of thunder and a flash of lightning outside, as if the powers that be had said Amen and Let's get on with it, gang. McQuaid kissed me again, brushed a tear off my cheek, and then released me. He turned to Brian and held out his hand.

"Come here, partner," he said. When Brian joined us, blushing beet-red, Mc-

Quaid stepped aside so the boy could stand between us. Then, holding hands, the three of us turned to say thank you to our families and friends as the triumphant notes of the *Ode to Joy* rang through the room. It was a glorious moment, and if the day had ended there, everything would have been hunky-dory.

It didn't.

By the time McQuaid and I had hugged and kissed everybody, snacked, cut the cake, and toasted one another with punch and glasses of bubbly — all to the delicate melodies of a Celtic harp — the wind was bending the trees double, the rain was pouring down in torrents, and the electric lights had gone out. Pecan River, now the color of frothy chocolate milk, was roaring past the windows of the Garden Room like a miniature Niagara. Awestruck and murmuring, the guests gathered to watch as limbs and whole trees, a shed roof, and a Porta-Potty were ferried downstream by the churning waters.

The Whiz had just said, "Wow, this is getting serious," when Linda Davis, carrying a flashlight, came into the room. She held her hands up for silence.

"I'm sorry to be the bearer of bad news," she said, when we had quieted down, "but the police have just closed the River Road. I'm afraid we're all going to be here until it's reopened."

"Oh, no!" Ruby exclaimed. "When?"

"When the police say so," Linda said. "It could be a while, unfortunately. The flood waters are chewing up bridge footings."

"The police?" Lurel asked. "But the chief is *here!* And so is the county sheriff. How could they do such a thing without notifying *them?*"

All eyes went to the groom and his best man.

Blackie shrugged. "Not my job."

"Don't look at me, either," McQuaid said. "The highway department is in charge of road closings."

"I've got to get to a phone," Hark said urgently. "The biggest natural disaster story in decades, and I'm missing it!"

"Looks to me like you're right in the middle of it," Sheila remarked grimly, as a flock of shingles swooped like errant blackbirds past the window.

"The phones are out," Linda said to Hark, "but I've got a cell phone in my office." To the others, she said, "It looks like we're stranded, folks. Sorry — but at least we're all in the same boat." Loud groans from the exasperated guests. She shrugged ruefully. "Sorry about that. Please hang tight. We'll try to make your stay as comfortable as possible."

"Comfort be damned!" the Whiz exclaimed hotly. "I've got a court date in the morning! I've got to get back to San Antonio."

"And Bertha and I need to get to Austin tonight," Betsy said. She looked at her watch. "Our plane leaves at seven tomorrow morning. We're due to catch a connecting flight in Houston."

"Houston!" Charlie Lipton hooted. "With this storm, the entire city of Houston will be running a couple of days late."

At the mention of the plane, McQuaid looked at me. "Hey, hon, what time is our Hawaii flight?"

My answer was lost in the explosive sound of breaking glass. We all jumped, and Leatha clutched Sam's arm with a shriek of surprise. At the far end of the room, away from the guests, a massive live oak limb had smashed through the window. Rain and wind howled in.

Linda, like a woman in charge of her safari, raised her voice. "That's it, folks. We're outta here. Into the hall, away from the windows. Come on, everybody move! *Now!*"

"But the cake!" Leatha cried. "We can't leave the cake. It'll be ruined!"

I put my arm around her shoulders. "Leave the cake, Mom. You can always bake me another one."

And that was the end of the wedding reception — officially, that is. I would like to report that the National Guard dispatched a helicopter to airlift McQuaid and me to Austin in time to catch our plane to Hawaii, but that didn't happen. (The airline canceled the flight and found seats for us on a plane leaving on Monday afternoon.) We spent our wedding night in the Honeymoon Suite of the Pack Saddle Inn, a crimson-flocked room of mammoth proportions with a large mirror, discreetly draped in red velvet, on the wall opposite the waterbed, which was roughly the size of Canyon Lake. Blackie had risked life and limb to retrieve my suitcase from McQuaid's truck, so I at least had Ruby's honeymoon nightgown. It got rave reviews from McQuaid before it fell in a heap on the floor and we fell into bed together, naked but legal, to make waves. We didn't bother to undrape the mirror. That's the virtue of having lived in sin before you're married. There are no disappointments, no uncomfortable discoveries, no unwelcome surprises.

The other guests spent our wedding night in various Pack Saddle accommodations. Since the inn had been close to capacity already, most people had to sleep several to a room, and a few of the more stalwart bedded down in the lobby. The party, however, went on until the wee hours, as the wind blew and the rain rained and the spiked punch and champagne were augmented from the emergency stock in the Pack Saddle's wine cellar. McQuaid and I crashed early, so we missed the entertainment. But a bleary-eyed, hungover Hark told us the next day that ours was the rowdiest wedding party anybody could remember.

On Monday morning, all those who were ambulatory breakfasted in the Pack Saddle dining room. When the rain tapered off around ten, we turned out to watch the highway crew repair the flood damage. After the inspector pronounced the bridge fit for use, people began to leave, hugging and congratulating us and vowing never to forget our wedding as long as they lived.

On our way out to the parking lot with armloads of flower containers, Ruby and I stopped in Linda's office. She looked tired but cheerful, the way a safari director ought to look at the end of a long and successful trip, having lost none of her tourists to the leopards.

"Thanks for the hospitality, Linda," I said. "You were wonderful."

"Right," Ruby said. "When I get married, I'll plan to hold the wedding here. You certainly know how to throw a party."

"Yeah. Life's a blast, isn't it?" Linda shook her head. "Hey, did you hear the latest? Both Pauline Perkins and Ken Bowman announced their resignations from the Council this morning."

"No kidding," Ruby said. She looked at me. "I'll bet they chose this morning to make the announcement because they figured the news would get buried in all the stuff about the storm."

"No doubt," I said, and picked up my suitcase. "Guess we'd better be on our way. Thanks again, Linda."

Linda grinned at me. "Have a great time on your honeymoon. Where are you and Mike headed?"

"Hawaii," I said expansively. "Blue skies, sweet breezes, days in the sun, sweet tropical nights. I can't wait."

"Blue skies?" Linda gave me a long look.

"Have you looked at the weather forecast for Hawaii?"

"Oh, no!" Ruby groaned. "Don't tell me — not another storm!"

"Hernando," Linda said. She gave me a thumbs-up. "Bon voyage!"

Resources, References, and Recipes

If you're a lavender lover, you're not alone in your passion. The sharply clean, refreshing scent of its delicate flowers and silver-gray foliage was cherished in early times by the Egyptians (who used it to make mummies), the Phoenicians, the Greeks, and the Romans, and by gardeners everywhere.

Lavender grows best under its native conditions — that is, where it can have bright sun and excellent drainage. If lavender doesn't like your moist, shady garden, try it in the hot, dry, gravelly space between the curb and the sidewalk where everything else fries to a crisp. If you live north of the Mason-Dixon line, you'll need to stick with one of the winter-hardy species and toss a mulch blanket around it in winter.

There are twenty to thirty different species of lavender (depending on who's counting) and lots of different varieties. The shrubby, thirty-inch plant you see most often is English lavender (*Lavandula angustifolia*), which tolerates cold weather. Its warm-weather friends are Spanish and French lavenders, and if you live in the South, they may do better for you. Lavender doesn't come in just lavender, of course: it comes in varying shades of white, pink, dark violet, and blue. You can grow it from seed, cuttings, or root divisions, or do it the easy way and buy plants from Wanda's Wonderful Acres (Wanda will love you for this) or your local nursery.

One of the greatest delights in the herb garden is harvesting lavender. Pick the spikes just as the flowers are about to open, watching for snakes, or fairies masquerading as snakes. (Sicilians used to believe that fairies took the form of snakes and draped themselves across the lavender branches.) Wrap the cut stems in a rubber band and hang upside down to dry in a warm, dark place so the color doesn't fade. Your closet is good, particularly because you can visit it often and sniff to your heart's content.

Once you've harvested your lavender, you'll find all sorts of ways to enjoy it. The plant has long been used to scent soaps, cosmetics, and potpourris, and sachets, many of which you can make for yourself

427

from the recipes and formulas in the books listed below. You can also use it in your bath and in footbaths, or put a few drops of the essential oil on your hair brush. While most people don't think of lavender as a culinary herb, you can use it to flavor cookies and cakes, make tangy vinegars and punches, and brew fragrant teas.

Lavender's healing properties have been known and exploited for centuries. It has been used to soothe headaches, calm the nerves, relieve anxiety, quiet indigestion, induce sleep, relax sore muscles, cool hot, tired feet, and kill germs. (During the dreadful plagues of the late Middle Ages, the robbers who plundered the personal belongings of the dead wore face masks dipped in Four Thieves Vinegar, which contained lavender.) Recent research shows that the plant contains a powerful antiseptic. Scientists have also confirmed that the scent of lavender lulls you to sleep by functioning as a central nervous system depressant. Other research suggests that the plant may have anticancer potential as well, triggering a mechanism that helps cancer cells destroy themselves.

All this, and pretty, too.

LOTS MORE ABOUT LAVENDER . . . AND WEDDINGS

The following books can help you learn more about lavender's many and various uses. And if there's a wedding in your future, you might want to consult a couple of experts.

The Bride's Herbal, by Bertha Reppert. Available from Rosemary House, 120 South Market St., Mechanicsburg, PA 17055.

A Cozy Book of Herbal Teas, by Mindy Toomay. Recipes, remedies, and bits of folk wisdom about many herbs, including lavender.

Lavender: Practical Inspirations for Natural Gifts, Country Crafts and Decorative Displays, by Tessa Evelegh. Lots of lavender lore, ideas for using lavender, gorgeous photographs.

Lavender, Lovage, & Lemongrass, by Hazel Evans. Recipes, crafts, beauty products, and lovely, lovely photographs. Learn how to make lavender syrup, lavender bubble bath, lavender sleep toys, and even (a Victorian necessity) lavender ink.

Lavender, Sweet Lavender, by Judyth A. McLeod. Information about lavender history, lore, cultivation, and use, abundantly illustrated.

Planning Your Herbal Wedding, by Betsy Williams. Valuable instructions and ideas for using herbs to celebrate your wedding. Available from Betsy Williams's The Proper Season, 155 Chestnut Street, Andover, MA 01810.

A COLLECTION OF LAVENDER CRAFTS & COOKERY

Traditional Lavender Wands

These little wands are often placed in drawers and on linen shelves, where the fragrance of lavender is especially welcome. Here's what you need:

9, 11, or 13 fresh, long lavender stems
1 yard 1/8" satin ribbon per wand

Strip the leaves from the stems (don't disturb the flowers). Bundle the stems together, lining up the lowest blossoms, and tie a string tightly around the stems just below the blossoms. Bend the stems over the blossoms to form a cage around them, and secure with a rubber band. Starting at the top of the cage, weave the ribbon in and out of the stems in a descending spiral, forming a woven basket around the flowers. Tie tightly at the bottom of the basket. Trim stems neatly and add a bow.

Lavender Madeleines

This delicate recipe comes from a fine book of original recipes called *Seasonal Herbal Favorites from Martha's Herbary*, Vol. 1, by cooking instructor Martha Paul. Martha says she's working on Volume 2, so ask her about it when you order her book. The address: Martha's Herbary, P.O. Box 236, Pomfret, CT 06258.

3/4 cup granulated sugar
3 tablespoons dried or 5 tablespoons fresh lavender flowers
3/4 cup unsalted butter, melted and cooled
2 large eggs, room temperature
1/2 teaspoon vanilla extract
1 cup unsifted all purpose flour
Confectioners' sugar
Madeleine cookie mold

In food processor, process granulated sugar and flowers until flowers are finely ground. Heat oven to 400°. In a large bowl beat eggs with lavender sugar mixture and vanilla until light and fluffy (about 4 minutes). Gradually beat in 3/4 cup melted butter. With wire whisk, fold in flour. Spoon a scant one tablespoon batter into each madeleine mold. Bake 8-10 minutes or until golden brown. Immediately remove from pan. Cool on wire rack. Store in airtight container. Dust with confectioners' sugar just before serving. (Martha suggests spraying the madeleine mold with cooking spray before filling. She says you might also try substituting rose water for the vanilla — a wonderful rose fragrance!)

Ruby's Lavender & Mint Tea Party Punch

For China's wedding, Ruby made this sparkling punch, using two favorite herbs. This recipe serves six; you can double or triple it to serve your guests. Double the herb quantities if you are using fresh herbs.

2 tablespoons dried mint
2 tablespoons dried lavender blossoms

6 cups boiling water
1 liter ginger ale
1 cup purple grape juice

In a teapot brew the mint in the hot water for 10 minutes. Add lavender, stir, and let cool. Strain, and add the grape juice. Chill. Just before serving, pour in ginger ale. Add ice cubes that have been frozen with a sprig of lavender or a mint leaf, or cool with a pretty ice ring. (Fill a ring mold half full of water, layer with roses and other edible flowers, then finish filling and freeze.)

Lavender Bath Tea

Mix two teaspoons each of these dried herbs: rosemary, thyme, marjoram, and sage. Add four teaspoons of lavender. Mix and store in a tightly capped jar. For each bath, brew a strong tea of two teaspoons of this mixture to one cup of boiling water. Steep 10 minutes and add to your bath.

Soothing Lavender Bath Oil

Mix 1 tablespoon lavender essential oil with 4 tablespoons almond oil and 1 tablespoon vodka. Add a few drops of rose or jasmine oil and mix. Store in a glass or plastic bottle. Add a few drops to your tub for a scented soak. To make your own massage oil, omit the vodka.

Lavender Bubble Bath

To make a mild bubble bath, grate one bar of castile soap into a quart of warm water. Mix well. To this liquid soap solution add 3 ounces of glycerin or coconut oil (either will make bubbles) and 2-4 drops lavender essential oil. Store in a glass or plastic container.

Kate Ardleigh's Victorian Secrets

Kate Ardleigh is the heroine of the Robin Paige Victorian mysteries (written by Susan and Bill Albert under the pseudonym of Robin Paige). Lavender sachet is a necessity in every drawer in Kate's home, and Lavender Lip Balm is always on her dressing table. Here are Kate's recipes for these truly Victorian pleasures.

Lavender and Rosemary Sachet

For a sweetly scented sachet, mix these ingredients, place in a lace sachet bag, and tie with a pretty ribbon.

2 tablespoons lavender flowers
2 tablespoons rosemary
10 whole cloves
1/4 teaspoon powdered dry orange peel

Lavender Lip Balm

1/2 cup cosmetic oil (apricot kernel,
    sweet almond, or grapeseed oil)
1/4 cup fresh lavender flowers
Lavender essential oil
1-2 teaspoons pure beeswax, grated

In a clean lidded jar, steep the lavender flowers in the oil for a week. Strain into a small saucepan, add 5-6 drops of essential oil, and place over low heat. When warm, begin adding the beeswax. When you've melted in the first teaspoon of wax, remove from heat and test for hardness by placing a little on a saucer and putting it in the refrigerator. After a couple of minutes, check to see if the gloss has congealed. If it isn't hard enough, add a little more wax and reheat. If it's too hard, add a few drops of oil and reheat. When done, pour into a small lidded jar and let cool.